Venom in Vanilla

Copyright © 2025 by Patti Petrone Miller
All rights reserved.

No part of this publication may be reproduced, stored in a retrieval system, or transmitted in any form or by any means—electronic, mechanical, photocopying, recording, or otherwise—without the prior written permission of the author, except in the case of brief quotations embodied in reviews, articles, or scholarly analysis.

This is a work of fiction. Names, characters, places, and incidents are either the product of the author's imagination or used fictitiously. Any resemblance to actual persons, living or dead, events, or locales is entirely coincidental.

Publisher: AP Miller Productions

Cover Design by: TMT Book Cover Design

Printed in the United States of America

For more information, visit:
https://pattipetronemillerexecutiveproducer.wordpress.com/

Patti Petrone Miller

Social Media Links
https://www.facebook.com/pattipetronemiller/
https://www.facebook.com/pattipetronemillerexecutiveproducer/
https://www.facebook.com/halloweenismyfavoriteholiday/
https://www.pinterest.com/pattipetmiller/
htps://www.threads.net/@pattipetronemiller
Website and Blog
https://pattipetronemillerexecutiveproducer.wordpress.com/2024/09/22/a-comprehensive-guide-to-crystals-history-magic-and-tinctures/

Venom in Vanilla

Praise For Author

Patti Petrone Miller's books hit different from your typical feel-good stories. Sure, Hallmark's got their formula down pat, but Miller brings something fresh to the table - authentic characters that actually feel like people you know, dealing with real-life stuff while still keeping things wonderfully uplifting.
I honestly get the same warm fuzzies reading her books as I do curling up with hot cocoa for a Hallmark marathon, but without all the predictable plot points we've seen a million times. She's nailed that sweet spot between heartwarming and genuine that's super hard to find these days. If you're looking for stories that'll leave you smiling but don't make you roll your eyes at how perfect everything is, Miller's your girl. She's got that special touch that makes you feel like you're hanging out with friends rather than just reading about characters. Move over, Hallmark - there's a new queen of wholesome in town!"

Authors Book List

Accidental Vows
A Very Merry Krampus Christmas
A Devil's Bargain
The Devilf of London
Sin Takes A Holiday
Barking Up The Wrong Bakery, Thankgiving
Barking Up The Wrong Bakery, Christmas
Best Served Dead
Bewitching Charms
Christmas at Hollybrook Inn
Christmas on Peppermit Lane
Cabinet of Curiosities
Krampus
Hex and the City
Love in Stitches
Pies and Perps
Spectres and Souffles
Mamma Mia It's Murder
Once Upon A Christmas
The Fatman
The Frosted Felony
The Purr-fect Suspect
The Boogeyman
The Gingerdead Men
Vikings Enchantress
Welcome to Scarecrow Hollow
The Pendleton Witches
Christmas In Pine Haven
Love in the Stacks
Once Upon A Christmas
Frosted Felony
Truth or Dare
Before the Fire
Heart of the Beast

Venom in Vanilla

Savage Bloodline
The Secret Ingredient, Mad Batter Bakery Mysteries Prequel
Drive By Pies, Mad Batter Bakery Mysteries Book 1
Venom in Vanilla, The Sundae of Secrets Series
The Big Bad, Wolf Lake Series Book 1

Patti Petrone Miller

VENOM IN VANILLA

Venom in Vanilla

For Tessa. The little love of my life

Patti Petrone Miller

Chapter 1
The Discovery

    The ocean breeze carried the scent of salt and sugar through the open windows of Salted Caramel's, the beloved ice cream shop nestled between the boardwalk and Main Street in Seabreeze Shores. Lila Montgomery wiped a bead of sweat from her brow with the back of her hand, careful not to disturb the delicate vanilla orchid tucked behind her ear—a morning ritual she'd picked up from her late father. The small, white flower was a reminder of her signature flavor and the legacy her family had built in this sleepy coastal town.

    "One scoop of salted caramel, one scoop of strawberry cheesecake, both in waffle cones," Lila announced, handing the treats to a pair of sunburned tourists. Her hazel eyes crinkled at the corners as she smiled. "Enjoy the rest of your day at the beach."

    The couple thanked her and made their way out, the little bell above the door jingling as they left. Lila glanced at the old nautical clock hanging above the register—a weathered piece that had once belonged on her father's fishing boat. It was just past noon, and already the day felt endless. Summer in Seabreeze Shores meant a constant stream of visitors seeking refuge from the heat in the form of her homemade ice cream.

    She tucked a stray strand of dark brown hair behind her ear and straightened her light blue sundress, smoothing down the front of her apron embroidered with the shop's logo—a scoop of ice cream nestled against a backdrop of ocean waves. The shop itself was a reflection of its owner: warm, inviting, with splashes of coastal blues and creams. Vintage photos of the town lined the walls, alongside snapshots of happy customers enjoying their frozen treats.

"You've been on your feet since six this morning," her mother, Eva, called from the back room. "Why don't you take a break? I can handle the counter for a bit."

Eva Montgomery emerged, wiping her hands on a small towel. At sixty-two, she still moved with the energy of someone decades younger. Her silver-streaked hair was pulled back in a neat bun, and her eyes—the same hazel as Lila's—were bright and alert despite the early morning start.

"I'm fine, Mom," Lila insisted, though her feet were beginning to ache in her well-worn sandals. "We've got a line starting to form outside. I'll take a break when the rush is over."

Eva sighed but didn't argue. She knew her daughter well enough to recognize the stubborn set of her jaw—a trait inherited from her father. Instead, she began restocking the display case with freshly made waffle cones, their sweet aroma mixing with the scent of churning ice cream.

The bell above the door chimed again, and Lila looked up to greet the next customer. Her practiced smile faltered slightly as a stranger walked in. In a town as small as Seabreeze Shores, unfamiliar faces were always noticed, especially those that seemed as out of place as this man.

He was tall with broad shoulders, dressed in a crisp white button-down shirt and pressed khaki slacks—far too formal for a day at the beach. His dark hair was neatly combed, and his blue eyes scanned the shop with an intensity that made Lila straighten her posture. There was something calculated about the way he moved, as if he were taking inventory of every detail.

"Welcome to Salted Caramel's," Lila greeted him, her voice carrying across the shop. "What can I get for you today?"

The man approached the counter, his leather shoes—not sandals, Lila noted—clicking against the weathered wooden floor. He offered a smile that didn't quite reach his eyes.

"Just a single scoop of vanilla bean, please," he said. His voice was deep and smooth, like good bourbon. "In a cup, not a cone."

"Plain vanilla? Are you sure?" Lila asked, raising an eyebrow. "We've got twenty-four flavors, all homemade. Our salted caramel is what put us on the map."

The man's smile tightened. "I prefer to keep things simple," he replied. He glanced at his watch—an expensive-looking timepiece that caught the sunlight streaming through the windows. "Just vanilla."

Lila nodded and scooped the ice cream, noticing how the man's eyes darted around the shop. He seemed distracted, his attention repeatedly drawn to the window overlooking the boardwalk.

"That'll be three fifty," she said, sliding the cup across the counter.

He handed her a crisp five-dollar bill. "Keep the change," he said, before taking his ice cream to a small table by the window.

As Lila watched him from behind the counter, she couldn't shake the feeling that he wasn't here for the ice cream. He'd barely touched it, instead focusing on the world outside the window, occasionally checking his phone with a furrowed brow.

"Who's the suit?" Eva whispered, sidling up next to Lila. "He looks like he's waiting for someone."

"No idea," Lila murmured. "Said his name is Graham Fox when he paid with card. First time I've seen him in here."

"Well, there's been talk about developers eyeing properties along the waterfront," Eva said, her voice dropping even lower. "Elliot Price mentioned something about it at the town meeting last week."

Lila frowned. The waterfront was the heart and soul of Seabreeze Shores. It was where local fishermen like Elliot had worked for generations, where families gathered for sunset picnics, and where the annual Seabreeze Festival was held each summer. The thought of developers transforming it into another soulless tourist trap made her stomach knot.

The bell above the door jingled once more, and Lila's best friend, Elsie Winters, breezed in. With her fiery red curls and emerald green sundress, she was impossible to miss. She carried a woven basket filled with fresh flowers, likely from her morning trip to the farmers' market.

"Lila Montgomery, please tell me you saved me some of that blackberry lavender ice cream from yesterday," Elsie called out, her voice carrying through the shop. She set her basket on the counter and leaned forward with a conspiratorial grin. "I've been dreaming about it all morning."

Lila laughed, the tension in her shoulders easing at the sight of her friend. "For you? Always." She reached below the counter for a special container she'd set aside. "I knew you'd be by, so I saved some before we sold out."

As Lila scooped the rich purple ice cream into Elsie's favorite ceramic bowl—a piece from Elsie's own pottery collection—she noticed Graham Fox watching them with interest.

"Who's the eye candy by the window?" Elsie whispered, following Lila's gaze. "New in town?"

"Seems like it," Lila replied, handing over the ice cream. "And I'm not sure 'eye candy' is the right term. There's something... off about him."

Elsie dug her spoon into the ice cream and took a bite, closing her eyes in obvious delight. "Mmm, this is divine," she murmured. Opening her eyes, she glanced back at Graham. "He's watching you, you know. Maybe he's interested in more than just the vanilla."

Lila rolled her eyes. "Don't start, Els. I'm not looking for a relationship, remember? Besides, he gives me a weird vibe. Too corporate, too..." she searched for the right word, "calculated."

"Your problem," Elsie said between spoonfuls, "is that you're too picky. When was the last time you went on a date? That disaster with the marine biologist last summer?"

"Oh, please don't remind me," Lila groaned, thinking back to the date that had ended with her date obsessively cataloging the various species of mollusks found along Seabreeze's coastline for three straight hours. "And I'm not picky. I'm just... selective."

Eva chuckled as she passed by. "That's what I used to say too, sweetie. And then I met your father and realized I'd been waiting for him all along." Her eyes misted over slightly at the mention of Jack Montgomery. Even after all these years, the wound of his loss remained fresh.

Lila squeezed her mother's hand briefly before turning her attention back to the shop. The lunch rush was beginning to pick up, with families fresh from the beach lining up for a cool treat. She pulled her hair back into a tighter ponytail and got to work, her movements fluid and practiced after years behind the counter.

Through the rush, she found her gaze repeatedly drawn to Graham Fox. He remained at his table, ice cream melting untouched, as he made several phone calls. His expression grew increasingly agitated, and at one point, he stood abruptly, as if ready to leave, only to sit back down and check his watch again.

By the time the rush ebbed, Elsie had taken up residence on a stool at the counter, chatting with customers and helping refill napkin dispensers—a voluntary role she'd assigned herself years ago as Lila's unofficial assistant.

"So," Elsie said, leaning across the counter after the last family had been served, "are you coming to the town meeting tonight? They're voting on the budget for the Seabreeze Festival."

Lila nodded, wiping down the counter. "Wouldn't miss it. I'm bringing samples of the new flavor I'm working on for the festival—blackberry mint. I want to get feedback before I commit to making gallons of it."

"Smart," Elsie replied. She lowered her voice, glancing toward Graham, who was now standing and gathering his things. "And it'll give us a chance to find out more about our mysterious visitor. I overheard Mira Douglas saying something about a meeting with a real estate developer this week. I bet that's him."

Lila frowned. Mira, who owned the charming Seabreeze Bed & Breakfast just up the street, was usually quite protective of the town's traditional character. If she was meeting with developers, it couldn't be good.

Graham Fox made his way to the door, pausing briefly to look back at Lila. Their eyes met, and he gave her a curt nod before exiting, the bell announcing his departure with a cheerful jingle that seemed at odds with the heavy atmosphere he left behind.

"Well, that was weird," Lila muttered, watching through the window as he strode purposefully down the boardwalk, phone pressed to his ear.

"Definitely weird," Elsie agreed. "But intriguing. Maybe he'll be at the meeting tonight."

The rest of the afternoon passed in a blur of scoops and smiles. As the sun began its descent toward the horizon, painting the sky in shades of orange and pink, Lila flipped the sign on the door to "Closed" and began the evening cleanup routine.

Eva had left hours earlier for her book club meeting, promising to see Lila at home for a late dinner. Elsie, true to form, had stayed to help, and was now carefully arranging the day's leftover ice cream into storage containers.

"Do you ever wonder what it would be like to leave Seabreeze Shores?" Elsie asked suddenly, breaking the comfortable silence that had settled between them. "Maybe open a shop in a big city, somewhere with actual nightlife?"

Lila paused, broom in hand, and considered the question. "Sometimes," she admitted. "After Dad died, I thought about selling the shop and starting fresh somewhere else. But this place..." she gestured around the ice cream parlor, with its weathered wooden floors and the faint smell of sugar and salt, "it's in my blood. I couldn't leave it behind."

Elsie nodded, understanding in her eyes. "I get it. This town might be small, but it's home."

They finished cleaning in companionable silence, and as Lila locked up the shop, the first stars were beginning to appear in the darkening sky. The boardwalk was quieter now, with just a few couples strolling hand in hand, enjoying the cool evening air.

"I need to stop by my place to change before the meeting," Elsie said, picking up her basket of now-wilted flowers. "Want me to swing by and pick you up at seven?"

"That'd be great," Lila replied, fishing her keys out of her apron pocket. "I need to get these ice cream samples ready anyway."

They parted ways at the corner of Main Street, Elsie heading toward her small cottage near the lighthouse, and Lila making her way to the modest two-bedroom house she shared with her mother, just a few blocks from the shop.

The sky had darkened considerably by the time Lila arrived home, and she was surprised to find the house empty. A note on the kitDabney counter explained that Eva had gone directly to the town hall from her book club to help set up for the meeting.

Lila showered quickly, changing into a fresh sundress—this one a pale yellow that complemented her sun-kissed skin—before heading to the kitDabney to pack up her ice cream samples. As she worked, she couldn't shake the unsettled feeling that had taken root when Graham Fox walked into her shop.

Something about his presence felt like a harbinger of change, and in a town as set in its ways as Seabreeze Shores, change was rarely welcomed. She made a mental note to ask Elliot Price if he knew anything about the developer's plans for the waterfront.

Just as she was placing the last sample container into a cooler, her phone rang. Lila glanced at the caller ID, expecting to see Elsie's name, but instead, an unfamiliar number flashed across the screen.

"Hello?" she answered, wedging the phone between her ear and shoulder as she continued packing.

"Is this Lila Montgomery?" a deep voice asked. It wasn't Graham Fox, but there was an official tone that made her pause.

"Yes, this is she. Who's calling?"

"This is Detective Marcus Cole with the Seabreeze Shores Police Department. I'm afraid there's been an incident behind your ice cream shop."

Lila's heart skipped a beat. "An incident? What kind of incident?"

There was a brief pause, and when the detective spoke again, his voice was grave. "A body was found in the alley behind your shop about twenty minutes ago. We need you to come down and answer some questions."

The cooler slipped from Lila's suddenly numb fingers, clattering to the floor. "A body? Who—"

"We're still working on a positive identification," Detective Cole cut in. "But preliminary evidence suggests it may be Graham Fox, a businessman who was seen in your shop earlier today."

Lila sank into a kitDabney chair, her legs no longer able to support her. "I... I don't understand. I just saw him a few hours ago. He was fine."

"Ms. Montgomery, I understand this is a shock, but we need you to come down to the scene as soon as possible. Your shop is currently part of an active investigation."

"I'll be right there," Lila managed to say, her voice barely above a whisper.

After hanging up, she sat motionless for several long moments, trying to process what she'd just heard. Graham Fox—dead? Behind her shop? It seemed impossible, yet the detective's serious tone left no room for doubt.

With trembling hands, she texted Elsie to meet her at the shop instead of picking her up, then grabbed her purse and headed out the door. The short walk to Salted Caramel's had never felt so long.

As she approached, Lila could see the flashing lights of police cars illuminating the darkened street. Yellow crime scene tape cordoned off the alley behind her shop, and a small crowd of curious onlookers had already gathered.

A tall man in a dark suit stepped forward as she approached, his expression unreadable in the harsh glare of the police lights.

"Ms. Montgomery? I'm Detective Marcus Cole. Thank you for coming."

Lila nodded numbly, taking in the scene before her. Several officers were moving around the alley, their flashlights cutting through the darkness. A white sheet covered what was unmistakably a body.

"Is that... is that really Graham Fox?" she asked, her voice barely audible.

Detective Cole's green eyes—almost hazel in this light—studied her face carefully. "We believe so. Can you confirm that Mr. Fox was in your shop today?"

"Yes, he came in around lunchtime," Lila replied, trying to keep her voice steady. "He ordered vanilla ice cream in a cup. He stayed for about an hour, but he barely touched it. He seemed distracted, kept looking out the window like he was waiting for someone."

The detective nodded, jotting down notes in a small black notebook. "Did he speak to anyone else while he was there?"

Lila shook her head. "No, he kept to himself. Made some phone calls, though. He seemed agitated."

"And what time did he leave?"

"Around two-thirty, I think. I didn't see which way he went after he left the shop."

Detective Cole's gaze was penetrating, as if he were trying to see beyond her words. "Did Mr. Fox say anything about why he was in Seabreeze Shores? Did he mention any business in town?"

"No, he didn't say much at all," Lila replied, wrapping her arms around herself against a sudden chill. "But there's been talk about developers looking at the waterfront. My mom mentioned that he might be connected to that."

The detective made another note before looking up at her again. "And where were you between the hours of three and five PM today, Ms. Montgomery?"

The question hit Lila like a bucket of ice water. "I was at the shop all day until closing at six. You can ask my friend Elsie Winters or any of the customers who came in. Are you... are you suggesting I had something to do with this?"

Before Detective Cole could respond, a commotion at the edge of the crowd caught their attention. Elsie was pushing her way through, her red curls wild and her face pale with worry. Behind her, Lila could see her mother rushing forward as well, concern etched on her face.

"Lila!" Elsie called out, ducking under the police tape despite an officer's protest. "What's happening? Your text scared me half to death!"

Detective Cole stepped forward, preventing Elsie from reaching Lila. "Ma'am, this is an active crime scene. I need you to step back."

"It's okay," Lila quickly interjected. "This is Elsie Winters, my friend. She was with me at the shop today. And that's my mother, Eva Montgomery, coming up behind her."

The detective's expression softened slightly, but he maintained his professional demeanor. "I understand your concern, but I need to ask Ms. Montgomery a few more questions. If you could please wait outside the perimeter..."

Elsie looked ready to argue, but Lila gave her a small nod. "It's okay, Els. I'll be right there."

As Elsie reluctantly stepped back, Detective Cole turned his attention back to Lila. "I'm not suggesting anything at this point, Ms. Montgomery. I'm simply gathering information. Did you notice anyone unusual hanging around your shop today, apart from Mr. Fox?"

Lila thought back through the busy day, trying to recall any faces that stood out. "No, just the usual mix of locals and tourists. It was a typical summer day."

"And the alley behind your shop—do you use it regularly?"

"Just to take out the trash at the end of the day, and for deliveries in the morning," Lila explained. "It's not really visible from inside the shop."

Detective Cole nodded, making one final note before closing his notebook. "Thank you for your cooperation, Ms. Montgomery. We'll need you to come by the station tomorrow morning to give a formal statement. In the meantime, your shop will remain closed as we process the scene."

The reality of the situation hit Lila with full force. Her ice cream shop—her livelihood and her legacy—was now a crime scene. And a man she'd served just hours ago was dead.

"How... how did he die?" she asked, unable to stop herself.

The detective hesitated, his expression guarded. "We're still determining the cause of death. The medical examiner is on the way."

But something in his eyes told Lila that he knew more than he was saying. A chill ran down her spine, and she suddenly felt very vulnerable standing in the shadow of her beloved shop.

As Detective Cole walked her back to where Elsie and Eva were waiting, a gust of wind swept through the alley, carrying with it the faint scent of vanilla. Lila couldn't help but look back at the sheet-covered form lying on the ground—a stark reminder that beneath Seabreeze Shores' picturesque façade, something dark and dangerous was lurking.

And somehow, she knew that her life and her beloved town would never be the same again.

Chapter 2
Suspicions and Secrets

The Seabreeze Diner had been serving the same blueberry pancakes since 1972, and according to the locals, not a single ingredient had changed in all that time. The worn vinyl booths, slightly sticky from decades of maple syrup, were filled with the usual morning crowd—fishermen grabbing a hearty breakfast before heading to their boats, retirees nursing cups of coffee while arguing over the daily crossword, and a few bleary-eyed tourists recovering from the previous night's beach bonfire.

Lila Montgomery sat in her usual corner booth, pushing a forkful of pancakes around her plate. She hadn't slept more than an hour or two. Every time she closed her eyes, she saw Graham Fox's body lying in the alley behind her shop, covered by that stark white sheet. The image wouldn't leave her, no matter how hard she tried to focus on something else.

"You haven't touched your food, honey," said Maggie Wilson, the diner's longtime waitress, as she stopped to refill Lila's coffee. Her gray hair was pulled back in a tight bun, and her eyes, lined with decades of laughter and worry, studied Lila with concern. "Still thinking about what happened yesterday?"

Lila nodded, taking a sip of the freshly poured coffee. It was strong and bitter, exactly what she needed. "It's not every day you find out someone was killed behind your business, Maggie."

"Killed?" Maggie's voice dropped to a whisper, and she leaned in closer. "The news said it was an accident—that he slipped and hit his head."

"That's what they're telling everyone," Lila murmured, careful to keep her voice low. Detective Cole had been vague about the cause of death, but something in his expression had told her it was no accident. "But I'm not so sure."

Before Maggie could respond, the bell above the diner's door jingled, and a hush fell over the room. Lila looked up to see two men entering—Elliot Price, the local fisherman whose family had worked Seabreeze's waters for generations, and Sheriff Sam Jennings, the town's longtime law enforcement official. Both men paused just inside the entrance, their eyes scanning the diner until they spotted Lila.

Elliot made his way over first, his weathered face set in a grim expression. At forty-five, he looked older than his years, his skin tanned and creased from decades under the sun, his dark hair streaked with premature gray. He wore his usual attire—faded jeans, a flannel shirt with the sleeves rolled up to reveal muscular forearms, and well-worn boots that had seen better days.

"Morning, Lila," he said, sliding into the booth across from her without waiting for an invitation. His voice was rough, like he'd spent the night shouting into the wind. "Heard about what happened at your shop. Terrible business."

Sheriff Jennings approached more slowly, tipping his hat to several patrons as he passed. Unlike Elliot, the sheriff was clean-shaven and meticulously groomed, his uniform pressed and his badge polished to a high shine. Despite being in his early fifties, he moved with the confidence of a much younger man.

"Mind if I join you folks?" he asked, though he was already pulling up a chair to the end of the booth.

"Of course not, Sheriff," Lila replied, setting down her coffee cup. "Though I'm not sure what else I can tell you that I didn't tell Detective Cole last night."

Sheriff Jennings offered a tight smile. "Actually, I came to share information, not ask for it. Thought you might want to know that the medical examiner confirmed the identity of the deceased. It was indeed Graham Fox, a real estate developer from the city."

"City folk," Elliot muttered, shaking his head. "Coming down here thinking they can just buy up our town and turn it into another overpriced tourist trap."

Lila's gaze shifted between the two men. "So it's true then? Fox was here to buy property?"

Sheriff Jennings nodded. "From what we've been able to gather, he represented a development company called Coastal Ventures. They've been eyeing the waterfront for some time now, looking to build a resort complex."

"A resort?" Lila echoed, her stomach twisting at the thought. "But that would mean—"

"It would mean the end of our fishing community," Elliot cut in, his voice rising enough to draw glances from nearby tables. "They've been pressuring all of us who own property along the water. Offering cash deals, talking about how much 'potential' the area has, as if we haven't been making our living there for generations."

Sheriff Jennings held up a placating hand. "Now, Elliot, no need to get worked up. Nothing's been decided yet, and with Fox's unfortunate passing, those plans might be on hold."

"Unfortunate?" Elliot scoffed. "Not from where I'm sitting. Man was a vulture, circling our town and waiting for someone to show weakness."

A chill ran down Lila's spine at Elliot's words. She'd known the fisherman all her life—he'd been her father's friend and had taught her how to cast a line when she was just a girl—but she'd never heard such bitterness in his voice before. Could his resentment toward Fox have run deeper than she realized?

"Elliot," she said carefully, "you didn't happen to see Fox yesterday, did you? After he left my shop?"

The fisherman's dark eyes narrowed. "What are you asking, Lila? You think I had something to do with what happened to him?"

"No, of course not," she backpedaled quickly. "I'm just trying to understand what happened."

Sheriff Jennings cleared his throat. "Speaking of which, the cause of death hasn't been officially determined yet. The detective handling the case wants to be thorough."

"Detective Cole," Lila supplied, unable to keep a slight edge from her voice. "He seemed quite... intense."

"Marcus Cole is one of the best," Sheriff Jennings said with a nod. "Transferred to our department from the city about six months ago. Wanted a quieter life, I guess, though this case might make him reconsider that decision."

The bell above the door jingled again, and as if summoned by their conversation, Detective Marcus Cole strode into the diner. He was even more imposing in the daylight than he had been the night before. Tall and broad-shouldered, he moved with the confident grace of a predator, his gaze sharp and assessing as it swept across the room. He wore a charcoal gray suit that fit his athletic frame perfectly, and a tie the color of stormy seas. His dark hair was neatly combed, though a single rebellious strand fell across his forehead, somehow making him look both professional and slightly disheveled at the same time.

The moment his green eyes landed on Lila, he made a beeline for their table.

"Ms. Montgomery," he said by way of greeting, his deep voice carrying an authority that seemed to quiet the entire diner. "I was hoping to find you here. I need to ask you a few more questions about yesterday."

Lila's heart skipped a beat, though whether from nervousness or something else entirely, she couldn't quite say. "Detective Cole. I was just about to head to the station, as you requested."

"Plans have changed. I'd like to speak with you at your shop, if you don't mind." His gaze shifted to the other two men at the table. "Sheriff. Mr. Price."

Sheriff Jennings stood, smoothing down his uniform. "Detective. I was just filling Ms. Montgomery in on what we know about Fox's identity and purpose in town."

"I see," Detective Cole replied, his expression unreadable. "I'd appreciate it if you'd let me handle the investigation from here, Sheriff. No offense intended, but this case requires a certain approach."

An awkward tension settled over the table. Sheriff Jennings' smile became strained, and Elliot looked between the two law enforcement officers with undisguised interest.

"No offense taken," Sheriff Jennings said finally, though his tone suggested otherwise. "I'll let you get on with it then." He tipped his hat to Lila. "You take care now, Lila. Don't let this business get you down."

As the sheriff walked away, Detective Cole turned his attention to Elliot. "Mr. Price, I understand you had some interactions with Mr. Fox regarding your waterfront property."

Elliot's jaw tightened. "Nothing unusual. He made an offer, I turned it down. End of story."

"And when was this?"

"Two days ago. He came by my boat, tried to charm me with talk of 'fair market value' and 'once-in-a-lifetime opportunities.' I told him my family's livelihood wasn't for sale at any price."

Detective Cole nodded, making a mental note. "And where were you yesterday afternoon, between three and six PM?"

Elliot's eyes flashed with indignation. "Out on my boat, like I am every afternoon. Ask any of the men at the dock—they'll vouch for me."

"I'll be sure to do that," Detective Cole replied evenly. He turned back to Lila. "If you're finished with your breakfast, Ms. Montgomery, we should get going. There's a lot of ground to cover."

Lila glanced down at her barely touched pancakes and nodded. She left enough cash on the table to cover her meal plus a generous tip for Maggie, then slid out of the booth. As she stood, she found herself much closer to Detective Cole than she'd anticipated. Up close, she could see the fine lines around his eyes—signs of someone who squinted into the sun, or perhaps frowned too often—and catch the faint scent of his cologne, something woody and subtle.

"After you," he said, gesturing toward the door.

As they stepped outside into the bright morning sunshine, Lila was acutely aware of the eyes following them from inside the diner. In Seabreeze Shores, news traveled faster than the tides, and by noon, everyone would know that Lila Montgomery was being escorted to her shop by the handsome detective investigating a suspicious death.

"You didn't eat much," Detective Cole observed as they walked down Main Street toward Salted Caramel's.

The comment surprised her. "I didn't think detectives noticed things like that."

"Detectives notice everything, Ms. Montgomery. It's part of the job." There was a hint of something in his voice—not quite warmth, but not the clinical detachment he'd shown the night before. "And lack of appetite is common after experiencing a traumatic event."

"Is that what this is? Trauma?" Lila asked, watching a seagull swoop low over a nearby trash can. "I didn't even know the man."

"You don't need to know someone for their death to affect you. Especially when it happens in a place you consider safe."

They walked in silence for a moment, the sounds of the waking town surrounding them—shopkeepers raising their awnings, car doors slamming as people arrived for work, the distant crash of waves against the shore.

"The crime scene team finished processing the alley early this morning," Detective Cole said as they approached Salted Caramel's. The yellow police tape was gone, but the shop remained closed, its cheerful blue awning providing shade to darkened windows. "You'll be able to reopen tomorrow, if you wish."

"Thank you," Lila said, fishing her keys from her purse. "Though I'm not sure how many customers will want ice cream from a shop where someone was just killed."

"You'd be surprised," Detective Cole replied dryly. "Some people are drawn to the macabre."

As Lila unlocked the front door, she was struck by how different the shop felt. The familiar space—with its blue and cream color scheme, the vintage photos on the walls, the gleaming display case—now seemed somehow tainted, as if Graham Fox's death had cast a shadow over everything she held dear.

Detective Cole followed her inside, his eyes scanning the shop with practiced efficiency. "Can you show me exactly where Mr. Fox sat while he was here?"

Lila pointed to the small table by the window. "There. He stayed for about an hour, hardly touched his ice cream. He seemed distracted, kept looking out the window and checking his phone."

"Was he meeting someone?"

"Not that I could tell. But he definitely seemed to be waiting for something or someone."

Detective Cole walked to the table and looked out the window, taking in the view of the boardwalk and, beyond it, the ocean. "Good vantage point," he murmured, almost to himself. "You can see most of Main Street from here."

He turned back to Lila. "Did Mr. Fox receive any letters or packages while he was here?"

The question caught her off guard. "Letters? No, I don't think so. Why?"

Instead of answering, Detective Cole moved to the counter. "According to your statement last night, Mr. Fox paid with a card. Do you keep copies of receipts?"

Lila nodded, moving behind the counter to her old-fashioned register. She pulled out a drawer and rifled through the receipts from the previous day. "Here," she said, handing one to Detective Cole. "It's not much, just shows he bought a single scoop of vanilla for $3.50 at 12:23 PM."

The detective studied the receipt, his brow furrowing. "Did you notice anything unusual about his credit card?"

"No, it looked like a standard card. Black, probably platinum or some high-end variety. Why? Is that important?"

"Everything is important at this stage," he replied, returning the receipt to her. "Now, can you show me the route you would take to dispose of trash in the alley?"

Lila led him through the shop to the back door, which opened into the alley where Graham Fox's body had been found. In the harsh light of day, the alley looked remarkably ordinary—just a narrow passage between buildings, lined with dumpsters and the occasional delivery entrance. The only sign that anything untoward had occurred was a faint dark stain on the asphalt, which Lila tried very hard not to look at.

"I usually take the trash out at closing," she explained, keeping her voice steady. "Around six or six-thirty, depending on how busy we've been."

"And did you take the trash out last night?"

"No, I was running late for the town meeting. I was planning to do it this morning."

Detective Cole nodded, making another mental note. "One more thing. After Mr. Fox left your shop, did you notice anyone else behaving unusually? Anyone watching the shop, or perhaps asking about him?"

Lila thought back to the busy afternoon. "Not that I recall. It was a typical summer day—lots of tourists, a few regulars. Nothing stood out."

"What about your friend, Elsie Winters? She was here yesterday, correct?"

"Yes, she came by for lunch. She stayed for about an hour, helping out a bit as she usually does."

"And what time did she leave?"

"Around three, I think. She had to get back to her shop." Elsie ran a small boutique on the other side of town, selling handmade jewelry and local artwork. "Why are you asking about Elsie?"

Detective Cole's expression remained neutral. "Just establishing a timeline, Ms. Montgomery. Everyone who interacted with the victim in his final hours is of interest to the investigation."

A chill ran down Lila's spine. "You don't think Elsie had anything to do with this, do you? That's absurd. She's my best friend."

"I'm not suggesting anything of the sort," Detective Cole replied, his tone softening slightly. "But in my experience, it's often the people closest to us who hold the most secrets."

Before Lila could respond, the front door of the shop opened with a jingle. Both of them turned to see a woman standing in the entrance—Mira Douglas, owner of the Seabreeze Bed & Breakfast. In her early forties, Mira was strikingly beautiful, with dark hair swept up in an elegant twist and a cream-colored sundress that highlighted her tanned skin. She carried herself with the poise of someone accustomed to being observed, but today, her usual confidence seemed diminished, her eyes red-rimmed as if she'd been crying.

"Lila, darling," she called out, her voice carrying a slight tremor. "I just heard about what happened. Are you alright?" Her gaze shifted to Detective Cole, and something flickered across her face—recognition, perhaps, or concern. "I'm sorry, I didn't realize you had company."

"It's fine, Mira," Lila replied, moving back toward the front of the shop. "This is Detective Marcus Cole. He's investigating what happened to Graham Fox."

At the mention of Fox's name, Mira's composure faltered. She reached out to steady herself against a nearby table. "Yes, I... I heard. It's just awful. I can't believe he's gone."

Detective Cole's attention was now fully focused on Mira. "You knew Mr. Fox, Ms. Douglas?"

Mira seemed to gather herself, straightening her spine and lifting her chin. "Yes, we were... acquainted. He was staying at my B&B during his visit to Seabreeze Shores."

"I see," Detective Cole said, his tone perfectly neutral even as his gaze intensified. "In that case, I'd like to ask you a few questions as well. Would you mind coming down to the station later today?"

"The station?" Mira echoed, a hint of panic creeping into her voice. "Is that really necessary? I mean, I hardly knew the man. He was just a guest."

"Standard procedure," Detective Cole assured her. "We're speaking with everyone who had contact with Mr. Fox in the days leading up to his death."

Mira nodded stiffly. "Of course. Whatever I can do to help."

"Excellent. Shall we say two o'clock?"

"That should be fine. I'll have my assistant cover the front desk." Mira turned to Lila, her smile not quite reaching her eyes. "I just wanted to check on you, dear. It must have been such a shock, finding him like that."

"I didn't actually find him," Lila clarified. "Someone else did. But yes, it's been... unsettling."

Mira reached out and squeezed Lila's hand. "If you need anything at all, you just let me know. We have to stick together in times like these." With a final nod to Detective Cole, she turned and left the shop, the bell jingling in her wake.

As the door closed behind her, Detective Cole turned to Lila with a raised eyebrow. "You mentioned earlier that your mother thought Mr. Fox might be connected to the waterfront development. Did Ms. Douglas ever mention anything about this to you?"

Lila shook her head. "No, but Mira keeps to herself when it comes to business matters. She's protective of the B&B—it's been in her family for three generations."

"Interesting," Detective Cole murmured. "She seemed quite affected by Mr. Fox's death for someone who 'hardly knew the man.'"

Lila hadn't missed that either. Mira's reaction had seemed disproportionate for a mere business acquaintance. "Maybe there was more to their relationship than she's letting on."

"Maybe indeed." Detective Cole checked his watch, a simple but elegant timepiece with a leather strap. "I should get going. I have several more interviews to conduct today." He reached into his jacket pocket and produced a business card, which he handed to Lila. "If you think of anything else, anything at all, call me directly. Even if it seems insignificant."

Lila took the card, noting the direct line and cell phone number written on the back in a neat, precise hand. "I will."

As Detective Cole headed for the door, he paused and turned back. "One more thing, Ms. Montgomery. You mentioned a letter addressed to Mira Douglas that you found yesterday. What happened to it?"

Lila blinked in surprise. She hadn't expected him to circle back to that detail. "I, um... I gave it to Elsie to deliver to Mira. Her shop is closer to the B&B than mine is."

"I see. And what did this letter look like? Anything distinctive about it?"

"It was in a plain white envelope, but there was a strange symbol on the seal—a sort of stylized wave or shell design. I thought it might be from the development company."

Detective Cole nodded, his expression thoughtful. "Thank you for your cooperation, Ms. Montgomery. I'll be in touch."

As he left, Lila couldn't help but watch him through the window as he strode purposefully down the boardwalk. There was something about Detective Marcus Cole that both unsettled and intrigued her. He had a presence that filled the room, an intensity in his gaze that made her feel simultaneously exposed and protected.

She glanced down at his business card in her hand, turning it over to see his handwritten numbers. The gesture seemed oddly personal for a man who otherwise maintained such professional distance. She tucked the card into her pocket, trying to ignore the fluttery feeling in her stomach.

With a sigh, Lila began the process of checking her inventory and preparing to reopen the shop the next day. As she worked, her mind kept returning to Graham Fox and the circumstances of his death. What had the developer been doing in Seabreeze Shores? Who had wanted him dead? And why leave his body behind her shop, of all places?

The questions swirled in her mind like storm clouds gathering on the horizon. Something told her that Graham Fox's death was just the beginning, that his presence in their peaceful town had stirred up secrets long buried beneath Seabreeze's tranquil surface.

As she was counting ice cream containers in the walk-in freezer, her phone buzzed with a text message from Elsie:

"We need to talk. Meet me at the lighthouse at sunset. I found something in that letter you gave me. Something bad."

Lila stared at the cryptic message, a chill running down her spine despite the freezer's cold. Whatever Elsie had discovered, it couldn't be good. And somehow, Lila knew that by meeting her friend at the lighthouse, she would be taking her first step down a path from which there would be no turning back.

With trembling fingers, she typed a reply: "I'll be there."

Then she closed the freezer door and tried to shake off the feeling that someone was watching her, waiting to see what she would do next in this dangerous game she didn't even know she was playing.

Chapter 3
The First Clue

Seabreeze Shores took on a different character at sunset. As the sky transformed into a canvas of orange, pink, and deepening purple, the tourists retreated from the beaches, and the locals emerged to reclaim their town. Fishing boats returned to harbor, their decks laden with the day's catch. Couples strolled along the boardwalk, hands entwined, while musicians set up for evening performances on the small stage near the pier.

Lila Montgomery walked briskly toward the lighthouse, her sandals slapping against the weathered wooden boards of the boardwalk. The historic lighthouse stood on a rocky outcropping at the northern edge of town, its white tower gleaming in the last golden rays of sunlight. Built in 1893, it had guided countless ships safely to shore and had become the unofficial symbol of Seabreeze Shores, appearing on everything from postcards to the town's official letterhead.

As she approached the narrow path that led up to the lighthouse, Lila couldn't shake the feeling of unease that had settled in her stomach since receiving Elsie's text. The cryptic message had occupied her thoughts all afternoon as she'd prepared her shop for reopening. What could Elsie have found in that letter that was so important—and so troubling—that they needed to meet in secret?

The lighthouse keeper's cottage sat at the base of the tower, a small, whitewashed building with blue shutters and a red door. It had been converted into a museum decades ago, showcasing the maritime history of Seabreeze Shores. Lila spotted Elsie sitting on a bench outside the cottage, her red curls blowing wildly in the sea breeze. She was wearing a flowing green sundress that matched her eyes, and she clutched her woven bag tightly in her lap, her knuckles white with tension.

"Elsie," Lila called out as she approached. "What's going on? Your message had me worried."

Elsie looked up, her normally cheerful face drawn with concern. "Lila, thank goodness. I've been going crazy waiting for you." She glanced around nervously, as if checking to make sure they were alone. "Let's walk up to the observation deck. I don't want anyone overhearing this."

Without waiting for a response, Elsie stood and headed toward the lighthouse entrance. Lila followed, her concern deepening at her friend's unusual behavior. Elsie was typically the epitome of bubbly optimism—to see her so agitated was alarming.

They climbed the spiral staircase in silence, their footsteps echoing against the stone walls. The lighthouse was officially closed for the day, but as a town council member, Elsie had a key. By the time they reached the observation deck, 128 steps later, Lila was slightly out of breath, and her mind was racing with possibilities.

The circular deck offered a panoramic view of Seabreeze Shores. From this height, the town looked like a picture postcard—quaint buildings with colorful awnings nestled between the deep blue of the ocean and the lush green of the hills beyond. In the fading light, Lila could make out her shop on Main Street, the town hall with its distinctive clock tower, and the marina where Elliot Price's fishing boat was now docked.

"Okay, we're alone," Lila said, turning to face her friend. "What's this all about? What did you find in that letter?"

Elsie reached into her bag and pulled out a white envelope—the same one Lila had given her the day before. The stylized shell or wave design on the seal was even more distinctive than Lila remembered. "I didn't deliver it," Elsie admitted. "After everything that happened with Graham Fox, I got curious. And worried. So I... well, I opened it."

"You opened someone else's mail?" Lila asked, unable to keep the surprise from her voice. Elsie had always been impulsive, but this seemed out of character even for her.

"I know, I know," Elsie said, waving away the concern. "Probably illegal, definitely immoral. But Lila, I'm glad I did." She pulled a folded document from the envelope. "This isn't just a letter. It's a contract. A property transfer agreement between Coastal Ventures—that's Fox's company—and Mira Douglas. She was selling the B&B to them."

"What?" Lila took the document, scanning its contents with growing disbelief. "But that doesn't make any sense. The B&B has been in Mira's family for generations. She's always said she'd never sell, no matter the price."

"Exactly," Elsie said, pointing to a figure near the bottom of the page. "And look at the amount they were offering—two million dollars. That's at least twice what the property is worth."

Lila whistled softly. "That's a lot of money. But why would they overpay by so much?"

"That's what I wondered," Elsie replied, pulling out another document from her bag. "So I did some digging at the town records office. The B&B isn't just any property—it sits on a plot of land that used to be the old harbor master's office in the 1800s. According to these records, there's a clause in the original deed that gives the owner certain rights to the adjacent waterfront."

Lila's eyes widened as the implications became clear. "So if Coastal Ventures owned the B&B..."

"They'd have leverage to push through their development plans for the entire waterfront," Elsie finished, nodding grimly. "Even if Elliot and the other property owners refused to sell."

"This is big, Els," Lila said, handing the documents back to her friend. "We need to tell someone. Detective Cole—"

"No!" Elsie interjected forcefully. "Not yet. There's more to this, Lila. Look at the signature page."

Lila flipped to the last page of the contract. Graham Fox's signature was there, along with the date—just three days ago. But where Mira's signature should have been, there was only a blank line.

"She hadn't signed it yet," Lila murmured.

"Exactly. Which means Fox might have been pressuring her, or maybe she was having second thoughts." Elsie lowered her voice, even though they were alone on the observation deck. "Don't you see? This gives Mira a motive. If she didn't want to sell but felt cornered..."

Lila shook her head, unwilling to jump to conclusions. "That's a big leap, Els. Just because she hadn't signed doesn't mean she killed him."

"Maybe not," Elsie conceded. "But it's suspicious, especially given how upset she was at the shop today. You said she seemed more affected by his death than a mere business acquaintance would be."

Lila couldn't argue with that. Mira's reaction had been notably intense. But was it grief or guilt that had caused those tears? Or something else entirely?

Before she could voice these thoughts, a noise from the staircase caught their attention—the unmistakable sound of footsteps climbing toward them. Elsie hastily shoved the documents back into her bag just as a familiar figure emerged onto the observation deck.

Frank Mitchell, owner of the general store on Main Street, paused at the top of the stairs, looking as surprised to see them as they were to see him. Frank was in his sixties, with a barrel chest and a shock of white hair that seemed perpetually windblown. His ruddy face suggested a lifetime spent outdoors, and the calluses on his hands spoke of hard work and self-reliance.

"Evening, ladies," he said, tipping his worn baseball cap. "Didn't expect to find anyone up here this time of day."

"Frank," Lila replied, forcing a casual tone. "What brings you to the lighthouse?"

The older man shrugged, his weathered face breaking into a smile that didn't quite reach his eyes. "Just watching the sunset. Best view in town up here." He moved to the railing, looking out over the town he'd called home his entire life. "Heard about what happened at your shop, Lila. Terrible business. How are you holding up?"

"As well as can be expected," Lila said, exchanging a quick glance with Elsie. Something about Frank's sudden appearance felt off, though she couldn't put her finger on why. "It's been a shock."

Frank nodded sympathetically. "Town's been buzzing with talk about it all day. Some folks saying it wasn't an accident—that someone might have wanted that developer out of the picture." He turned to face them, his expression unreadable in the deepening twilight. "What do you think? You talked to the man, didn't you?"

The directness of the question caught Lila off guard. "I didn't know him, Frank. He was just a customer."

"Hmm." Frank seemed to consider this, his gaze shifting between Lila and Elsie. "Well, whatever happened, I hope they figure it out soon. Don't need that kind of cloud hanging over our town during tourist season."

An awkward silence settled over the observation deck. Frank continued to watch the horizon, though Lila had the distinct impression that his attention remained fixed on them. After a few uncomfortable moments, Elsie spoke up.

"Well, we should probably head back down," she said, tugging gently on Lila's arm. "Getting dark, and I've got to open the shop early tomorrow."

Frank nodded but made no move to leave himself. "You girls be careful. Strange things happening in town these days."

As they descended the spiral staircase, neither Lila nor Elsie spoke until they were well away from the lighthouse, walking along the darkening beach toward town.

"That was weird, right?" Elsie whispered. "Frank showing up like that?"

Lila nodded, glancing back toward the lighthouse. Frank Mitchell had always been a fixture in Seabreeze Shores, his general store the go-to place for everything from fishing tackle to emergency groceries. He knew everyone in town and their business—sometimes before they knew it themselves. But his appearance at the lighthouse had felt too convenient, too coincidental.

"Do you think he overheard us?" Lila asked.

"I don't know," Elsie replied. "But I'm starting to think we need to be more careful about who we trust."

They walked in silence for a few minutes, the soft sand crunching beneath their feet. The beach was nearly deserted now, with just a few die-hard surfers catching the last waves of the day.

"What should we do with the information about the contract?" Lila finally asked.

Elsie sighed, adjusting her bag on her shoulder. "I still think we should investigate more before going to the police. If Mira is involved, she might have allies we don't know about."

"Like who? Frank?"

"Maybe. Or Sheriff Jennings. He and Mira have always been close."

Lila considered this. The connections in Seabreeze Shores ran deep, with friendships and rivalries spanning generations. If Mira was involved in Graham Fox's death, and if she had powerful friends in town, going directly to the authorities might complicate matters.

"Let's sleep on it," Lila suggested. "Tomorrow, I'll reopen the shop and keep my ears open. People talk when they're comfortable, and there's nothing that makes people more comfortable than ice cream."

Elsie smiled for the first time since they'd met at the lighthouse. "Your dad used to say that. 'Ice cream loosens lips faster than liquor,' he'd tell us."

"And at a much earlier hour," Lila added with a laugh. The memory of her father—his booming voice, his calloused hands, the way his eyes crinkled when he smiled—brought a bittersweet ache to her chest. He'd been gone for five years now, but sometimes the loss still felt as fresh as yesterday.

They reached the end of the beach, where a set of wooden stairs led up to the boardwalk. As they climbed, Lila noticed a familiar figure leaning against the railing, looking out at the darkened ocean—Detective Marcus Cole.

He turned at the sound of their approach, his expression unreadable in the dim light cast by the boardwalk lamps. He wore the same suit as earlier, though his tie was now loosened, and that rebellious strand of hair still fell across his forehead, softening his otherwise austere appearance.

"Ms. Montgomery. Ms. Winters," he greeted them, his deep voice carrying in the quiet evening air. "Enjoying an evening stroll?"

"Detective Cole," Lila replied, trying to keep her voice neutral despite the spike of adrenaline that shot through her at his unexpected appearance. "What brings you to the boardwalk at this hour?"

"Same as you, I imagine. Trying to clear my head." His gaze shifted to Elsie, who clutched her bag more tightly. "Ms. Winters, I've been meaning to speak with you. I understand you were at Salted Caramel's the day Graham Fox visited."

Elsie nodded, her knuckles white around the strap of her bag. "That's right. I had lunch there, like I do most days."

"Did you interact with Mr. Fox at all?"

"No," Elsie said, a bit too quickly. "I mean, I saw him sitting by the window, but we didn't speak. I was at the counter with Lila the whole time."

Detective Cole studied her for a moment, his green eyes reflecting the gentle glow of the boardwalk lights. "I see. And where were you between three and six PM yesterday?"

Elsie stiffened beside Lila. "At my shop. The Salty Mermaid Boutique, on Harbor Street. I was there until closing at six, then I went home to change before the town meeting."

"Can anyone vouch for your presence at the shop during those hours?"

"I had customers in and out all afternoon," Elsie replied, her voice tight. "And my assistant, Jenny, was there until five."

Detective Cole nodded, making a mental note. "Thank you. I'll be following up with her to confirm."

The implication—that he needed to verify Elsie's alibi—hung in the air between them. Lila felt a surge of protectiveness toward her friend. "Elsie had nothing to do with what happened to Graham Fox," she said firmly.

"I'm not suggesting she did, Ms. Montgomery," Detective Cole replied, his tone softening slightly. "But I have to follow every lead, question every person who might have information. That's how investigations work."

Lila wanted to argue further, but something in his expression stopped her. Despite his professional demeanor, there was a weariness in his eyes that suggested the weight of the case was already taking its toll.

"Of course," she conceded. "We all want to find out what happened."

"Indeed." His gaze shifted between the two women, lingering on Elsie's bag before returning to Lila's face. "Have either of you remembered anything else that might be relevant to the investigation? Any detail, no matter how small?"

The contract in Elsie's bag felt like a physical presence between them, its implications burning in Lila's mind. She should tell him, she knew. Withholding evidence was probably a crime. But Elsie's earlier warnings echoed in her thoughts. What if Mira did have powerful allies in town? What if sharing this information now, before they understood its full context, did more harm than good?

"Nothing specific," Lila said finally, the lie tasting bitter on her tongue. "But if we think of anything, you'll be the first to know."

Detective Cole held her gaze for a moment longer than necessary, and Lila had the unsettling feeling that he could see right through her deception. But he merely nodded and pushed himself away from the railing.

"I appreciate that," he said. "Good evening, ladies."

As he walked away, his tall figure soon swallowed by the deepening darkness of the boardwalk, Elsie let out a shaky breath. "He knows something," she whispered. "Did you see how he looked at my bag? It's like he knew exactly what was in it."

"That's just his way," Lila replied, though she wasn't entirely convinced. "He's a detective. They're trained to be observant."

"Maybe," Elsie conceded. "But I still think we should keep this between us for now, at least until we have more information."

Lila nodded reluctantly. "Alright. But we need to be careful, Els. If Graham Fox was murdered, we could be putting ourselves in danger by investigating on our own."

"I know," Elsie said, her voice small. "But what choice do we have? Seabreeze Shores is our home. If someone's trying to take advantage of that—or worse, if someone in town is a killer—we need to know."

They parted ways at the corner of Main Street and Harbor, with Elsie heading toward her small cottage near the marina, and Lila continuing on to the two-bedroom bungalow she shared with her mother. As she walked, Lila couldn't shake the feeling that she was being watched, that eyes followed her progress through the darkened streets of the town she'd known all her life.

The bungalow was dark when she arrived, save for a single lamp glowing in the living room. Her mother must have already gone to bed, exhausted from the emotional toll of the past day. Lila moved quietly through the house, navigating by memory more than sight, until she reached the sanctuary of her bedroom.

Only after she'd closed the door did she allow herself to exhale fully. She kicked off her sandals and sank onto the edge of her bed, her mind whirling with everything she'd learned. The contract in Mira's letter, Frank's suspicious appearance at the lighthouse, Detective Cole's penetrating gaze—it was all too much to process.

Almost without thinking, she reached for the business card Detective Cole had given her earlier, running her fingers over the embossed letters of his name and the handwritten numbers on the back. There was something reassuring about his directness, his unwavering focus on finding the truth. But there was also something intimidating about it—the sense that nothing would escape his notice, including her own deceptions.

A soft sound from outside her window startled her from her thoughts. Lila rose and moved to the window, peering out into the moonlit yard. Nothing seemed amiss, just the familiar outline of her mother's garden and, beyond it, the silhouette of the old oak tree that had stood sentinel over their home for decades.

As she was about to turn away, something caught her eye—a flash of movement near the garden gate. She strained to see in the darkness, but whatever it was had vanished. A cat, perhaps, or a late-night wanderer taking a shortcut through their yard.

Still, the moment left her unsettled. Lila crossed to her bedroom door and checked the lock, something she rarely did in the safety of Seabreeze Shores. Then, on second thought, she moved to her dresser and pulled out the small notebook she used for developing new ice cream recipes. Flipping to a blank page, she began to write down everything she knew about Graham Fox, Mira Douglas, and the waterfront development plans.

If she and Elsie were going to investigate this on their own, they needed to be organized. Methodical. They needed to approach it like Detective Cole would—with careful attention to detail and a commitment to finding the truth, no matter where it led.

As she wrote, a plan began to form in her mind. Tomorrow, she would reopen Salted Caramel's and, as she'd told Elsie, keep her ears open for gossip. But she would also make a point of visiting key locations around town—the marina where Elliot Price docked his boat, the general store owned by Frank Mitchell, and perhaps even the B&B run by Mira Douglas. She would observe, ask casual questions, and piece together a clearer picture of the connections between these people and Graham Fox.

It was nearly midnight when Lila finally set down her pen, several pages filled with notes and questions. She changed into her pajamas—a soft cotton tank top and shorts—and was about to turn out the light when her phone buzzed with an incoming text.

Unknown Number: Be careful who you trust, Ms. Montgomery. Not everything in Seabreeze Shores is as sweet as it seems.

Lila stared at the message, a chill running down her spine despite the warm summer night. She didn't recognize the number, and there was no signature. It could be anyone—Detective Cole warning her about her own investigation, Mira or Frank having somehow overheard her conversation with Elsie, or even the killer, watching her movements and sending a warning.

With trembling fingers, she deleted the message and set her phone on the nightstand. Tomorrow, she would begin her investigation in earnest. But tonight, sleep would be a long time coming, as the shadows in her room seemed to deepen and shift with each passing moment, harboring secrets she could only begin to imagine.

The alley behind Salted Caramel's looked different in the harsh light of morning. Lila arrived early, well before her usual opening time, determined to search the area where Graham Fox's body had been found. Detective Cole and his team had already processed the scene, but Lila couldn't shake the feeling that they might have missed something—something that only a local, someone intimately familiar with the shop and its surroundings, would notice.

She unlocked the back door and set down her bag inside before stepping into the alley. The morning air was crisp, carrying the scent of salt and seaweed from the nearby harbor. Gulls circled overhead, their cries echoing off the buildings that lined the narrow passage.

The dark stain on the asphalt where Graham's body had lain was still visible, though someone had made an attempt to clean it. Lila forced herself to look at it, to acknowledge the reality of what had happened here. A man had died—possibly been murdered—right outside her beloved shop. The thought made her stomach clench, but she pushed through the discomfort, focusing instead on the task at hand.

She began a systematic search of the alley, starting from the spot where the body had been found and working outward in concentric circles. Most of the debris was typical of a commercial alley—cigarette butts, candy wrappers, a few discarded receipts from neighboring businesses. Nothing stood out as unusual or connected to Graham Fox.

As she was about to give up, something caught her eye—a small, rectangular object partially hidden beneath a dumpster. Lila crouched down and reached for it, her fingers closing around what turned out to be a small leather notebook, its edges worn and softened with use.

Heart pounding, she flipped it open. The first few pages contained what appeared to be business notes—figures, initials, and brief annotations that meant little to her. But as she continued turning pages, she found a hand-drawn map of Seabreeze Shores' waterfront, with several properties marked with X's and annotations.

The B&B was circled in red, with the notation "Priority acquisition—leverage clause in deed." Elliot Price's property was marked with "Resistant—apply pressure through marina access?" And there, near the edge of the map, was her own shop, Salted Caramel's, with the cryptic note: "Secondary target—historical significance?"

Lila frowned. Historical significance? The shop had been in her family for two generations, but it was hardly a historical landmark. What could Graham Fox have meant by that?

A noise at the entrance to the alley startled her. Lila quickly tucked the notebook into her pocket and stood, brushing off her hands on her sundress. She turned to find Detective Marcus Cole watching her, his expression a mixture of curiosity and suspicion.

"Ms. Montgomery," he said, approaching with measured steps. "You're here early."

"I wanted to get the shop ready for reopening," she replied, trying to keep her voice steady despite the damning evidence now burning a hole in her pocket. "It's been closed for two days. There's a lot to do."

Detective Cole glanced around the alley, his gaze lingering on the area where she'd been crouching. "And that preparation involves searching the alley where a man was found dead?"

Lila felt her cheeks flush. "I was just... I wanted to make sure the area was clean before customers started coming around." The lie sounded weak even to her own ears.

"I see." Detective Cole moved closer, his tall figure casting a shadow over her in the morning light. "Find anything interesting?"

The notebook felt like a brick in her pocket. She should give it to him. It was evidence, potentially crucial to his investigation. But the notation about her shop—"Secondary target"—nagged at her. What did it mean? And why would Graham Fox have been targeting her family's business?

"No," she said finally, the lie coming easier this time. "Just the usual trash."

Detective Cole studied her face for a long moment, and Lila had the distinct impression that he knew she was lying. But rather than call her on it, he simply nodded and changed the subject.

"I've been meaning to ask you more about your interactions with Frank Mitchell," he said. "He mentioned stopping by your shop the day of Fox's death, but you didn't include that in your statement."

Lila blinked, caught off guard by the shift in conversation. "Frank? He comes by the shop almost every day for a scoop of butter pecan. It's nothing unusual."

"And did he speak with Mr. Fox during his visit?"

"Not that I noticed. Frank was only there for a few minutes, and he sat at the counter, not near the window where Fox was."

Detective Cole made a noncommittal sound, his gaze still penetrating. "Ms. Montgomery, I get the distinct impression that you're not telling me everything you know. I understand your desire to protect your town and its residents, but withholding information only hampers my investigation."

Guilt twisted in Lila's stomach, but she stood her ground. "I'm telling you what I can, Detective. If I think of anything else that might be relevant, you'll be the first to know."

"Will I?" he asked, one eyebrow raised slightly. "Because I've been in law enforcement long enough to recognize when someone is conducting their own parallel investigation. It's dangerous, Ms. Montgomery. And it rarely ends well for amateur detectives."

Lila bristled at the condescension in his tone. "I'm not playing detective, Detective Cole. I'm trying to understand why a man was killed behind my shop. Why my business was apparently a 'target' for whatever scheme Graham Fox was planning."

The words slipped out before she could stop them, and she saw the immediate flash of interest in Detective Cole's eyes.

"Target?" he repeated, taking another step toward her. "And how would you know that your shop was a target, Ms. Montgomery, unless you found something you're not sharing with me?"

Lila swallowed hard, realizing her mistake too late. She could continue to lie, to deny finding the notebook, but something told her that Detective Cole wouldn't believe her. And more importantly, a part of her didn't want to lie to him. Despite her reservations, despite her desire to protect her town, she found herself wanting to trust him.

Slowly, she reached into her pocket and pulled out the notebook. "I found this under the dumpster just now," she admitted, holding it out to him. "I was going to bring it to you after I'd had a chance to look through it."

Detective Cole took the notebook, his fingers brushing against hers in the process. The brief contact sent an unexpected jolt of electricity up her arm, and she quickly withdrew her hand, hoping he hadn't noticed her reaction.

"You should have come to me immediately," he said, his voice stern but not unkind. He flipped through the pages, his expression growing more serious with each turn. When he reached the map of the waterfront, he paused, studying the notations carefully.

"This is significant evidence, Ms. Montgomery," he said, looking up at her. "It confirms that Fox was indeed planning a major development of the waterfront, and that he was willing to use leverage—possibly even underhanded tactics—to acquire the properties he needed."

Lila nodded, pointing to the notation beside her shop. "But what does he mean by 'historical significance'? Salted Caramel's has been in my family for two generations, but it's hardly a historical landmark."

Detective Cole studied the map again, his brow furrowed in concentration. "Perhaps there's something about the property itself that made it valuable to Fox's plans. Something beyond the building."

The thought had occurred to Lila as well, but she couldn't imagine what it could be. The shop was just that—a shop. It had been a small grocery store before her father converted it into an ice cream parlor in the 1980s. Nothing historically significant about it at all.

"I'll have my team look into the history of all these properties," Detective Cole said, carefully closing the notebook. "In the meantime, I'd appreciate it if you'd leave the investigating to the professionals, Ms. Montgomery. If Fox was murdered—and this notebook certainly suggests he had enemies—then whoever killed him wouldn't hesitate to silence anyone else who got too close to the truth."

The warning was clear, and Lila felt a chill run down her spine despite the morning sun now warming the alley. But she also felt a flicker of defiance. This was her town, her shop, her life that had been disrupted. She couldn't simply stand by and wait for Detective Cole to solve the case.

"I understand your concern," she said carefully. "But I can't promise to stay completely uninvolved. Not when my business is apparently part of whatever Fox was planning."

Detective Cole sighed, tucking the notebook into his jacket pocket. "I figured you'd say that. Just... be careful. And if you do find anything else, come to me first next time. Not after you've examined it yourself."

Lila nodded, though they both knew it wasn't a promise. As Detective Cole turned to leave, she called after him. "Why were you here this morning anyway? The crime scene has already been processed."

He paused, glancing back at her over his shoulder. "Same as you, Ms. Montgomery. Looking for something I might have missed the first time around." A ghost of a smile touched his lips. "Great minds think alike, it seems."

As he walked away, Lila couldn't help but watch him go, noting the confident set of his shoulders and the purposeful stride that seemed to define him. Despite his warnings, despite the professional distance he maintained, there was something about Detective Marcus Cole that intrigued her—something beyond his role in the investigation.

She shook off the thought and headed back into her shop. She had ice cream to make, a business to run, and now, more questions than ever about Graham Fox and his plans for Seabreeze Shores. The notebook had provided some answers, but it had also raised new mysteries—mysteries that Lila was determined to solve, with or without Detective Cole's approval.

Little did she know that the clue she'd just discovered was merely the first thread in a complex web of secrets that would soon unravel, threatening to tear apart the peaceful facade of Seabreeze Shores and everyone she held dear.

Chapter 4
Digging Deeper

    The smell of freshly churned vanilla bean ice cream filled Salted Caramel's as Lila wiped down the counters for the third time that morning. Despite reopening, customers had been scarce. A few brave souls had ventured in, ordered quickly, and left with darting glances toward the back alley, as if expecting to find crime scene tape or, worse, a lingering ghost of Graham Fox. Word had spread fast about the death, and the gossip mill of Seabreeze Shores was working overtime.
    Lila sighed, tucking a loose strand of hair behind her ear. The shop felt different somehow—tainted by association with death. She wondered if her father had ever imagined his beloved ice cream parlor would become the site of a potential murder investigation. Jack Montgomery had been a simple man with simple pleasures: fishing at dawn, crafting ice

cream flavors by day, and playing his guitar on the porch at sunset. The complexity of murder would have been foreign to him.

The bell above the door jingled, pulling Lila from her thoughts. She looked up, expecting another hesitant tourist, but instead found herself face to face with her younger brother, Kyle Montgomery.

"Kyle!" Lila exclaimed, rushing around the counter to embrace him. "What are you doing here? I thought you weren't coming home until next week!"

Kyle returned the hug with equal enthusiasm, lifting her slightly off her feet. At twenty-six, he was four years younger than Lila but stood a full head taller, with the same hazel eyes and an easy smile that had broken multiple hearts in Seabreeze Shores before he'd left for graduate school.

"Changed my plans when Mom called about what happened," he said, releasing her and glancing around the shop. "Figured you could use some family support. Plus, I was curious. It's not every day your sister's ice cream shop becomes a crime scene."

Despite the grim subject, Lila couldn't help but smile at her brother's presence. Kyle had always had that effect on her, bringing levity to even the most somber situations. He was dressed in his typical attire—khaki shorts, a faded blue t-shirt with some obscure marine biology joke printed on it, and boat shoes that had seen better days. His dark brown hair was longer than when she'd last seen him at Christmas, now curling slightly over his ears.

"I'm glad you're here," she admitted, moving back behind the counter. "It's been... intense. Want your usual?"

"Is that even a question?" Kyle grinned, taking a seat at the counter. His "usual" was a double scoop of salted caramel in a waffle cone, a preference that hadn't changed since he was twelve.

As Lila prepared his ice cream, she studied her brother. Despite his casual demeanor, there was tension in the set of his shoulders, and his eyes kept darting to the window, much like Graham Fox's had done.

"So," Kyle said, accepting the cone, "Mom gave me the basics, but I want to hear it from you. What happened with this developer guy?"

Lila hesitated, unsure how much to share. Kyle's field was marine biology, with a focus on coastal ecosystems. The waterfront development that Graham Fox had been planning would have directly impacted his research areas. Would that give him a motive for wanting Fox gone?

The thought startled her. Was she really considering her own brother as a suspect? Detective Cole's warnings about trust came flooding back, but Lila pushed them aside. This was Kyle—her little brother who had cried when their father died, who sent her silly memes at odd hours, who still built sand castles with their mother during family beach days.

"He came into the shop two days ago," Lila began, keeping her voice low despite the empty store. "Ordered vanilla ice cream, barely touched it. Kept watching out the window like he was expecting someone. The next thing I know, Detective Cole is calling me to say Fox was found dead in the alley."

Kyle's expression grew serious as he licked his ice cream. "And they think it was murder, not an accident?"

"They haven't officially said, but..." Lila glanced around, then lowered her voice even further. "I found something, Kyle. Fox's notebook. It had plans for the waterfront, including targeting specific properties. The B&B, Elliot's fishing dock, and... our shop."

Kyle's eyebrows shot up. "Our shop? Why would he care about an ice cream parlor?"

"That's what I can't figure out. He made a note about 'historical significance,' but as far as I know, there's nothing historically significant about this place except to our family."

"Hmm." Kyle seemed lost in thought, absently licking his cone as melted ice cream threatened to drip onto his fingers. "Did you tell the detective about this?"

"I did. Well, after he caught me finding the notebook in the alley this morning." Lila grimaced at the memory. "He wasn't thrilled that I was poking around the crime scene."

Kyle snorted. "I bet not. Is he as uptight as Mom described? She said he looked like he had a ruler down his spine."

"He's... intense," Lila admitted, feeling a flush creep up her neck that had nothing to do with the heat. "Very focused on the case. Not exactly the warm and friendly type."

"But handsome?" Kyle teased, noticing her blush.

"I didn't say that," Lila protested, though she couldn't deny the objective truth of the observation. "Anyway, he's warned me to stay out of the investigation, but I can't just sit back, Kyle. Not when our shop is somehow involved."

Kyle finished his ice cream and wiped his hands on a napkin. "I don't blame you. And I want to help. My advisor at the marine institute has been tracking Coastal Ventures for months. They've tried to develop protected coastline in three other towns up and down the Eastern Seaboard. Always with the same MO—find a legal loophole, pressure local owners, offer way above market value to get what they want."

"That fits with what we've found," Lila nodded, thinking of the contract Elsie had discovered. "They were offering Mira Douglas twice what the B&B is worth, apparently to get access to some waterfront rights connected to her property."

"Classic Coastal Ventures," Kyle muttered. "They did the same thing in Hampton Cove last year. Bought an old lighthouse keeper's cottage because it came with riparian rights that gave them leverage over neighboring properties."

Lila leaned against the counter, processing this new information. "So Fox's death might be connected to these development plans? Maybe someone who didn't want to sell decided to take extreme measures?"

"Maybe," Kyle agreed. "Or maybe someone from a rival development company? The waterfront here is prime real estate. Coastal Ventures wouldn't be the only ones interested."

The bell above the door jingled again, cutting their conversation short. This time, it was Elliot Price who entered, looking even more weathered than usual. His dark hair was windblown, his face reddened from a morning on the water, and his clothes carried the distinct smell of fish and salt.

"Lila," he nodded in greeting, then brightened when he saw Kyle. "Well, look who's back in town! The marine scientist himself! How's university treating you, kid?"

Kyle stood to shake Elliot's hand. "Can't complain. About to finish my thesis on coastal ecosystem preservation. How's the fishing business?"

A shadow crossed Elliot's face. "Been better. This development business has everyone on edge. Even the fish are swimming scared." He turned to Lila. "Speaking of which, that's why I stopped by. Heard you talked to the detective about Fox. What'd you tell him?"

The directness of the question caught Lila off guard. "Just what I knew—that Fox came into the shop, that I didn't know him. Why?"

Elliot rubbed the back of his neck, his weathered fingers working at a knot of tension. "No reason. Just curious. Sheriff Jennings has been asking around about who had contact with Fox in his final days. Seems everyone who owns waterfront property is on his list."

"Including you?" Kyle asked, his tone carefully neutral.

"Especially me," Elliot confirmed with a grim laugh. "I made no secret of my opposition to Fox's plans. Told him to his face I'd never sell, no matter what he offered."

Lila moved to the ice cream display. "Can I get you anything, Elliot? On the house."

"Nah, I can't stay. Got to get the morning catch to market before it spoils." He hesitated, then added, "But listen, both of you. Be careful stirring up this business about Fox. Some folks in town aren't too broken up about his passing, if you catch my drift. Might not appreciate anyone asking too many questions."

The warning hung in the air, ambiguous yet pointed. Was Elliot trying to protect them, or warn them off a trail that might lead back to him?

After he left, Kyle turned to Lila with raised eyebrows. "Well, that was subtle. Think he's involved?"

"I don't know what to think anymore," Lila admitted. "Everyone in town seems to have a reason to want Fox gone, but murder? That's a big leap, even for someone as passionate as Elliot."

Kyle checked his watch. "I promised Mom I'd help her with some repairs at the house this afternoon. Want to grab dinner later? We can compare notes on all this."

"Sure," Lila agreed. "The Lobster Pot at seven? I'm closing early today anyway—not exactly fighting off customers."

After Kyle left, Lila spent the next few hours mechanically going through the motions of running the shop—serving the few customers who ventured in, making fresh batches of ice cream for the next day, and cleaning equipment that was already spotless. All the while, her mind was racing, trying to connect the dots between Graham Fox, the waterfront development, and her shop's mysterious "historical significance."

By mid-afternoon, she couldn't stand the inactivity any longer. She flipped the sign to "Closed," locked up, and headed toward the town's historical society building, housed in a Victorian mansion on a hill overlooking the harbor.

The Seabreeze Shores Historical Society was a passion project for many of the town's older residents, particularly Daisy Clark, the local librarian. At sixty-eight, Daisy had lived in the town her entire life and knew more about its history than anyone else. If there was something historically significant about the ice cream shop, Daisy would know.

The historical society occupied a three-story Victorian house that had once belonged to the town's founder, Captain Jeremiah Seabreeze. Its wrap-around porch, turrets, and gingerbread trim had been meticulously maintained, making it one of the town's most photographed landmarks. Inside, the rooms were filled with artifacts, photographs, and documents chronicling the town's evolution from a small fishing village to the tourist destination it was today.

Lila found Daisy in the research room, surrounded by stacks of leather-bound ledgers and faded maps. Her silver hair was pulled back in its usual bun, and her bifocals perched precariously on the end of her nose as she squinted at a particularly ancient document.

"Lila, dear!" Daisy exclaimed when she looked up. "What brings you to our dusty archives? Not that I'm not delighted to see you, of course."

"I need your help, Daisy," Lila said, pulling up a chair next to the older woman. "I'm trying to understand something about my shop. Someone mentioned it might have historical significance beyond being a family business. Does that ring any bells for you?"

Daisy removed her glasses, letting them hang from the chain around her neck. "Historical significance? Well, the building itself dates back to the 1920s. It was originally Wilson's General Store, then became Montgomery's Grocery when your grandfather bought it in the 1950s, and finally Salted Caramel's when your father converted it in the 1980s."

"Nothing special about the property itself? No historical events or legal quirks?"

Daisy's eyes narrowed slightly. "This wouldn't have anything to do with that developer who died, would it? The one asking about waterfront properties?"

Lila hesitated, then decided honesty was the best approach. "Yes, actually. I found some notes suggesting he was interested in my shop because of some historical significance. I can't figure out why."

"Hmm." Daisy rose from her chair with surprising agility for her age. "Let me check something in the archives. Your shop is at 237 Main Street, correct?"

"That's right."

Daisy disappeared into a back room filled with filing cabinets, returning several minutes later with a large, leather-bound book and a rolled-up map. She spread the map on the table, revealing a detailed survey of Seabreeze Shores from 1872.

"Look here," she said, pointing to a section of the map where Main Street met the harbor. "Your shop sits on land that was once part of the original harbor. When they expanded Main Street in the 1920s, they filled in part of the harbor to create more land for businesses."

Lila leaned in, studying the old map. Sure enough, where her shop now stood had once been underwater, part of the natural harbor that had made Seabreeze Shores an ideal location for a fishing community.

"I'm not seeing the significance," she admitted. "Lots of coastal towns have expanded by filling in waterfront areas."

"True," Daisy agreed, opening the leather-bound book. "But what makes your property special is this—the Harbor Act of 1873." She pointed to a passage in the book. "It established that any land reclaimed from the harbor would retain certain water rights in perpetuity. Specifically, the owners of such properties have the right to veto any major changes to the harbor's use or structure if those changes would impact access to their property."

Lila's eyes widened as the implications became clear. "So if someone wanted to develop the waterfront..."

"They would need your approval, along with the approval of anyone else owning property built on the reclaimed harbor land," Daisy finished. "It's an old law, rarely invoked these days, but still legally binding."

"Who else owns property on this reclaimed land?"

Daisy consulted the map again. "Let's see... There's your shop, of course. Frank Mitchell's general store next door. The old boat repair shop that's now a souvenir stand. And... the Seabreeze Bed & Breakfast, though that's only partially on reclaimed land."

The pieces were falling into place. Fox's company had been trying to buy Mira's B&B, likely because its partial position on the reclaimed land gave it the same veto rights as Lila's shop. And Frank Mitchell's general store—that explained his sudden appearance at the lighthouse when she and Elsie were discussing the contract. He had a stake in this too.

"Daisy, this is incredibly helpful," Lila said, her mind racing. "Do you have any records of Graham Fox or Coastal Ventures researching this information recently?"

The older woman nodded. "As a matter of fact, a young woman came in about two weeks ago, asking very similar questions. Said she was a law student researching coastal property rights. Spent hours going through these same records."

"Did she give a name?"

"Nina West, I believe. Left a business card." Daisy rummaged through a drawer and produced a small white card with the name 'Nina West, Legal Research Associate' printed on it, along with a phone number.

Lila had never heard of Nina West, but the timing was too perfect to be coincidental. She must have been working for Fox, researching the legal leverage they would need to push through their development plans.

"May I take a picture of this?" Lila asked, and when Daisy nodded, she quickly snapped a photo of the card with her phone.

"Be careful, dear," Daisy warned as Lila prepared to leave. "People have killed for less than what that historical clause is worth. If developers want to build on the waterfront badly enough, the owners of those veto rights become obstacles—obstacles that some might find easier to remove than to work around."

The warning sent a chill down Lila's spine. "I'll be careful, Daisy. And thank you."

Outside, the afternoon sun was beginning to dip toward the horizon, casting long shadows across Main Street. As Lila walked back toward her shop, she couldn't shake the feeling that she was being watched. She glanced over her shoulder several times but saw nothing out of the ordinary—just tourists browsing shop windows, locals going about their business, and a few seagulls squabbling over discarded food.

When she reached Salted Caramel's, she was surprised to find Detective Marcus Cole waiting outside the locked door. He was leaning against the wall, one ankle crossed over the other, his suit jacket draped over his arm in concession to the afternoon heat. Without the jacket, the holster at his hip was visible, a stark reminder of the seriousness of his profession.

"Detective," Lila greeted him, fishing her keys from her purse. "Looking for more ice cream?"

"Looking for you, actually," he replied, straightening as she approached. "I've been trying to reach you for the past hour."

Lila checked her phone and realized she had three missed calls from an unknown number. "Sorry, I was at the historical society. What's so urgent?"

"We've identified a person of interest in Fox's death, and I wanted to give you a heads up before we brought them in for questioning." His green eyes were intense, focused entirely on her face. "It's someone you know."

Lila's heart skipped a beat. "Who?"

"Elsie Winters." The name hung in the air between them, heavy with implication. "We found her fingerprints on Fox's briefcase, which was discovered in a dumpster three blocks from your shop. When questioned about it, she denied ever touching his belongings."

"That's impossible," Lila protested immediately. "Elsie wouldn't lie about something like that. And she certainly wouldn't kill anyone!"

"I'm not saying she killed Fox," Detective Cole clarified. "But she's clearly withholding information, which makes her a person of interest. We'll be bringing her in for formal questioning tomorrow morning."

Lila's mind raced. Elsie's fingerprints on Fox's briefcase? How was that possible unless... unless she had taken something from it. Like the contract that she'd shown Lila at the lighthouse.

"Detective, there might be an explanation for this," Lila began carefully. "But I need to speak with Elsie first. Can you give me that much?"

"Ms. Montgomery," Detective Cole's voice took on a warning tone. "If you're planning to tip her off—"

"I'm not," Lila interrupted. "I just want to understand what's happening before my best friend gets dragged into a murder investigation."

Detective Cole studied her face for a long moment, then sighed. "You have until nine tomorrow morning. After that, we're bringing her in—with or without an explanation."

"Thank you," Lila said, relief flooding through her. "I promise I'll find out the truth."

"See that you do," he replied, but his expression had softened slightly. "Because right now, all the evidence points to Elsie having a direct connection to Fox—a connection she's deliberately hiding."

As he turned to leave, Lila called after him. "Wait. What about what I found out today? About the historical significance of my shop?"

Detective Cole paused, turning back with interest. "What did you find?"

Lila explained what Daisy had shown her—the Harbor Act, the veto rights, the connection between her shop, Frank's general store, and Mira's B&B. As she spoke, she could see the detective making mental connections, fitting this new information into the puzzle he was assembling.

"That's significant," he acknowledged when she finished. "It gives multiple people a motive to either want Fox gone or to protect their property rights. I'll need to follow up with the historical society myself."

"And there's something else," Lila added, showing him the photo of Nina West's business card. "This woman was researching the same information two weeks ago, claiming to be a law student. But Daisy's never seen her before, and neither have I. Could she be working for Fox?"

Detective Cole studied the photo, his brow furrowed. "Possibly. Or for a competitor. I'll run the name and number through our databases." He looked up at Lila with newfound respect. "This is good work, Ms. Montgomery. But it still doesn't explain why Elsie's fingerprints are on Fox's briefcase."

"I'll find out," Lila promised. "By nine tomorrow."

As Detective Cole walked away, Lila unlocked her shop and went inside, her mind whirling with new questions. She needed to find Elsie immediately, to warn her and to understand what was happening. But first, she needed to call Kyle and cancel their dinner plans. Family would have to wait—her best friend's freedom might be at stake.

She pulled out her phone and dialed Kyle's number, but it went straight to voicemail. Frowning, she tried again with the same result. Maybe he was helping their mother with repairs and had his phone off. She left a brief message explaining that something had come up and she needed to reschedule.

Just as she was about to call Elsie, her phone buzzed with an incoming text. She expected it to be from Kyle, but instead, it was from the same unknown number that had messaged her the night before:

Unknown Number: Your friend is in danger. Meet at the old boathouse at the end of Harbor Street. Come alone.

A chill ran down Lila's spine. The old boathouse was in a secluded area of the marina, rarely used these days except for storage. It was exactly the kind of place someone would choose for an ambush.

But if Elsie was in danger...

Lila's fingers hovered over Detective Cole's number. She should call him, tell him about the text. But what if it was a trap meant to frame Elsie further? What if the sender was watching, waiting to see if Lila involved the police?

Making a decision, Lila grabbed her purse and headed for the door. She would go to the boathouse—but not alone, not entirely. She quickly texted Kyle again, this time with her destination and the cryptic message she'd received. If she didn't contact him within the hour, he was to call Detective Cole.

It wasn't much of a safety net, but it was better than nothing. And if Elsie was truly in danger, there wasn't time to wait for the proper authorities.

As Lila stepped out into the fading light of early evening, the weight of Graham Fox's death and all its complications settled heavy on her shoulders. She was no longer just an ice cream shop owner in a small coastal town. She was now caught in a web of secrets, property rights, and possible murder—a web that seemed to be tightening around her with each passing hour.

The marina was mostly deserted as she approached, the day's fishing boats already docked and secured for the night. The old boathouse loomed at the end of a rickety pier, its weathered boards gray with age and sea spray. No lights shone from its windows, and the door hung slightly ajar, creaking in the gentle evening breeze.

Lila hesitated at the entrance to the pier, her heart pounding in her chest. Was she walking into a trap? Or was Elsie truly in danger, waiting for her friend to come to the rescue?

Taking a deep breath, she stepped onto the pier, the boards groaning beneath her weight as she moved toward the boathouse and whatever—or whoever—waited inside.

Chapter 5
Old Town Secrets

The old boathouse creaked and groaned as the evening wind picked up, its weathered boards protesting against the salty air that had been wearing them down for decades. Lila paused at the entrance, her heart hammering against her ribs. The door hung slightly ajar, revealing nothing but darkness within. She pulled out her phone and switched on its flashlight, the beam cutting through the gloom like a knife.

"Elsie?" she called, her voice wavering slightly. "Are you in there?"

No response came from the shadowy interior. Lila took a deep breath and pushed the door open wider, wincing at the loud creak of rusted hinges. The smell hit her immediately—damp wood, old rope, and something metallic that reminded her uncomfortably of blood. She swallowed hard and stepped inside, the beam of her flashlight sweeping across abandoned fishing equipment, coils of rope, and stacks of wooden crates.

"Elsie? It's Lila. If you're in here, please say something."

The silence was broken only by the gentle lapping of waves against the pilings beneath the boathouse and the distant cry of a night bird. Lila moved deeper into the space, her sandals crunching on sand and broken shells that had been tracked in over the years. Something rustled in the far corner, and she swung her light toward the sound, half-expecting to find Elsie bound and gagged.

Instead, a large rat scurried away from the sudden brightness, disappearing behind a stack of lobster traps. Lila let out a shaky breath, relief and disappointment mingling in her chest. The boathouse appeared to be empty—no Elsie, no mysterious messenger, no obvious danger.

As she turned to leave, her light caught something out of place among the nautical debris—a white envelope resting on top of an overturned rowboat. Lila approached cautiously, noting the same shell or wave design on the seal that had been on the letter addressed to Mira Douglas. With trembling fingers, she picked it up and broke the seal.

Inside was a single sheet of paper, and unlike the contract Elsie had found, this contained just a few lines of typed text:

The truth about Graham Fox is buried in old town soil. Ask your mother about Jack Montgomery's debt and why the Seabreeze land deal failed in 1995. Not everyone in this town is who they claim to be. Trust no one—especially those closest to you.

Lila read the note twice, her confusion growing with each word. Her father, Jack Montgomery, had died five years ago after a lifetime spent fishing and making ice cream. He'd been beloved in Seabreeze Shores, known for his generosity and warm laugh. What debt? What land deal? And what did any of this have to do with Graham Fox?

The sound of footsteps on the pier outside froze her in place. Someone was approaching the boathouse—slowly, deliberately, as if trying not to be heard. Lila quickly folded the note and tucked it into her pocket, then killed her phone's flashlight and pressed herself against the wall beside the door, heart pounding so loudly she was sure it could be heard across the marina.

The footsteps stopped just outside. A shadow fell across the threshold as someone peered inside. Lila held her breath, mentally calculating her chances of escaping if the intruder turned out to be dangerous. The door creaked open wider, and a tall figure stepped inside.

"Ms. Montgomery? Are you in here?"

Detective Marcus Cole's deep voice sent a wave of relief washing over Lila. She stepped away from the wall, switching her phone light back on. "Detective! How did you know I was here?"

Cole squinted against the sudden brightness, his hand instinctively moving toward his holster before he recognized her. In the harsh light, his features looked sharper, more severe, though there was no mistaking the concern in his green eyes.

"Your brother called the station," he explained, his voice tight with barely contained frustration. "Said you'd texted him about meeting someone at the old boathouse after receiving a threatening message. What were you thinking, coming here alone?"

"I wasn't alone," Lila defended herself. "I told Kyle where I was going. And I was worried about Elsie."

"Elsie isn't here," Detective Cole stated the obvious, glancing around the empty boathouse. "Was she supposed to be?"

Lila hesitated, unsure how much to reveal. The note in her pocket seemed to burn against her thigh, its warning to trust no one echoing in her mind. But the alternative—lying to a detective in the middle of a murder investigation—seemed even riskier.

"I received a text saying my friend was in danger and to meet here," she admitted, pulling out her phone to show him the message. "I thought it might be about Elsie, given what you told me earlier about her being a person of interest."

Detective Cole took the phone, studying the message with a frown. "This is the second anonymous text you've received. Why didn't you report the first one?"

"I didn't think it was important," Lila replied, avoiding his gaze. "Just someone being cryptic. But when this one mentioned danger..."

"You should have called me immediately," he said, his tone softening slightly as he handed back the phone. "This is exactly the kind of situation I warned you about. Whoever sent this message clearly wanted to lure you to an isolated location. If I hadn't arrived when I did—"

"Nothing happened," Lila interrupted. "I'm fine. And I found this." She pulled out the note, her conscience winning over caution. "It was waiting for me on that boat."

Detective Cole read the note quickly, his expression growing more serious with each line. "Your father had a debt? And what's this about a land deal in 1995?"

"I have no idea," Lila confessed. "My father was the most honest man I knew. If he had debts or was involved in some failed land deal, he never mentioned it to me." She hesitated, then added, "But my mother might know something."

"We need to speak with her," Detective Cole said decisively, pocketing the note. "And Ms. Montgomery, from now on, you come to me first with any communication like this. Is that clear?"

His authoritative tone should have irritated her, but instead, Lila found herself nodding in agreement. There was something reassuring about his take-charge attitude, especially in the eerie confines of the abandoned boathouse.

"Crystal clear," she replied. "But you have to promise to keep me in the loop. This involves my family now, Detective. I have a right to know what's going on."

Detective Cole studied her face for a long moment, the beam of her phone's flashlight casting dramatic shadows across his features. Finally, he nodded. "Fair enough. But we do this by the book. No more solo investigations or meeting anonymous messengers in deserted buildings. Deal?"

"Deal," Lila agreed, surprising herself with how readily she conceded.

They left the boathouse together, the warm evening air a welcome relief after the musty interior. The marina was quiet now, most of the day's fishermen and tourists long gone. A few lights twinkled on boats moored in the distance, and the moon had begun its ascent, casting a silver path across the dark water.

Detective Cole's unmarked police car was parked at the entrance to the pier. He opened the passenger door for Lila, a surprisingly gentlemanly gesture that made her pause. She was not used to seeing this side of the stern detective.

"I can drive myself," she said, though without much conviction. The events of the day had left her shaken, more than she wanted to admit.

"I'd prefer to keep you where I can see you," Detective Cole replied, his voice softer than usual. "At least until we've spoken with your mother. This case is taking a personal turn, Ms. Montgomery, and I don't like coincidences."

The concern in his eyes made something flutter in Lila's chest. She slid into the passenger seat without further protest, oddly comforted by the idea of not being alone.

As they drove through the quiet streets of Seabreeze Shores toward her mother's house, Lila found herself stealing glances at Detective Cole's profile. In the dim light from the dashboard, his face seemed less severe, the lines around his eyes more like evidence of laughter than frowning. His hands rested lightly on the steering wheel, long fingers tapping occasionally to some internal rhythm.

"Why did you become a detective?" she asked suddenly, breaking the comfortable silence that had settled between them.

Detective Cole glanced at her, surprise evident in his raised eyebrows. "That's a change of subject."

"Just curious," Lila shrugged. "You don't seem like the small-town police type. Sheriff Jennings said you transferred from the city. There must be a story there."

He was quiet for so long that Lila thought he might not answer. When he finally spoke, his voice had a distant quality to it, as if he were remembering something from long ago.

"My father was a cop in Boston. Good at his job, respected in the community. When I was twelve, he was killed during a routine traffic stop. The driver had a warrant out for his arrest and panicked." He paused, his fingers tightening almost imperceptibly on the steering wheel. "After that, I knew I'd follow in his footsteps. Not just to honor him, but because I'd seen firsthand what happens when justice isn't served."

"I'm sorry about your father," Lila said softly. "I lost mine too, though not so suddenly. Cancer, five years ago."

Detective Cole nodded, a silent acknowledgment of their shared experience with loss. "The ice cream shop was his, wasn't it?"

"Yes. He started it when I was little, converted it from the family grocery store. He used to say life was too short not to have something sweet in it every day." The memory made her smile despite the heaviness of the moment. "That's why this note about debts and land deals doesn't make sense. My father wasn't involved in real estate or development. He was happy with his shop and his fishing boat."

"People can surprise you," Detective Cole said, his tone gentle rather than accusatory. "Sometimes they keep parts of themselves hidden, even from those they love most."

The words hung between them as they pulled up to Eva Montgomery's neat bungalow. The porch light was on, casting a warm glow over the well-tended garden that had been Jack Montgomery's pride and joy. Eva had maintained it meticulously after his death, as if keeping the flowers blooming was a way of keeping him close.

Eva opened the door before they could knock, her expression a mixture of concern and confusion. At sixty-two, she was still a striking woman, with silver-streaked dark hair pulled back in a loose bun and the same hazel eyes as Lila. She wore a simple floral dress and reading glasses perched on top of her head, a book clutched in one hand.

"Lila? Kyle called and said you were in some kind of trouble at the marina." Her gaze shifted to Detective Cole, and her forehead creased with worry. "Detective? What's going on?"

"May we come in, Mrs. Montgomery?" Detective Cole asked. "We have some questions that you might be able to help us with."

Eva hesitated only briefly before stepping aside to let them enter. The living room was cozy and lived-in, with comfortable furniture and walls lined with family photographs. A half-finished cup of tea sat on the coffee table beside Eva's reading chair, a pair of slippers tucked neatly underneath.

"Is this about that poor man who died behind Lila's shop?" Eva asked as they sat down, Lila and Detective Cole on the sofa, Eva returning to her armchair. "I don't see how I could help with that."

"Actually, Mrs. Montgomery, it's about your late husband, Jack," Detective Cole began, his tone professional but gentle. "We've come across some information suggesting he may have been involved in a land deal back in 1995, possibly involving the waterfront."

Eva's face paled visibly, her fingers tightening around the book in her lap. "Where did you hear about that?"

The reaction confirmed what the note had implied. Lila leaned forward, studying her mother's face. "Mom? What land deal? Dad never mentioned anything like that."

Eva was quiet for a long moment, her gaze fixed on the family portrait hanging above the fireplace—Jack Montgomery smiling broadly, one arm around his wife and the other around a teenage Lila, with young Kyle grinning in front. It had been taken just before Jack's diagnosis, when life was simpler, sweeter.

"He wouldn't have mentioned it," Eva finally said, her voice soft but steady. "It wasn't his proudest moment, and it nearly cost us everything—the shop, this house, our reputation in town."

"What happened?" Lila asked, struggling to reconcile this new information with her memories of her father—the man who had taught her to fish at dawn, who sang off-key while churning ice cream, who never missed a school event or family dinner.

Eva set her book aside and removed her reading glasses, rubbing the bridge of her nose as if warding off a headache. "It was a different time, Lila. The town was struggling economically. The fishing industry was in decline, tourism hadn't picked up yet, and many businesses were barely staying afloat—including your father's ice cream shop."

"I remember those years," Lila nodded. "Dad was always worried about money, always checking the books late at night."

"What you don't know is that he was approached by a development company called Maritime Ventures. They wanted to build a resort complex on the waterfront, much like what this Graham Fox was planning. They offered generous compensation to property owners willing to sell, especially those with rights under the Harbor Act."

Detective Cole leaned forward, his interest clearly piqued. "Your family's shop was built on reclaimed harbor land, giving it veto rights over waterfront development."

Eva looked surprised. "You know about that?"

"We discovered it today," Lila explained. "But what was Dad's involvement? Did he agree to sell?"

"Not exactly," Eva sighed. "Maritime Ventures needed unanimous agreement from all Harbor Act properties to push through their development plans. Most owners were on board, tempted by the money. Your father initially resisted—he loved that shop, loved the town as it was. But times were tough, and they kept increasing their offer."

She paused, her eyes growing distant with memory. "Eventually, he agreed to be the deal broker. He would convince the remaining holdouts to sell, and in return, he'd receive a substantial commission on top of what they paid for our property. It seemed like the answer to our financial problems."

"So what went wrong?" Detective Cole asked.

"Elliot Price," Eva replied simply. "His family owned the largest fishing operation in town, and their property was crucial to Maritime Ventures' plans. Elliot's father, Samuel Price, refused to sell at any price. He and Jack had been friends since childhood, but this deal came between them. There were arguments, threats..." She trailed off, shaking her head.

"And then?" Lila prompted, unable to believe what she was hearing about her father.

"Then Samuel Price died in a boating accident," Eva said quietly. "It was ruled accidental—a storm came up suddenly, capsized his boat. But there were whispers in town, suggestions that it wasn't entirely accidental, that maybe Maritime Ventures had something to do with it."

"Did they?" Detective Cole's voice was carefully neutral.

Eva shook her head. "I don't know. But Jack was devastated. He backed out of the deal immediately, forfeiting his commission and turning down their offer for our property. By then, other owners were getting cold feet too, worried about the rumors. The entire development plan collapsed."

"And the debt mentioned in the note?" Lila asked, pulling the paper from Detective Cole's pocket and showing it to her mother. "What's this about?"

Eva scanned the note, her face growing increasingly troubled. "Where did you get this?"

"It was left for me at the old boathouse," Lila explained. "Someone's been sending me cryptic messages about Graham Fox's death, and now about Dad's past."

"The debt was to Maritime Ventures," Eva said after a moment's hesitation. "When Jack backed out of the deal, they claimed he owed them for expenses already incurred based on his promise to deliver the necessary properties. It was a substantial amount—nearly two hundred thousand dollars."

Lila gasped. "How did he ever pay that?"

"He didn't, not entirely," Eva admitted. "He worked out a payment plan, stretched over twenty years. He took out loans, worked double shifts at the docks in addition to running the shop. It's why he was always so tired, why he never took vacations. He was still paying it off when he died."

A heavy silence fell over the room as Lila absorbed this new reality. Her father, the man she had idolized, had nearly made a decision that would have changed Seabreeze Shores forever, profiting from the destruction of its traditional character. But he had also chosen to bear an enormous financial burden rather than follow through with something he believed was wrong.

"Mrs. Montgomery," Detective Cole broke the silence, his tone thoughtful, "do you know if there's any connection between Maritime Ventures and Coastal Ventures, the company Graham Fox represented?"

Eva shook her head. "I wouldn't know. After Jack died, the debt was considered cleared. I haven't heard anything about Maritime Ventures in years."

"Could there be documentation of the deal somewhere? Papers, contracts, anything that might shed light on who was behind Maritime Ventures?"

"Jack kept everything related to the deal in a lockbox," Eva replied. "He never wanted to look at those papers again, but he couldn't bring himself to destroy them either. Said they were a reminder of how close he came to betraying his principles."

"Do you still have this lockbox?" Detective Cole asked, an edge of excitement creeping into his voice.

Eva nodded. "In the attic. I haven't opened it since Jack died. It felt wrong somehow, like invading his privacy even though he was gone."

"Mom," Lila said gently, "I think we need to see what's in that box. It might help us understand what's happening now, why someone is bringing up the past after all these years."

Eva hesitated, then nodded and rose from her chair. "I'll get it. It'll take me a few minutes to find it in all the clutter up there."

As Eva left the room, Lila turned to Detective Cole, her mind racing with implications. "Do you think there's a connection between what happened in 1995 and Graham Fox's death?"

"It's too much of a coincidence not to be connected," he replied, his eyes intense. "Fox shows up with plans to develop the waterfront, just like Maritime Ventures did twenty-five years ago. He targets the same properties governed by the Harbor Act. And now someone is leaving notes about your father's involvement in the old deal."

"But why kill Fox? And why involve me?"

"That's what we need to find out," Detective Cole said, his voice lowering as he leaned closer to her. "Someone in town doesn't want these connections made. Someone who might have been involved in both situations. Someone who has secrets to protect."

Their faces were inches apart now, close enough that Lila could see flecks of gold in his green eyes, could feel the warmth of his breath. For a moment, the investigation, the notes, even her father's surprising past faded into the background, replaced by an acute awareness of Detective Marcus Cole as a man, not just a detective.

The moment was broken by the sound of Eva's footsteps on the stairs. Detective Cole straightened up, clearing his throat slightly, though Lila noticed a faint flush coloring his neck just above his shirt collar.

Eva returned carrying a small metal box, its surface dusty from years in the attic. She set it on the coffee table, her hands lingering on the lid as if still reluctant to open it. "The key should be taped to the bottom," she said, turning the box over to reveal a small key secured with yellowing tape.

With careful fingers, Eva removed the key and unlocked the box. Inside were several folders of papers, a few photographs, and what appeared to be a small recording device.

"I didn't know he kept a recorder in here," Eva murmured, lifting it out carefully. "It's one of those old microcassette types he used for dictating notes about ice cream recipes."

Detective Cole took the device, examining it closely. "The battery's probably dead after all these years, but we might be able to retrieve whatever's on the tape. May I take this with me?"

Eva nodded, then began sorting through the folders. "Here's the contract with Maritime Ventures. And these are letters threatening legal action when Jack backed out." She handed the documents to Detective Cole, who began scanning them quickly.

"Coastal Acquisitions Group," he read aloud from the letterhead. "A subsidiary of... Marigold Holdings." He looked up, excitement in his eyes. "This could be the connection we're looking for. If Coastal Ventures is also linked to Marigold Holdings, it would explain why Fox's plans mirrored the 1995 attempt so closely."

"And why someone might want to stop history from repeating itself," Lila added, the pieces starting to fit together in her mind.

"Someone who was involved twenty-five years ago and is still in Seabreeze Shores today."

"But who?" Eva asked, looking troubled. "Most of the key players from back then are gone now. Samuel Price died in that boating accident. The Maritime Ventures representatives never lived in town—they just came for meetings and left. And Jack..." Her voice caught on her late husband's name.

"What about Elliot Price?" Detective Cole suggested. "He would have inherited his father's property and presumably his father's stance against development."

"Elliot was away at college when all this happened," Eva shook her head. "He came back for his father's funeral, of course, but he wasn't directly involved in the disputes."

"Frank Mitchell?" Lila offered. "His store is on Harbor Act land too. And he's been acting strangely since Fox's death."

"Frank was one of the holdouts, like Jack," Eva confirmed. "He refused to sell even after most others had agreed. But after Samuel's death, when the deal fell apart, Frank actually seemed disappointed. Said the town had missed an opportunity for growth."

Detective Cole was making notes in a small notebook he'd pulled from his pocket. "What about Sheriff Jennings? Was he involved back then?"

Eva considered this. "Sam Jennings was a deputy at the time, not yet sheriff. I don't recall him being particularly vocal about the development one way or another. His family didn't own Harbor Act property."

"And Mira Douglas? The B&B has been in her family for generations, right?"

"Yes, but Mira was just a teenager then. Her parents ran the B&B, and they were initially in favor of selling. They changed their minds after Samuel's death, like many others."

They continued through the documents, finding mention of various town residents and their positions on the 1995 development plan. Some names Lila recognized as people still living in Seabreeze Shores—business owners, retired fishermen, local politicians. Others had moved away or passed on in the intervening years.

As they worked, Lila couldn't help noticing how Detective Cole had subtly shifted closer to her on the sofa, their shoulders occasionally brushing as they leaned over documents together. Each brief contact sent a small thrill through her, despite the serious nature of their task. She found herself watching his hands as he carefully turned pages—strong hands with long fingers, a small scar across the right knuckles, nails neatly trimmed.

Eva yawned, drawing Lila's attention away from the detective's hands. "It's getting late," she said, glancing at the clock on the mantel, which showed it was past midnight. "And we've gone through most of the papers. Should we continue this tomorrow?"

Detective Cole nodded, gathering the documents they'd set aside as potentially relevant. "I'll take these to the station for further analysis, if that's alright with you, Mrs. Montgomery. They might help us establish a connection between the old case and current events."

"Of course," Eva agreed, rising from her chair with a slight wince that suggested her back was stiff from sitting too long. "I hope they help. Jack would want his mistakes to mean something, to prevent someone else from making similar ones."

As they prepared to leave, Eva pulled Lila aside briefly. "Will you be staying here tonight, dear? I'd feel better knowing you're not alone, especially after what happened at the boathouse."

Lila hesitated, glancing toward Detective Cole, who was waiting by the door, giving them privacy. "I should be fine at my place, Mom. It's just a few blocks away."

"Actually," Detective Cole interjected, having overheard, "I'd recommend staying with your mother tonight, Ms. Montgomery. Until we understand who's sending these messages and why, it's better to be cautious."

The concern in his voice warmed something in Lila's chest. "Alright," she conceded. "I'll stay. But I need to stop by my apartment to get a few things first."

"I'll drive you," Detective Cole offered immediately.

Eva smiled, a knowing look in her eyes that made Lila blush slightly. "That's very kind of you, Detective. I'll make up Lila's old room while you're gone."

The drive to Lila's small apartment above the hardware store on Main Street was brief and quiet, both of them lost in their own thoughts about the revelations of the evening. When they arrived, Detective Cole insisted on accompanying her inside, checking each room before allowing her to pack an overnight bag.

"You don't have to wait," Lila told him as she gathered toiletries from her bathroom. "I can walk back to Mom's. It's not far."

"I'll wait," he replied firmly, standing in her living room with his hands clasped behind his back, surveying the cozy space with interest. His gaze lingered on the bookshelves filled with cookbooks and mystery novels, the collection of seashells on the windowsill, the framed photographs of her family displayed on the walls.

When Lila emerged with her bag packed, she found him examining a picture of her father, taken on his fishing boat with a teenaged Lila proudly holding up a large bass.

"He taught you to fish?" Detective Cole asked, a softness in his voice she hadn't heard before.

"Every Sunday at dawn," Lila nodded, a bittersweet smile tugging at her lips. "Rain or shine, summer or winter. Said a Montgomery had to know how to catch dinner in case the ice cream business went bust."

Detective Cole smiled, the expression transforming his usually serious face, making him look younger, more approachable. "My father taught me too. Not many good fishing spots in the city, but we'd drive out to a lake upstate a few times each summer. Best memories of my childhood."

The shared moment of connection hung between them, unexpectedly intimate in the quiet of her apartment. Lila found herself wanting to prolong it, to learn more about the man behind the detective's badge.

"Ready to go?" he asked, breaking the spell and returning to his professional demeanor.

Lila nodded, suddenly self-conscious about the messy bun she'd pulled her hair into and the faded sundress she'd been wearing all day. "Thank you for staying. And for everything today. I know I haven't made your job any easier by poking around on my own."

"You've actually been quite helpful," he admitted as they headed down the exterior stairs to his car. "Your knowledge of the town and its history has given us leads we might not have found otherwise."

They drove back to Eva's house in comfortable silence, the streets of Seabreeze Shores almost entirely deserted at this late hour. When they arrived, Detective Cole walked Lila to the door, the porch light casting warm shadows across his face.

"I'll call you tomorrow with any updates," he promised. "In the meantime, stay alert. Whoever sent those messages knows a lot about your family's past and seems intent on involving you in whatever is happening now."

"I will," Lila assured him. "And you'll let me know if you find anything in those documents? Or on the recording device?"

"You'll be my first call," he nodded, then hesitated, as if wanting to say something more. Instead, he simply added, "Goodnight, Ms. Montgomery."

"Lila," she corrected him with a small smile. "After everything today, I think we're past formalities, Detective Cole."

A smile tugged at the corner of his mouth. "Marcus," he offered in return. "Sleep well, Lila."

As he turned to go, Lila impulsively reached out and touched his arm. "Be careful, Marcus. If someone in town is willing to kill once to protect their secrets, they won't hesitate to do it again."

His expression softened, and for a moment, she thought he might reach for her hand. Instead, he gave a small nod. "Always am. Lock up behind me."

Lila watched from the porch as he walked back to his car, his tall figure silhouetted against the moonlit street. Only when his taillights had disappeared around the corner did she go inside, locking the door as instructed and making her way to her childhood bedroom, where Eva had indeed prepared the bed with fresh sheets.

As she changed into her pajamas and slipped between the cool cotton sheets, Lila's mind raced with everything she'd learned. Her father, the man she'd idolized, had nearly been party to the very sort of development that Graham Fox had been pushing. The debt that had weighed him down for years, the extra jobs he'd taken, the vacation they'd never had—all consequences of his choice to back out of the deal.

Yet despite this new, more complicated view of her father, Lila found herself proud of his final decision. When faced with the consequences of his actions—the death of his friend, the potential destruction of the town's character—he had chosen the harder path. He had chosen to make amends, to bear the burden of his mistake rather than profit from it.

Venom in Vanilla

As sleep began to claim her, Lila's thoughts drifted to Detective Marcus Cole—to the flecks of gold in his green eyes, to the rare smile that transformed his face, to the shared connection of fathers who taught their children to fish. There was more to him than the stern, by-the-book detective he presented to the world. And despite the danger surrounding them, despite the warnings to trust no one, Lila found herself wanting to know that man better.

Outside the Montgomery home, a figure watched from the shadows of the oak tree, noting the detective's departure and the darkening of lights within the house. Patience had always been their strong suit, and now more than ever, caution was essential. The past was rising to the surface, threatening to expose long-buried secrets. Something would have to be done about Lila Montgomery and her detective—and soon.

Chapter 6
Breaking Point

Morning light filtered through the lace curtains of Lila's childhood bedroom, casting dappled patterns across the quilt her grandmother had made decades ago. Lila stirred, momentarily disoriented by the familiar-yet-forgotten surroundings—the bookshelf still lined with her teenage novels, the collection of seashells on the windowsill, the faded blue walls she'd once insisted on painting herself.

The events of the previous day came rushing back: the mysterious message, the abandoned boathouse, the revelations about her father's past, and most persistently, the memory of Detective Marcus Cole's green eyes in the soft porch light as he'd said goodnight.

Marcus, she reminded herself. Not Detective Cole anymore. The shift to first names felt significant, a tentative step across the professional boundary he'd maintained since they met.

The smell of coffee and bacon wafted up from the kitDabney, along with the murmur of voices. Lila slipped from bed, pulled on a light robe over her pajamas, and padded barefoot down the hall to the bathroom. After a quick shower, she changed into a fresh sundress—a pale yellow one with tiny embroidered daisies along the hem—and headed downstairs, her wet hair twisted into a loose bun.

She paused at the kitDabney doorway, surprised to find not just her mother at the breakfast table, but Kyle as well. They both looked up as she entered, their conversation abruptly halting.

"Morning, sleepyhead," Kyle greeted her, raising his coffee mug in salute. He looked tired, dark circles under his eyes suggesting he hadn't slept well. "I was starting to think you'd sleep through the excitement."

"What excitement?" Lila asked, helping herself to coffee from the pot on the counter. She added a splash of cream and a teaspoon of sugar, stirring absently as she waited for an explanation.

Kyle and Eva exchanged a look that immediately put Lila on edge. "What is it? What's happened?"

"They arrested Elsie this morning," Eva said gently, pushing a plate of bacon and scrambled eggs toward Lila as she sank into a chair. "It's all over town. Sheriff Jennings and that detective came for her at her shop around seven."

"What?" Lila nearly dropped her mug. "But Marcus—Detective Cole promised he wouldn't bring her in until nine! He said I had until then to talk to her!"

"Well, plans change, I guess," Kyle shrugged, though his expression was sympathetic. "Sheriff Jennings was the one who made the arrest. Your detective was just along for the ride."

Lila's mind raced. Why would Marcus go back on his word? Just last night, he'd seemed to be trusting her more, even partnering with her to uncover the truth about her father's connection to the old land deal. Had it all been a ploy to keep her distracted while they built a case against Elsie?

"What are they charging her with?" she demanded, ignoring the breakfast in front of her.

"Not murder, if that's what you're worried about," Kyle replied. "Obstruction of justice and tampering with evidence, from what I heard at the docks this morning. Apparently, they found some contract in her shop that she'd taken from Fox's briefcase."

The contract that Elsie had shown her at the lighthouse—the one outlining the sale of Mira's B&B to Coastal Ventures. Lila closed her eyes briefly, guilt washing over her. She should have insisted they turn it over to the police immediately. Now Elsie was paying the price for what had been a joint decision.

"I need to go see her," Lila said, standing up so abruptly that her chair scraped against the wooden floor.

"Honey, you haven't even touched your breakfast," Eva protested. "And I don't think they'll let you visit Elsie right away. These things take time."

"I'm not hungry," Lila stated, already heading for the door. "And I'm not going to see Elsie first. I'm going to have a word with Detective Cole about keeping his promises."

Kyle rose to follow her. "I'll drive you. You're in no state to be behind the wheel right now."

Lila didn't argue. Her hands were shaking with a mixture of anger and fear—anger at Marcus for the perceived betrayal, fear for Elsie and what this meant for their investigation.

They drove in silence to the Seabreeze Shores Police Station, a modest brick building just off Main Street. Inside, the reception area was empty except for a young officer behind the desk who looked up with a startled expression as Lila burst through the door.

"I need to see Detective Marcus Cole," she demanded without preamble. "Now."

The officer—his nameplate identified him as Officer Jensen—blinked in surprise. "Uh, Detective Cole is in a meeting right now. If you'd like to wait—"

"I don't want to wait," Lila cut him off. "Please tell him Lila Montgomery is here and it's urgent."

Officer Jensen looked like he wanted to argue but thought better of it after taking in Lila's determined expression. "One moment," he said, picking up the phone on his desk and speaking quietly into it.

Kyle placed a calming hand on Lila's shoulder. "Take it easy, sis. Getting worked up won't help Elsie."

"He lied to me, Kyle," Lila whispered fiercely. "He said I had until nine to talk to Elsie, and instead, he arrested her at seven."

"Maybe there's an explanation," Kyle suggested. "Don't jump to conclusions until you hear his side."

Before Lila could respond, a door opened at the far end of the reception area, and Marcus appeared. He looked even more tired than Kyle, his suit slightly rumpled as if he'd been wearing it for too long, the shadow of stubble darkening his jaw. When he saw Lila, a flicker of something crossed his face—guilt, perhaps, or resignation.

"Ms. Montgomery," he said, his tone professional once more, the intimacy of the previous night seemingly forgotten. "I was about to call you."

"Were you?" Lila replied coldly. "Before or after you finished processing my best friend for a crime we both know she didn't commit?"

Marcus glanced at Kyle, then at Officer Jensen, who was pretending not to listen. "Let's talk in my office," he suggested, holding open the door he'd just emerged from.

Lila turned to Kyle. "Wait here. I won't be long."

Her brother nodded, settling into one of the plastic chairs in the reception area and picking up a dog-eared fishing magazine.

Marcus's office was small and sparsely decorated, with a desk covered in neat stacks of papers, a pair of chairs for visitors, and a large whiteboard on one wall covered with notes and photographs related to Graham Fox's death. Lila noticed her own name there, connected by lines to several other names—Elsie, Mira, Elliot, Frank, and Jack Montgomery.

"Have a seat," Marcus offered, closing the door behind them.

"I'll stand," Lila replied, crossing her arms. "You lied to me. You promised I had until nine to talk to Elsie."

Marcus sighed, running a hand through his dark hair, which only made it stand up in a way that would have been endearing under different circumstances. "I didn't lie. Plans changed. Sheriff Jennings received an anonymous tip early this morning about evidence in Elsie's shop. He insisted on moving immediately, and as the lead detective on this case, I had no choice but to accompany him."

"What evidence?" Lila demanded, though she already suspected the answer.

"The contract between Coastal Ventures and Mira Douglas," Marcus confirmed. "The one your friend removed from Graham Fox's briefcase after his death. The one neither of you saw fit to mention to me."

Guilt flashed through Lila again, but she pushed it aside. "We were going to tell you. We just wanted to understand what it meant first."

"That's not how this works, Lila," Marcus said, his voice softening slightly as he used her first name. "You can't withhold evidence in a murder investigation, no matter your intentions. Elsie took that contract from a dead man's belongings, and then you both concealed it from the police. That's obstruction of justice at minimum."

"Is that what she's being charged with?" Lila asked, some of her anger deflating in the face of his reasonable explanation.

"Yes, along with tampering with evidence. She's not being charged with Fox's murder, if that's what you're worried about." He gestured to the chair again. "Please, sit. You look like you might fall over."

This time, Lila complied, sinking into the chair across from his desk. "Can I see her?"

"Not yet. She's still being processed and questioned." Marcus sat down as well, his chair creaking slightly under his weight. "But I can tell you she's cooperating now, telling us everything she knows about the contract and Fox's plans for the waterfront."

"What about the connection to my father? The 1995 land deal?"

Marcus leaned forward, his expression serious. "That's what I was working on when you arrived. I've been going through the documents from your father's lockbox all night. There's definitely a connection between Maritime Ventures from 1995 and Coastal Ventures today."

"What kind of connection?"

"Both are subsidiaries of the same parent company—Marigold Holdings. And both used the same playbook: target properties protected by the Harbor Act, offer above-market prices, use legal pressure when necessary." He pulled a folder from one of the stacks on his desk and opened it, revealing a sheet of paper with a company logo at the top. "What's even more interesting is the leadership. In 1995, Marigold Holdings was run by a man named Victor Caldwell. Today, the CEO is his son, Lawrence Caldwell."

"Caldwell," Lila repeated, the name unfamiliar. "I don't know anyone in town by that name."

"They're not local," Marcus explained. "Based in Boston, with development projects all along the Eastern Seaboard. But here's where it gets interesting." He turned the paper around so she could see it better. "The local representative for Maritime Ventures in 1995 was this man."

He pointed to a signature at the bottom of a document. The name was illegible, but next to it was a printed version: *Samuel Jennings, Regional Acquisitions Manager*.

"Samuel Jennings?" Lila echoed in disbelief. "As in Sheriff Sam Jennings?"

"His father," Marcus confirmed grimly. "Who, according to these records, was not just representing Maritime Ventures but was a minority shareholder in the company. He stood to make a significant profit if the 1995 development went through."

Lila's mind raced, connecting dots rapidly. "And when the deal fell apart after Samuel Price's death..."

"The Jennings family lost a lot of money," Marcus finished. "Which gives Sheriff Jennings a potential motive for wanting the new development to succeed where his father's failed."

"You think he killed Graham Fox?" Lila asked, struggling to reconcile this theory with the Sheriff Jennings she'd known all her life—the man who handed out candy on Halloween, who coached the high school baseball team, who had been one of the first to offer condolences when her father died.

"I don't know yet," Marcus admitted. "But I do know he's been interfering with my investigation since day one, insisting Fox's death was an accident despite evidence to the contrary. And this morning, he was adamant about arresting Elsie immediately, despite our agreement that you could talk to her first."

Lila sat back, absorbing this new information. "I owe you an apology. I thought you'd gone back on your word."

"I understand why you'd think that," Marcus said, his expression softening. "But Lila, I need you to trust me. We're on the same side here—trying to find out who killed Graham Fox and why."

The sincerity in his green eyes made something flutter in Lila's chest. Despite everything—the tension, the misunderstandings, the secrets—she found herself wanting to trust him. Needing to trust him.

"I do trust you," she said quietly. "But I need to know Elsie will be alright. She didn't kill Fox. She just made a stupid mistake taking that contract."

"I know," Marcus nodded. "And once she's finished her statement, I'll push to have her released on bail. The charges aren't severe enough to keep her locked up, especially given her ties to the community."

Relief washed over Lila. "Thank you."

"Don't thank me yet," he cautioned. "We still have a killer to catch, and now we have to consider that it might be the town's sheriff. That complicates things considerably."

"What's our next step?" Lila asked, the 'our' slipping out naturally.

Marcus raised an eyebrow at her automatic inclusion of herself in the investigation but didn't object. "We need to find out if Sheriff Jennings had contact with Graham Fox before his death. And we need to understand the current connection between Jennings and Coastal Ventures. Is he just facilitating their plans because of his father's old ties, or is he actively involved in the company like his father was?"

"I can help with that," Lila offered. "People talk in my shop. I could ask around, see if anyone remembers seeing the Sheriff with Fox."

"Carefully," Marcus warned. "If Jennings is involved in Fox's death, he won't hesitate to silence anyone he sees as a threat—including you."

The concern in his voice was unmistakable, and Lila felt a warmth spread through her that had nothing to do with the summer heat filtering through the office blinds. "I'll be careful," she promised. "I'm not planning to accuse the Sheriff of murder over ice cream cones."

A small smile tugged at the corner of Marcus's mouth. "I should hope not. Might be bad for business."

The moment of levity eased the tension between them. Lila found herself studying his face—the stubble darkening his jaw, the faint lines around his eyes that deepened when he smiled, the way his hair fell across his forehead in defiance of his otherwise neat appearance.

"You look exhausted," she observed. "Did you sleep at all last night?"

"Not much," he admitted. "After I left your mother's house, I came straight here to go through those documents. And then at dawn, Sheriff Jennings came in with his tip about Elsie, and things got... complicated."

"You should get some rest," Lila said, concern coloring her voice. "You can't solve a murder if you're falling asleep on your feet."

"I'll rest when we catch the killer," Marcus replied, though his expression softened at her concern. "But I could use some coffee that doesn't taste like it was brewed last week. The station coffee is notorious."

"My shop makes excellent coffee," Lila said before she could think better of it. "I was planning to open for a few hours this afternoon. You could stop by."

Was she imagining it, or did a faint flush color his neck just above his shirt collar? "I might do that," he said, his tone carefully neutral despite the warmth in his eyes.

A knock at the door interrupted the moment. Officer Jensen poked his head in. "Detective Cole, Sheriff Jennings is looking for you. Says it's urgent."

Marcus nodded, his expression immediately shifting back to professional detachment. "Tell him I'll be right there." As Jensen withdrew, Marcus turned back to Lila. "I need to go. We'll talk more later."

"About Elsie?" Lila pressed, rising from her chair.

"Among other things," Marcus agreed, standing as well. "I'll call you as soon as she's processed."

Lila nodded, suddenly aware of how close they were standing in the small office. She could smell his cologne—something subtle and woody—and see the faint shadow of stubble on his jaw. For a wild moment, she thought he might lean in, close the distance between them. Instead, he stepped back, maintaining a professional space.

"Be careful today," he said, his voice low. "And if you learn anything about Sheriff Jennings, call me immediately. Don't confront him yourself."

"I promise," Lila assured him, though her mind was already racing with possibilities for discreet inquiries around town.

When she rejoined Kyle in the reception area, her brother took one look at her face and raised an eyebrow. "Well, you don't look like you're ready to commit murder anymore. I take it Detective Handsome had a good explanation?"

"Detective Cole," Lila corrected automatically, feeling a blush rise to her cheeks. "And yes, he explained what happened with Elsie. She's being charged with obstruction and tampering, but not murder. They'll probably release her on bail once she's finished giving her statement."

"That's a relief," Kyle said as they walked out to his car. "So what now? Back to Mom's?"

Lila shook her head. "I need to open the shop for a few hours. We're losing too much business being closed, and I could use the normalcy of scooping ice cream and chatting with customers."

Kyle gave her a knowing look. "And this has nothing to do with inviting a certain detective for coffee?"

"I don't know what you're talking about," Lila replied primly, though her blush deepened. "Just drive, please."

The drive to Salted Caramel's was short, the streets of Seabreeze Shores bustling with the usual mix of locals and tourists enjoying the perfect summer weather. As they passed the marina, Lila noticed Elliot Price's fishing boat docked in its usual spot, the man himself unloading crates of fresh catch with practiced efficiency.

"Can you pull over for a minute?" she asked Kyle. "I want to talk to Elliot."

Kyle frowned but complied, easing the car to the curb across from the marina. "Is that wise? Especially if Sheriff Jennings might be involved in all this? Elliot isn't exactly subtle—if you start asking questions, the whole town will know within an hour."

"I'll be careful," Lila promised, already opening her door. "I just want to see if he knows anything about Sheriff Jennings' connection to the land deals. His father was the key holdout in 1995, after all."

Before Kyle could object further, Lila crossed the street to the marina, weaving between parked cars and tourists taking photos of the picturesque harbor. Elliot looked up as she approached, setting down a crate of still-glistening fish.

"Lila," he greeted her, wiping his hands on a rag tucked into his belt. "Didn't expect to see you today, what with all the excitement about your friend Elsie."

News traveled fast in Seabreeze Shores, as always. "That's actually why I'm here," Lila said, trying to sound casual. "I'm trying to understand what's happening. It all seems connected to these development plans—both Fox's and the ones from 1995."

Elliot's weathered face darkened. "Bad business, both times. Nearly tore the town apart back in '95. Seems like history's repeating itself."

"You were away at college then, right?" Lila asked, remembering what her mother had said. "But your father was involved?"

"Involved?" Elliot gave a bitter laugh. "My father was the entire reason the deal fell apart. He refused to sell no matter what they offered—said the Price family had fished these waters for five generations and wouldn't be the ones to end that tradition."

"And then he died in that boating accident," Lila said carefully. "Right when the pressure to sell was at its highest."

Elliot's eyes narrowed slightly. "That's right. Convenient timing, some might say. Though the official report called it an accident—sudden squall, capsized boat, nobody to blame."

"Who was pushing hardest for your father to sell?" Lila asked, trying not to sound too eager for the answer.

Elliot seemed to consider whether to answer, his gaze drifting out to the harbor where a few fishing boats were returning with their morning catch. Finally, he sighed. "Samuel Jennings was the main man—Sheriff Jennings' father. Came around almost daily near the end, making offers, then threats when offers didn't work. Said my father was holding up progress, costing people jobs and opportunities."

"Samuel Jennings worked for Maritime Ventures?" Lila pressed, though she already knew the answer from what Marcus had shown her.

"Worked for them? He practically was Maritime Ventures in Seabreeze Shores," Elliot scoffed. "Had a financial stake in the deal too, from what my father said. Was set to make a fortune if it went through."

"And his son? Was Sam Jennings involved back then?"

Elliot's expression grew guarded. "Sam was a deputy at the time. Young, ambitious. Why all the questions, Lila? This is ancient history."

"Maybe not so ancient," Lila replied carefully. "Graham Fox was here with almost identical plans to what Maritime Ventures proposed in 1995. Don't you find that strange?"

"Strange isn't the word I'd use," Elliot muttered. "Dangerous, maybe. For everyone involved." He picked up another crate, clearly ready to end the conversation. "Look, Lila, I liked your father. Jack was a good man who made some mistakes but tried to fix them. You'd do well to remember that not everyone gets a second chance to make things right. Some people hold grudges for a very long time."

With that cryptic warning, he turned and headed toward the fish market at the end of the pier, leaving Lila with more questions than answers.

When she returned to Kyle's car, her brother gave her a questioning look. "Learn anything useful?"

"Maybe," Lila said thoughtfully. "Elliot confirmed that Sheriff Jennings' father was heavily involved with Maritime Ventures and stood to profit significantly from the 1995 deal. And he hinted that some people might still hold grudges over what happened back then."

"Like who?" Kyle asked, starting the car and pulling back into traffic.

"That's what I need to find out," Lila replied, her mind already racing ahead to her next steps. "Let's get to the shop. I need to talk to Frank Mitchell too. His store is on Harbor Act land, just like ours."

Frank's General Store sat right next to Salted Caramel's, the two businesses sharing a common wall that had once been removed to connect them when both were part of the original Montgomery's Grocery. When Lila's father converted half the space into an ice cream shop, the wall had been rebuilt, but the businesses remained close neighbors in more ways than one.

As Kyle parked behind Salted Caramel's, Lila noticed that Frank's was unusually quiet for a summer morning. Normally, tourists would be streaming in and out, purchasing beach supplies, snacks, and souvenirs. Today, a handwritten "Back in 15 minutes" sign hung on the door.

"I'm going to check on Frank," Lila told Kyle, handing him the keys to her shop. "Can you start opening up? Everything should be ready to go—just flip the sign and turn on the lights."

Kyle took the keys with a concerned frown. "Are you sure that's a good idea? Going alone, I mean?"

"Frank's harmless," Lila assured him. "Besides, I've known him my whole life. He was Dad's friend."

"So was Sheriff Jennings," Kyle reminded her grimly. "And look how that's turning out."

Lila hesitated, then nodded. "Fair point. But I'll be careful, and Frank's store has a big front window. You can literally see me from our shop the entire time."

With a reluctant nod, Kyle headed to Salted Caramel's while Lila approached Frank's General Store. Despite the sign, the door was unlocked, the bell above it jingling cheerfully as she entered. The familiar smell of the store—a mixture of candy, sunscreen, and the faintly musty scent of beach supplies—brought back countless childhood memories of shopping trips with her father.

"Frank?" she called out, making her way past displays of sunglasses, flip-flops, and souvenir t-shirts. "It's Lila Montgomery. Are you here?"

The sound of something falling in the back room was followed by muttered cursing. A moment later, Frank Mitchell emerged, looking flustered. At sixty-three, he was still robust and active, his shock of white hair the only real concession to age. Today, however, he seemed agitated, his usually ruddy face pale, his hands fidgeting with the hem of his store apron.

"Lila," he said, sounding surprised. "Didn't expect to see you today. Heard about what happened with your friend Elsie. Terrible business."

"That's why I'm here," Lila said, deciding on a direct approach. "I'm trying to understand what's happening, Frank. It all seems connected to these waterfront development plans—both now and back in 1995."

Frank's eyes darted to the window, as if checking to see if anyone was watching. "Not sure what I can tell you about that. It was a long time ago."

"But you were involved," Lila pressed. "Your store is on Harbor Act land, just like my shop. You would have had the same veto rights my father had."

Frank sighed, moving behind the counter as if seeking the safety of a barrier between them. "Look, Lila, some things are better left in the past. Yes, I was approached by Maritime Ventures. Yes, I initially refused to sell. But after Samuel Price died and the whole deal fell apart, I realized we'd missed an opportunity for the town to grow, to evolve."

"And now? With Graham Fox and Coastal Ventures making the same pitch?"

Frank's gaze dropped to the counter. "I was in favor of the new development. Seabreeze Shores needs this—new jobs, more tourism, year-round income instead of just seasonal profits. Fox's plans were good for the town."

"Even if it meant destroying the character of the waterfront? The fishing community that's been here for generations?"

"Progress always has costs," Frank replied, a defensive edge creeping into his voice. "We can't stay stuck in the past forever, clinging to tradition while the world moves on without us."

Lila studied the older man, noting the way his hands continued to fidget, the slight sheen of sweat on his forehead despite the store's air conditioning. "Frank, were you working with Graham Fox? Did you agree to sell your property to Coastal Ventures?"

For a long moment, Frank was silent, his gaze fixed on some middle distance beyond Lila's shoulder. When he finally spoke, his voice had dropped to almost a whisper. "Yes. I signed a preliminary agreement the day before he died. Fox was just waiting on a few other properties—Mira's B&B, Elliot's fishing dock, and... your shop."

"My shop?" Lila repeated, though she'd suspected as much since finding Fox's notebook. "But I never spoke to him about selling."

"He was planning to approach you next," Frank explained. "Said he had leverage he could use if you proved difficult. Something about your father's old debt to Maritime Ventures possibly transferring to you."

Anger flared in Lila's chest. "That debt died with my father. My mother confirmed it was cleared after his death."

"Fox seemed to think otherwise," Frank shrugged. "But it doesn't matter now, does it? With Fox dead, the whole deal is probably off the table again."

"Unless someone else from Coastal Ventures takes over," Lila suggested. "Or unless Fox's death was meant to stop the development, not facilitate it."

Frank's eyes widened slightly. "What are you suggesting? That someone killed Fox to prevent the development? Who would do that? Everyone stood to benefit, even the holdouts. The offers were incredibly generous."

"Not everyone measures benefit in dollars, Frank," Lila replied, thinking of Elliot's determination to continue his family's fishing tradition, of her own attachment to her father's ice cream shop. "Some things can't be bought."

Before Frank could respond, the bell above the door jingled again. Lila turned to see Sheriff Sam Jennings entering the store, his uniform crisp, his badge gleaming in the morning light. He paused when he saw Lila, surprise flickering across his face before his expression settled into a practiced smile.

"Lila Montgomery," he greeted her. "Just who I was hoping to find. I stopped by your shop, but your brother said you were over here."

"Sheriff," Lila nodded, trying to keep her voice steady despite the sudden pounding of her heart. After what Marcus had told her about the Jennings family connection to the development deals, the Sheriff's presence seemed far more ominous than it would have just a day ago. "What can I do for you?"

"Just wanted to let you know we've processed your friend Elsie Winters," Jennings replied smoothly. "She's being released on bail as we speak. Thought you'd want to know."

"Thank you," Lila said cautiously. "That's good news."

"She's not out of the woods yet," Jennings warned. "Obstruction of justice is a serious charge. But given her ties to the community, the judge agreed to release her pending trial."

"I appreciate you coming to tell me in person," Lila said, wondering what his real motive was for seeking her out.

Jennings glanced at Frank, then back to Lila. "Actually, I was hoping to have a private word with you. About your father's connection to the 1995 development plan. I understand Detective Cole has been asking questions about my father's involvement."

The direct mention of what she'd just been discussing with Marcus sent a chill down Lila's spine. Had someone at the station told Jennings about their conversation? Was her suspicion of the Sheriff now common knowledge?

"Perhaps we could talk in my office," Jennings continued when Lila didn't immediately respond. "It's a sensitive matter, and I'd prefer not to discuss it in public."

Warning bells clanged in Lila's mind. Marcus's caution echoed in her memory: *If Jennings is involved in Fox's death, he won't hesitate to silence anyone he sees as a threat—including you.*

"Actually, Sheriff, I need to open my shop," Lila replied, trying to sound regretful rather than alarmed. "I've lost too much business being closed these past few days. But I'd be happy to talk later, perhaps with Detective Cole present since he's leading the investigation."

Jennings' friendly expression faltered for just a moment, a flash of something harder and colder showing through before the smile returned. "Of course, I understand. Business comes first. We can catch up later."

He tipped his hat to Frank, then turned and left the store, the bell jingling with artificial cheerfulness in his wake.

"You should be careful, Lila," Frank said quietly once the Sheriff was gone. "Sam Jennings has a long memory and isn't known for forgiving people who cross him. His father was the same way."

"I'm not crossing anyone," Lila defended herself. "I'm just trying to understand what happened to Graham Fox and how it connects to the past."

"Some connections are better left unexplored," Frank replied cryptically. "Now, if you'll excuse me, I have inventory to finish."

As Lila left the general store, her mind was spinning with new information and theories. Frank had admitted to signing a deal with Fox. Sheriff Jennings was clearly concerned about the investigation into his father's involvement with Maritime Ventures. And someone—perhaps Jennings himself—knew that she and Marcus were digging into the old case.

She crossed quickly to Salted Caramel's, where Kyle had turned on the lights and was wiping down the already spotless counters. A few customers had wandered in, examining the ice cream flavors displayed in the gleaming case.

"Everything okay?" Kyle asked in a low voice as she joined him behind the counter. "You look like you've seen a ghost."

"More like the potential killer," Lila murmured, quickly filling him in on her conversation with Frank and the Sheriff's ominous visit. "I need to call Marcus—Detective Cole," she corrected herself hastily. "He needs to know about this."

As she reached for her phone, the bell above the shop door jingled. Lila looked up, expecting to see another tourist, but instead found herself face to face with Elsie Winters. Her best friend looked tired and disheveled, her normally vibrant red curls limp, her green eyes shadowed with exhaustion and worry.

"Elsie!" Lila exclaimed, rushing around the counter to embrace her. "I'm so glad you're okay! I was so worried."

Elsie returned the hug fiercely, her slim frame trembling slightly. "It was awful, Lila. They kept asking me about the contract, about Fox, about why I took it from his briefcase." She pulled back, her expression haunted. "I told them everything—about finding the briefcase in the alley when I went to leave you a note the night Fox died, about seeing the contract inside and taking it when I realized it involved Mira's B&B."

"It's okay," Lila assured her, guiding her to a seat at the counter. "You're out now. That's what matters."

"But the charges are still pending," Elsie said miserably. "And Sheriff Jennings made it very clear that they could add more serious charges if they find evidence I was involved in Fox's death."

"You weren't," Lila stated firmly. "And we're going to prove it. In fact, I think we're getting closer to understanding who was really behind everything."

She quickly brought Elsie up to speed on what she'd learned about the Jennings family connection to both development projects, Frank's admission about signing a deal with Fox, and the strange warning in the note left at the boathouse about her father's past.

"So you think Sheriff Jennings might have killed Fox?" Elsie asked, her eyes wide. "But why? If his family stood to profit from the development, wouldn't he want it to proceed?"

"That's what doesn't make sense yet," Lila admitted. "Unless Fox discovered something about the old deal, something that Jennings didn't want brought to light."

"Like what happened to Samuel Price?" Kyle suggested, joining the conversation as he served a customer a double scoop of chocolate chip. "If Fox was digging into the history of the 1995 deal, he might have found evidence that Price's death wasn't an accident after all."

The implications hung in the air between them. If Samuel Price's boating "accident" had actually been murder, and if the Jennings family was somehow involved, it would give Sheriff Jennings an extremely powerful motive to silence Graham Fox before he could expose the truth.

"We need to talk to Marcus," Lila said decisively. "He needs to know about Frank's admission and the Sheriff's strange visit."

"Marcus?" Elsie raised an eyebrow, a ghost of her usual teasing smile appearing despite her exhaustion. "Is that what we're calling Detective Cole now?"

Lila felt heat rising to her cheeks. "It's his name."

"Mmhmm," Elsie hummed knowingly. "And the way your face lights up when you say it is purely professional, I'm sure."

"Leave her alone, Elsie," Kyle chuckled, though his eyes held the same knowing look. "She can't help it if she's developing a crush on the handsome detective who's investigating a murder case connected to our family."

"I do not have a crush," Lila protested weakly, though the blush creeping up her neck betrayed her. "We're working together to solve this case, that's all."

"Sure," Elsie and Kyle said in unison, exchanging amused glances.

Lila was saved from further teasing by the shop door opening again. This time, it was her mother, Eva, looking concerned as she made her way to the counter.

"Elsie, dear!" she exclaimed, enveloping the younger woman in a warm hug. "I'm so relieved you're alright. What a terrible ordeal for you."

"I'm okay, Mrs. Montgomery," Elsie assured her, returning the hug. "Just tired and a little shaken up."

Eva studied her with motherly concern. "You look exhausted. Have you eaten anything today?"

When Elsie shook her head, Eva immediately took charge. "Kyle, get her a bowl of that blackberry lavender ice cream she loves. Lila, there's homemade chicken salad in my bag—make her a sandwich. The poor girl needs sustenance after what she's been through."

No one argued with Eva Montgomery when she was in caretaking mode. Within minutes, Elsie was settled at a back table with ice cream, a chicken salad sandwich, and a large glass of iced tea, Eva sitting beside her and ensuring she ate every bite.

As Lila returned to serving customers—a steady trickle had begun to come in, curious to see the shop where a murder investigation had begun—her phone buzzed with a text message. She checked it discreetly, her heart skipping a beat when she saw it was from Marcus.

Need to speak with you urgently. Found something on your father's recording device. Can you meet at the station in 30 minutes? -MC

Lila quickly texted back: *Yes. Something to tell you too. About Frank Mitchell and Sheriff Jennings.*

His response came almost immediately: *Don't put details in text. And don't tell anyone where you're going. Trust no one right now.*

The ominous warning sent a chill down her spine. Whatever Marcus had found on her father's old recording device must be significant —and potentially dangerous.

Lila approached Kyle, who was cheerfully scooping strawberry ice cream for a family of tourists. "I need to step out for a bit," she said quietly when the customers moved away. "Can you handle things here?"

Kyle's easy smile faded as he noted her serious expression. "What's going on?"

"Marcus found something on Dad's recording device. I need to go to the station."

"Want me to come with you?"

Lila shook her head. "Better if you stay here with Mom and Elsie. I'll be fine—it's broad daylight, and I'm going straight to the police station."

Kyle looked reluctant but nodded. "Okay, but text me when you get there and when you're heading back. And if you're not back in an hour, I'm coming to find you."

"Deal," Lila agreed, touched by her brother's protective instinct.

She slipped out of the shop without alerting her mother or Elsie, not wanting to worry them or answer questions about where she was going. The walk to the police station was short, just a few blocks along Main Street, but Lila found herself glancing over her shoulder more than once, an unsettling feeling of being watched creeping over her.

The reception area of the station was busier than it had been earlier that morning. Officer Jensen was still at the desk, now joined by another young officer who was processing paperwork for a tourist reporting a stolen beach bag. Lila caught Jensen's eye and mouthed "Detective Cole?" The officer nodded toward the back hallway, indicating she could go through.

Marcus's office door was slightly ajar. Lila knocked lightly before pushing it open, finding him hunched over his desk, headphones on, listening intently to something. He looked up at her knock, removing the headphones and motioning her inside.

"Close the door," he said by way of greeting, his expression grave.

Lila complied, then took the seat across from his desk. "What did you find?"

Marcus ran a hand through his dark hair, making it stand up in that appealingly disheveled way that made Lila's heart flutter despite the seriousness of the situation. "Your father recorded a conversation with Samuel Jennings—Sheriff Jennings' father—shortly before Samuel Price's death in 1995. Listen to this."

He adjusted the old microcassette player and handed her the headphones. Lila put them on, and Marcus pressed play.

At first, the recording was difficult to make out—decades old, captured on outdated technology, with the hiss and pop of magnetic tape. But then her father's voice came through, unmistakable despite the years and the poor quality: "I'm not comfortable with the direction this is taking, Sam. The threats against Price have to stop."

Another voice—presumably Samuel Jennings—responded with a dismissive laugh. "They're not threats, Jack. Just business reality. Price is holding up a multi-million dollar deal because of some misguided family tradition. He's costing all of us money—you included."

"I signed on to broker a fair deal, not to intimidate people into selling," her father's voice insisted. "And these 'accidents' at Price's dock—equipment failures, vandalism—they've gone too far."

"Those are just coincidences," Jennings replied, though his tone suggested otherwise. "But Price needs to understand that his stubbornness has consequences. One way or another, Marigold Holdings will have that waterfront property."

"What does that mean, Sam? What are you planning?"

"Nothing you need to worry about, Jack. Just do your job and convince Price to sell. If you can't do that, then stay out of the way. There's too much money at stake to let one stubborn fisherman ruin everything."

The recording ended abruptly there. Lila removed the headphones, her hands shaking slightly. "My father was worried that Samuel Jennings was planning something against Price," she said, the implications making her stomach twist. "And then Price died in a boating accident just days later."

"Exactly," Marcus nodded grimly. "Your father suspected foul play but couldn't prove it. Based on the other documents in the lockbox, I think that's why he backed out of the deal—he couldn't be part of something that might have involved murder, even if it meant taking on enormous debt."

"And now history is repeating itself," Lila murmured. "Another Jennings, another development deal, another suspicious death."

"Yes, but with a twist," Marcus said, leaning forward. "I think Graham Fox may have discovered this recording, or at least uncovered evidence about what really happened to Samuel Price. That's why he was interested in your shop's 'historical significance'—not just because of the Harbor Act rights, but because your father had evidence connecting the Jennings family to a potential murder."

Lila's mind raced, connecting dots rapidly. "And if Sheriff Jennings discovered that Fox was digging into his father's past..."

"He'd have a powerful motive to silence him," Marcus finished. "Now, tell me what you found out about Frank Mitchell and the Sheriff. You mentioned something in your text."

Lila quickly relayed her conversations with both men—Frank's admission that he'd already signed a deal with Fox, the Sheriff's unexpected attempt to get her alone to discuss the past, and the warning signals she'd felt during that interaction.

"So Frank sold out," Marcus mused, making notes in his small notebook. "That's not surprising, given what the documents show about his stance in 1995. He was disappointed when the original deal fell through. As for Jennings wanting to talk to you privately..." His expression darkened. "That's concerning. He knows we're digging into his family's connection to both development deals."

"Someone must have told him about our conversation this morning," Lila suggested.

"Or he's been monitoring my investigation more closely than I realized," Marcus replied, his tone grim. "Either way, you were right to refuse to meet with him alone. From now on, don't go anywhere with him, no matter what he says."

The seriousness in his voice sent a shiver down Lila's spine. "You really think he killed Fox, don't you?"

"I think it's a strong possibility," Marcus admitted. "But we still don't have enough evidence to make an arrest, especially given his position as Sheriff. We need more proof connecting him directly to Fox's death."

"What about the recording? Isn't that evidence that his father might have been involved in Samuel Price's death?"

"It's suspicious, certainly, but not definitive. And it happened twenty-five years ago—the statute of limitations on most crimes would have expired, except for murder. But to prove murder, we'd need a lot more than a vague recorded conversation." Marcus tapped his pen against the desk, thinking. "What we need is evidence that Sheriff Jennings met with Fox before his death, ideally something that shows a confrontation or threat."

"Maybe Mira Douglas would know something," Lila suggested. "Fox was staying at her B&B, after all. And we still don't understand her connection to all this. Why was Fox offering her twice what the B&B was worth?"

"Good point," Marcus nodded. "I've been trying to interview her again, but she's been surprisingly difficult to track down for someone who runs a business in a small town."

"I could talk to her," Lila offered. "Woman to woman. She might be more willing to open up to me than to an official police detective."

"Absolutely not," Marcus replied firmly. "It's too dangerous. If Jennings is our killer, and if Mira knows something about his connection to Fox, she could be in danger too—or she could be working with him. Either way, I don't want you anywhere near her without backup."

The protective edge in his voice sent a warm flutter through Lila's chest, though she tried to focus on the case rather than her growing feelings for the detective. "Then what's our next move?"

Marcus checked his watch, frowning slightly. "I have to meet with the District Attorney in thirty minutes to discuss Elsie's case. After that, I plan to interview Mira Douglas again, with or without her cooperation. In the meantime, I want you to go back to your shop and stay there. Don't go anywhere alone, don't talk to Sheriff Jennings, and don't mention what we've discovered to anyone."

"Not even Kyle or Elsie?" Lila protested. "They're already involved in this."

"The fewer people who know about the recording, the safer everyone will be," Marcus insisted. "If Jennings killed Fox to protect his family secret, he won't hesitate to silence anyone else who threatens to expose it."

The gravity of the situation settled over Lila like a weight. This wasn't just about saving her friend from an obstruction charge anymore, or protecting her shop from developers. It was about uncovering a potential double murder spanning twenty-five years, with the town's top law enforcement officer as the prime suspect.

"I'll be careful," she promised. "But you need to be careful too. If Sheriff Jennings suspects you're investigating him..."

"I know the risks," Marcus assured her, his expression softening slightly. "I've dealt with corrupt officers before. It's part of the job."

"Not usually when they're your boss, I imagine," Lila pointed out.

A wry smile crossed Marcus's face. "No, that does complicate things a bit."

Their eyes met across the desk, and for a moment, the tension of the case seemed to fade, replaced by a different kind of tension altogether. Lila was acutely aware of the small office, of how close they were sitting, of the way Marcus's green eyes seemed to see straight through her professional facade to the worry—and the attraction—beneath.

"I should get back to the shop," she said finally, breaking the charged silence. "Kyle will be wondering where I am."

Marcus nodded, though he made no move to stand. "Text me when you get there safely."

"I will," Lila promised, rising from her chair. "And you'll let me know what happens with the DA and Mira?"

"As soon as I can," he agreed.

At the door, Lila paused, turning back to him. "Marcus? Be careful. Please."

The use of his first name seemed to affect him, a flicker of something warm passing through his eyes. "You too, Lila."

The walk back to Salted Caramel's gave Lila time to process everything she'd learned. Her father's recording had confirmed what they'd already begun to suspect—that Samuel Price's death in 1995 might not have been an accident after all, and that the Jennings family had been directly involved in pressuring him to sell. If Graham Fox had discovered this connection, it would explain why Sheriff Jennings might have wanted him silenced permanently.

But questions still remained. How had Fox learned about the old case? What evidence had he found that linked the Sheriff to his father's potential crimes? And what role did Mira Douglas play in all this? The B&B owner was still a mystery—her property was valuable to the developers, but her personal connection to Fox remained unclear.

Lost in thought, Lila almost didn't notice the black SUV that slowed beside her as she approached her shop. The passenger window rolled down, revealing Sheriff Jennings behind the wheel.

"Lila," he called out, his tone friendly though his eyes were cold. "Just the person I was looking for. Could I have a moment of your time? It's about your friend Elsie."

Warning bells clanged in Lila's mind. Marcus's caution echoed in her memory: *Don't go anywhere with him, no matter what he says.*

"Actually, Sheriff, I'm in a bit of a rush," she replied, continuing to walk toward her shop, now just half a block away. "Elsie's at my shop right now if you need to speak with her."

"That's just it," Jennings said, keeping pace with her in the SUV. "There's been a development in her case. Something she should know immediately. I'd be happy to drive you back to your shop—it'll only take a minute."

The invitation—to get into his vehicle, to be alone with him—sent a chill down Lila's spine. "That's kind of you, but I'm almost there anyway," she said, quickening her pace slightly. "I'll let Elsie know you're looking for her."

Sheriff Jennings' friendly expression hardened. "Lila, I really think you should reconsider. This is important police business."

"Then I'm sure Detective Cole would want to be involved as well," Lila countered. "Why don't I call him right now?"

She pulled out her phone demonstratively, her finger hovering over Marcus's number. For a moment, she thought Jennings might actually get out of the car and force her to come with him. But then his expression shifted, the mask of friendliness returning.

"No need to bother the detective," he said smoothly. "I'll catch up with Elsie later. You have a good day now, Lila."

The SUV accelerated away, leaving Lila standing on the sidewalk with her heart pounding. The encounter had confirmed her worst fears—Sheriff Jennings was actively trying to get her alone, using Elsie as bait. Whatever he was planning, it couldn't be good.

She hurried the remaining distance to Salted Caramel's, relieved to see the shop busy with customers, Kyle efficiently serving scoops while Elsie and her mother chatted at a back table. The normalcy of the scene was reassuring after the tense encounter with Jennings.

"Everything okay?" Kyle asked as she joined him behind the counter, quickly washing her hands and donning an apron. "You look spooked."

"I'll tell you later," Lila murmured, not wanting to discuss it in front of customers. "For now, just be aware that Sheriff Jennings might stop by, supposedly looking for Elsie. If he does, don't let her go anywhere with him alone."

Kyle's eyebrows shot up, but he nodded, understanding the seriousness of her warning.

For the next hour, Lila threw herself into the familiar rhythm of running the shop—scooping ice cream, chatting with customers, restocking napkins and spoons. The mundane tasks helped calm her frayed nerves, though she found her gaze drifting to the door each time it opened, half-expecting to see Sheriff Jennings return.

Instead, just after three o'clock, it was Marcus who walked through the door. He was still in his suit, though he'd loosened his tie slightly, and there was a tension in his shoulders that hadn't been there earlier. He caught Lila's eye immediately, giving her a small nod that somehow managed to convey both relief at seeing her safe and an urgency to speak privately.

"I'll take care of the counter," Kyle offered, noticing the exchange. "Go talk to your detective."

Lila didn't bother correcting the possessive pronoun this time. She removed her apron and moved around the counter to meet Marcus, leading him to a small table in the corner, as far from other customers as possible.

"I was just about to text you," she said as they sat down. "Sheriff Jennings approached me on my way back from the station. Tried to get me into his car, claiming he had news about Elsie's case."

Marcus's expression darkened, his jaw tightening visibly. "I knew it. He's getting desperate. Did anyone see this interaction?"

"Several people were on the street, though I don't know if anyone was paying attention," Lila replied. "I made it clear I wasn't going anywhere with him, especially when I mentioned calling you. That seemed to change his mind pretty quickly."

"He knows we've been working together," Marcus said grimly. "And he probably suspects we've found the recording. My meeting with the DA was canceled at the last minute—apparently at Sheriff Jennings' request. He claimed new evidence had come to light that needed to be processed before any decisions were made about Elsie's case."

"What new evidence?"

"That's just it—there is no new evidence. It was a stalling tactic, and I'm now certain it's because he's trying to figure out how much we know about his family's connection to both Fox's death and what happened in 1995."

Lila's stomach twisted with anxiety. "What do we do now? We can't just wait for him to make another move, especially if he's targeting me or Elsie."

"We're not waiting," Marcus assured her, his voice low but intense. "I've contacted an old colleague at the State Police. Explained the situation and the evidence we've uncovered. They're sending investigators tomorrow to look into Sheriff Jennings and his connection to both cases."

Relief flooded through Lila. "So it's almost over? They'll arrest him?"

"Not quite that simple," Marcus cautioned. "We still need solid evidence connecting Jennings directly to Fox's death. The recording and circumstantial evidence about his father's involvement in 1995 isn't enough for an arrest, much less a conviction."

"So what's our next step?"

"Our next step is to keep you and Elsie safe until the State Police arrive," Marcus replied firmly. "Which means neither of you should be alone at any point. In fact, I think it would be best if you both stayed somewhere unexpected tonight—not at your apartment, not at your mother's house, and definitely not at Elsie's place."

"Where, then?" Lila asked, a chill running down her spine at the implication that they were in immediate danger.

"My place," Marcus said, then hastily added, "I have a spare bedroom. And my apartment building has security. Sheriff Jennings doesn't know where I live, and he won't expect either of you to be there."

The suggestion brought a flush to Lila's cheeks despite the seriousness of the situation. Staying at Marcus's apartment, seeing his personal space, spending the evening in his company outside the context of the investigation—it was both thrilling and terrifying.

"I'll check with Elsie," she said, trying to keep her voice steady. "But I think that's a good plan. Safety in numbers, right?"

"Exactly," Marcus nodded, though there was a hint of color on his neck just above his shirt collar. "Besides, I could use your help reviewing the evidence we've collected. Fresh eyes might catch something I've missed."

They were interrupted by Kyle approaching the table, his expression concerned. "Sorry to break up the detective meeting, but there's someone here asking for you, Lila. Says it's urgent."

Lila looked past her brother to see Daisy Clark, the town librarian and historical society curator, standing near the counter. The older woman looked agitated, clutching her purse tightly to her chest, her eyes darting nervously around the shop.

"Daisy?" Lila rose from the table, Marcus following suit. "Is everything alright?"

"No, it most certainly is not," Daisy replied, her voice quavering slightly. "I've found something in the archives that I think you and the detective need to see immediately. Something about the 1995 development project and Samuel Price's death. Something that might explain why Graham Fox was killed."

The direct mention of the connection between the two deaths—a connection that wasn't public knowledge—sent a jolt of alarm through Lila. "How do you know about that?"

Daisy's eyes widened slightly, as if realizing she'd said too much. "I... I pieced it together from what you asked me earlier, about your shop's historical significance. And then when I heard about Sheriff Jennings questioning your friend Elsie..." She trailed off, glancing nervously toward the door. "Please, we shouldn't discuss this here. Can you come to the historical society? I've found documentation that I think proves what really happened to Samuel Price. And why history seems to be repeating itself now."

Lila exchanged a look with Marcus, seeing her own wariness reflected in his eyes. Could they trust Daisy? The elderly librarian had always seemed harmless, dedicated to preserving the town's history. But in light of everything they'd discovered, everyone in Seabreeze Shores was a potential suspect or ally of Sheriff Jennings.

"Let me get my jacket," Lila said finally, making a quick decision. "Detective Cole and I will come with you right now."

As Daisy moved toward the door, Marcus gripped Lila's arm gently, his voice a low whisper. "Are you sure about this? It could be a trap."

"Daisy's seventy years old and has spent her life surrounded by dusty books," Lila whispered back. "If she's setting a trap, I'll eat my apron. Besides, you'll be with me. And if she really has found evidence about Samuel Price's death, it could be the proof we need to connect Jennings to both murders."

Marcus didn't look entirely convinced, but he nodded. "Alright. But we stay together, and at the first sign of anything suspicious, we leave immediately. Deal?"

"Deal," Lila agreed.

She quickly informed Kyle and her mother of where they were going, ignoring Kyle's concerned frown and her mother's knowing smile at the fact that she was leaving with Marcus yet again. Elsie, still exhausted from her ordeal at the police station, had fallen asleep in a chair by the window, sunlight streaming across her pale face.

"Don't wake her," Lila told her mother. "She needs the rest. We'll be back soon, and then I need to talk to both of you about plans for tonight."

As they left the shop to follow Daisy to the historical society, Lila felt a strange mixture of anticipation and dread. They were on the verge of uncovering the truth—about her father's past, about Samuel Price's death, about Graham Fox's murder. But the closer they came to the truth, the more dangerous their situation became.

The weight of Marcus's hand at the small of her back as they walked was reassuring, a silent reminder that she wasn't facing this alone. Whatever revelations awaited them at the historical society, whatever danger might still lie ahead, they would face it together. The thought gave her courage, even as she wondered what secrets Daisy had uncovered about Seabreeze Shores' troubled past—and whether those secrets might finally bring a killer to justice.

Chapter 7
Turning Tides

The Seabreeze Shores Historical Society stood on Lighthouse Hill, its Victorian architecture a testament to the town's once-prosperous shipping era. Late afternoon sunlight gilded its gingerbread trim and reflected off mullioned windows as Lila, Marcus, and Daisy Clark climbed the front steps. The wraparound porch, with its white rocking chairs and hanging ferns, seemed inviting despite the ominous purpose of their visit.

Daisy's silver key ring jingled as she unlocked the heavy oak door, her hands trembling slightly. At sixty-eight, she remained spry, with the ramrod-straight posture of someone who had spent decades reminding visitors to respect the treasures of the past. Today, however, she moved with an uncharacteristic urgency, ushering them inside with nervous glances over her shoulder.

"I've left everything laid out in the research room," she explained, leading them through the foyer with its display of maritime artifacts—

ships' wheels, navigational instruments, a captain's log from 1876. The floorboards creaked beneath their feet, the sound amplified in the hushed interior.

Lila had visited the historical society countless times—for school projects as a child, later for research on local recipes that might inspire new ice cream flavors. She'd always found comfort in the building's quiet dignity, the sense of connection to Seabreeze Shores' past. Today, however, the shadows seemed deeper, the silence more oppressive, as if the house itself knew they were disturbing long-buried secrets.

Marcus walked beside her, his hand occasionally brushing against hers, the brief contact sending warmth through her despite the tension of the moment. He took in their surroundings with the practiced eye of a detective, noting exits, sightlines, potential hiding places. Even here, pursuing historical evidence, he remained vigilant.

The research room occupied what had once been the mansion's library, its walls lined with built-in bookshelves housing leather-bound volumes, archival boxes, and carefully preserved documents. A massive oak table dominated the center of the room, its surface now covered with maps, photographs, and yellowed newspaper clippings arranged in a careful pattern.

"Please, close the door," Daisy requested, moving to the windows to draw the heavy velvet curtains, shrouding the room in dim, filtered light. She switched on a brass reading lamp, its warm glow illuminating the documents on the table. "What I'm about to show you... well, it could be quite dangerous if certain people knew I'd found it."

Lila and Marcus exchanged glances, his subtle nod encouraging her to take the lead with the elderly librarian. "Daisy," Lila began gently, "what exactly have you found? And how is it connected to Graham Fox's death?"

Daisy adjusted her bifocals, her thin fingers smoothing the edge of a newspaper. "It started when you asked about your shop's historical significance. That got me thinking about the Harbor Act properties and their importance to development plans. So I began digging through our archives, looking for connections between the 1995 project and what Mr. Fox was proposing."

She gestured toward the table. "What I found was... troubling. A pattern of suspicious accidents involving property owners who opposed development. Not just in 1995, but stretching back decades in Seabreeze Shores' history."

Marcus leaned forward, his interest clearly piqued. "What kind of accidents?"

"Boating mishaps, falls, apparent heart attacks at convenient moments," Daisy replied, pointing to various newspaper clippings. "In 1975, Harold Jenkins—who owned the largest stretch of undeveloped beachfront—drowned after his boat capsized in calm waters. In 1982, Martha Wilcox—whose family estate overlooked the harbor—fell down her stairs the day before she was to speak at a town meeting opposing a marina expansion."

Lila studied the articles, noticing small notations in Daisy's neat handwriting beside each one. "You think these weren't accidents? That they were somehow connected to development plans?"

"I didn't, initially," Daisy admitted. "But the pattern became impossible to ignore, especially when I found these." She carefully slid forward a manila folder labeled "Price Investigation—Unofficial."

Inside were photocopies of handwritten notes, what appeared to be a partial autopsy report, and several photographs of Samuel Price's fishing boat after the accident that claimed his life. "These belonged to Officer Thomas Reed," Daisy explained. "He was a rookie on the police force in 1995, assigned to take routine photographs at the scene of Samuel Price's accident. He wasn't satisfied with the quick ruling of accidental death and continued investigating privately."

Marcus examined the notes with professional interest. "Reed suspected foul play?"

"More than suspected," Daisy confirmed. "Look at his notes about the boat's outboard motor."

Marcus read aloud: "'Evidence of tampering. Fuel line appears deliberately damaged. Cut is clean, not consistent with wear or accident.'" He looked up sharply. "If this is accurate, someone sabotaged Price's boat."

"Exactly," Daisy nodded. "Reed brought his concerns to his superior—Deputy Sam Jennings at the time. The next day, Reed was reassigned to traffic duty, and the investigation was officially closed as an accident. A week later, Reed resigned from the force and left town."

Lila's mind raced with implications. "So Sam Jennings effectively shut down an investigation that might have implicated his own father in Samuel Price's death?"

"It certainly appears that way," Daisy agreed. "And here's where it connects to Graham Fox." She pulled out another folder, this one newer. "Two weeks ago, a young woman came to the historical society asking about accidents related to development disputes in Seabreeze Shores. She claimed to be a law student researching property rights, but she was particularly interested in Samuel Price's death and the abandoned 1995 development project."

"Nina West," Lila guessed, remembering the business card Daisy had shown her earlier.

"Yes," Daisy confirmed. "She spent hours going through our archives, taking notes and photographs. I didn't think much of it at the time—we get researchers fairly regularly. But after Graham Fox's death, I remembered something odd."

"What was that?" Marcus prompted.

"She received a phone call while she was here. She stepped outside to take it, but I overheard part of the conversation when she returned. She said, 'Yes, Mr. Fox, I've found it. The evidence is here, just like you suspected.'" Daisy's expression grew troubled. "Two days later, she checked out of her motel and left town abruptly. Three days after that, Graham Fox arrived in Seabreeze Shores."

Marcus was already making notes in his small notebook. "Did this Nina West leave any contact information? An address, phone number?"

"Just the business card I showed Lila," Daisy replied. "I tried calling the number yesterday, but it's disconnected."

"She was working for Fox," Lila murmured, the pieces falling into place. "Researching the town's history, looking for leverage he could use in his development plans. And she found evidence that Samuel Price's death wasn't an accident—evidence that implicated the Jennings family."

"Which gave Sheriff Jennings a powerful motive to silence Fox," Marcus added, his voice low. "If Fox had proof that Jennings' father was involved in a murder twenty-five years ago..."

"It would ruin him," Daisy finished. "His career, his reputation, his family legacy—all destroyed if the truth came out."

Lila moved to the window, carefully edging the curtain aside to peer at the street below. The historical society sat on a hill overlooking much of Seabreeze Shores. From this vantage point, she could see Main Street, the harbor with its bobbing fishing boats, and beyond, the blue expanse of the Atlantic. It all looked so peaceful, so normal—belying the dark secrets they were uncovering.

"There's one more thing you should see," Daisy said, her voice lowered though they were alone in the building. "Something I found just this morning, hidden in a false bottom of an old filing cabinet."

She produced a small leather journal, its pages yellowed with age. "This belonged to Samuel Jennings—the Sheriff's father. I believe he hid it here himself, in a moment of conscience or fear. You see, before he worked for Maritime Ventures, Samuel Jennings was on the historical society board. He had a key to the building and unrestricted access to our archives."

With reverent care, she opened the journal to a page marked with a faded ribbon. "Read this," she said, sliding it toward Lila and Marcus.

The handwriting was cramped but legible, the entry dated three days before Samuel Price's death:

Price remains stubborn despite increased offer. Caldwell growing impatient, threatening to pull entire project if we can't secure all Harbor Act properties. Too much at stake to fail now. Montgomery doing his part with most owners, but useless with Price—their friendship complicates matters. Discussed final contingency plan with L. If accident occurs as planned, investigation must be contained quickly. J. positioned to handle official response if necessary.

Lila read the entry twice, her blood running cold. "L must be Lawrence Caldwell—Victor Caldwell's son, the current CEO of Marigold Holdings. And J..."

"Sam Jennings," Marcus concluded grimly. "The current Sheriff, who was a deputy at the time. This journal entry strongly suggests that Samuel Price's 'accident' was premeditated, with the younger Jennings positioned to ensure it would be ruled accidental."

"And my father," Lila said softly, the revelation hitting her anew. "He was helping them convince other owners to sell, but he wouldn't pressure Price because they were friends."

"Which explains why he backed out of the deal completely after Price died," Marcus nodded. "He must have suspected what had happened, even if he couldn't prove it."

Daisy carefully took back the journal. "There's more. Entries that suggest a long-standing relationship between the Jennings family and Marigold Holdings, spanning decades. The 1995 development wasn't their first attempt to reshape Seabreeze Shores, nor was Price's death the first suspicious accident benefiting their plans."

"This is the evidence we need," Marcus said, his tone shifting to professional urgency. "Daisy, I need to take that journal, along with Officer Reed's notes and the other documentation you've collected. This could be enough to convince the State Police to move against Sheriff Jennings immediately, rather than waiting until tomorrow."

Daisy hesitated, her archivist's instinct to preserve historical documents warring with the gravity of the situation. "Of course," she finally agreed. "But please be careful with them. These aren't just evidence—they're part of our town's history, however dark that history might be."

As she gathered the documents into a portfolio, Lila returned to the window, drawn by movement on the street below. A black SUV had parked across from the historical society—the same vehicle Sheriff Jennings had been driving earlier when he tried to get her into his car. As she watched, the driver's door opened, and a familiar figure emerged.

"Marcus," she called softly, her voice tight with alarm. "Sheriff Jennings is here."

Marcus was at her side in an instant, peering through the gap in the curtains. "How did he know we'd be here?" he muttered, his expression darkening.

"Perhaps he followed you from the ice cream shop," Daisy suggested, her face paling. "Or someone told him where you were going."

"We need to leave, now," Marcus said decisively. "Is there a back exit?"

Daisy nodded. "Through the service hallway, past the maritime exhibit. It leads to a door opening onto Lighthouse Path—a walking trail that connects to Main Street behind the shops."

"Perfect," Marcus said, taking the portfolio of documents from her. "Daisy, you should come with us. If Jennings realizes you've shared this evidence with us, you could be in danger too."

The elderly librarian straightened her spine, a flash of steel showing beneath her gentle exterior. "This is my post, Detective Cole. I've been custodian of this society for thirty-two years, and I will not abandon it now. Besides," she added with a small smile, "I know every hiding place in this building. If necessary, I can make myself scarce until you've dealt with the Sheriff."

Lila touched the older woman's arm. "Are you sure? We could come back for your car later."

"Quite sure, dear," Daisy replied firmly. "Now go, quickly. I'll delay him if he comes to the door."

With a final grateful nod to the librarian, Lila and Marcus slipped from the research room and down the service hallway, past glass cases displaying harpoons, compasses, and the personal effects of long-dead sea captains. The back door, rarely used, protested with a creak as Marcus pushed it open, revealing a narrow dirt path winding down the hill between ancient oak trees draped with Spanish moss.

They had barely closed the door behind them when the muffled sound of the front doorbell echoed through the old house. Sheriff Jennings had reached the historical society.

"Move quickly but quietly," Marcus murmured, taking Lila's hand as they made their way down the path. The late afternoon sun filtered through the oak canopy, dappling the ground with shifting patterns of light and shadow. In other circumstances, it might have been a romantic walk; now, it was a tense escape.

Lila's sandals were not ideal for the uneven terrain, and she stumbled once on an exposed tree root. Marcus caught her before she could fall, his arm sliding around her waist to steady her. The contact, brief though it was, sent a flutter through her stomach that had nothing to do with their precarious situation.

"Sorry," she whispered, acutely aware of his closeness, the faint woodsy scent of his cologne.

"I've got you," he replied, his voice low, his eyes meeting hers for a moment that seemed to stretch beyond the seconds it actually occupied. Then, with a slight shake of his head as if to clear it, he released her waist but kept hold of her hand. "Come on, we're almost to Main Street."

The path wound down the hill, eventually emerging behind a row of shops about three blocks from Salted Caramel's. As they stepped onto the pavement of the back alley, Marcus pulled out his phone. "I need to call my contact at the State Police immediately. This evidence changes everything."

While he made the call, speaking in low, urgent tones, Lila kept watch on both ends of the alley, alert for any sign of the Sheriff's black SUV. Her mind raced with implications of what they'd discovered. Her father had been more deeply involved in the 1995 development than she'd realized, though he'd ultimately made the right choice in backing out. Samuel Price's death had indeed been murder, orchestrated by the Jennings family and Marigold Holdings. And now, history had nearly repeated itself with Graham Fox.

"They're sending a team immediately," Marcus reported as he ended the call. "Should be here within the hour. In the meantime, we need to get somewhere safe and secure this evidence." He held up the portfolio Daisy had given them. "If Jennings realizes what we have, he'll stop at nothing to destroy it."

"What about Daisy?" Lila asked, concern for the elderly librarian gnawing at her. "She's alone with him."

"Jennings doesn't know what she's found yet," Marcus reasoned. "And he's too smart to harm her without knowing exactly what she knows and who she's told. For now, our priority is protecting this evidence and getting you somewhere safe."

"My shop," Lila suggested. "Kyle and my mother are there, and Elsie too. We need to warn them about Jennings."

Marcus considered this, clearly weighing the risks. "It might be the last place Jennings would expect us to go, precisely because it's so obvious. And there's safety in numbers. Let's head there, but carefully—stay in the back alleys as much as possible."

They moved swiftly but cautiously through the network of service alleys that ran behind Main Street's shops. Seabreeze Shores had grown organically over centuries, resulting in a maze of narrow passages, courtyards, and cut-throughs known mainly to locals. Lila led the way, drawing on a lifetime of shortcuts discovered during childhood games of hide-and-seek.

As they approached the alley behind Salted Caramel's, Lila felt a growing sense of unease. The normally bustling back area, where deliveries arrived and shopkeepers took breaks, was unusually quiet. No one sat on the wooden benches where locals often gathered to smoke or chat, and even the resident alley cat—a ginger tom named Captain that all the shopkeepers fed—was nowhere to be seen.

Marcus sensed her hesitation, placing a restraining hand on her arm. "Wait," he whispered, his eyes scanning the alley with professional wariness. "Something's not right."

No sooner had he spoken than the back door of Salted Caramel's opened, and Kyle stepped out, followed closely by Sheriff Jennings. The Sheriff's hand rested casually on his holstered weapon, a gesture that might have seemed natural if not for the tight expression on Kyle's face.

"Just checking the trash bins like I said, Sheriff," Kyle called over his shoulder, his voice unnaturally loud, as if trying to alert someone inside the shop. "Won't take but a minute."

As he turned toward the alley, Kyle caught sight of Lila and Marcus partially concealed in the shadow of a delivery truck. His eyes widened fractionally, and he gave an almost imperceptible shake of his head—a warning not to approach.

"Take your time, son," Sheriff Jennings replied, leaning against the doorframe with deceptive casualness. "I'm enjoying catching up with your mother and Ms. Winters. Fascinating conversation about old times in Seabreeze Shores."

Lila felt her blood run cold. Her mother and Elsie were inside with Jennings, who was clearly using them to lay a trap for her and Marcus. Kyle's warning had potentially saved them from walking right into it.

Marcus pulled her gently back into the deeper shadows of the adjoining alley. "We need another plan," he whispered close to her ear, his breath warm against her skin. "My apartment. We'll be safe there until the State Police arrive."

"But my mother, Elsie, Kyle—"

"Are in a public place with witnesses," Marcus finished reassuringly. "Jennings won't risk anything with so many eyes around. Right now, his focus is on finding us and the evidence we have. The best way to protect everyone is to keep that evidence secure until the authorities arrive."

Though it pained her to leave her family and friend with the man they now knew was almost certainly a murderer, Lila recognized the logic in Marcus's plan. "Okay," she agreed reluctantly. "How do we get to your apartment without being seen?"

"My car is parked behind the police station," Marcus replied, thinking aloud. "But that's too risky—Jennings might have someone watching it. We need another vehicle."

Lila thought quickly. "What about Kyle's car? He usually parks in the municipal lot behind the hardware store. I have a spare key on my keyring."

Marcus nodded approvingly. "Good thinking. Let's go—but stay in the alleys until we reach the lot."

They retraced their steps, moving carefully through the back passages of Seabreeze Shores, alert for any sign of pursuit. The municipal lot was blessedly quiet when they arrived, most tourists preferring the more convenient beachfront parking during summer months. Kyle's blue Honda Civic sat in its usual spot, partially hidden by a delivery van.

Lila unlocked the car, and they slipped inside, ducking low in case anyone was watching the lot. "Where to?" she asked as Marcus took the driver's seat, adjusting it to accommodate his longer legs.

"Lighthouse Point Apartments, on the north side of town," he directed, starting the engine and carefully pulling out of the lot. "It's about ten minutes from here, assuming we don't encounter any unwanted attention."

As they drove through the streets of Seabreeze Shores, Lila found herself studying Marcus's profile in the golden late afternoon light. The strong line of his jaw, now showing a shadow of stubble; the intent focus in his green eyes as he navigated; the way his hands gripped the steering wheel with controlled strength. In the midst of danger and revelations, she was still acutely aware of him as a man, not just a detective—a realization that both surprised and unsettled her.

"What?" he asked, glancing her way, clearly sensing her gaze.

"Nothing," she replied quickly, then reconsidered. "Actually, I was just thinking how strange it is—a week ago, my biggest concern was deciding on the special flavor for the Seabreeze Festival. Now I'm fleeing a murderous sheriff with stolen historical documents and breaking into my brother's car with a detective I barely know."

A small smile tugged at the corner of Marcus's mouth. "When you put it that way, it does sound rather dramatic. Though for the record, it's not breaking in if you have a key. And as for barely knowing me..." He paused, his expression softening slightly. "Sometimes circumstances accelerate relationships. Crisis has a way of revealing character more quickly than casual interaction."

"And what has this crisis revealed about my character?" Lila asked, curious despite the gravity of their situation.

Marcus considered this as he navigated a turn, his eyes briefly meeting hers. "That you're fiercely loyal, surprisingly resourceful, and braver than you give yourself credit for. Most people would have backed away from this investigation long ago, especially once it became dangerous. You've persisted because you care about the truth and the people affected by it."

The assessment, delivered in his straightforward manner, warmed Lila from within. "And what about you, Detective Cole? What has this crisis revealed about your character?"

"That's for you to decide," he replied with that hint of a smile again. "Though I hope it's shown I can be trusted, even if I sometimes seem... intense."

"Intense is putting it mildly," Lila teased gently. "But yes, I do trust you. I wouldn't be in this car otherwise."

The moment of connection hung between them, a brief respite from the tension of pursuit and revelation. Then Marcus's expression grew serious again as he checked the rearview mirror. "I think we have company. Black SUV, two cars back. Been following the same turns as us for the last three blocks."

Lila twisted in her seat to look, her heart rate accelerating. "Is it Sheriff Jennings?"

"Can't tell from this distance, but the vehicle matches," Marcus replied, his voice calm despite the implication. "Let's find out for sure." He made a sudden right turn onto a residential street, then another quick left into an alley, accelerating slightly.

The black SUV followed the same pattern, confirming their suspicions.

"Definitely following us," Marcus concluded grimly. "Hold on. We're going to have to lose them before heading to my apartment."

What followed was a tense game of cat and mouse through the less-traveled streets of Seabreeze Shores. Marcus drove with the skill of someone professionally trained in evasive maneuvers, taking sudden turns, doubling back, and once cutting through the parking lot of the elementary school to emerge on an entirely different street.

Lila gripped the door handle as they navigated a particularly sharp turn, the portfolio of evidence secure in her lap. "Where did you learn to drive like this?" she asked, equal parts impressed and terrified.

"Advanced training at the academy," Marcus replied, his focus unwavering as he checked mirrors and calculated routes. "Plus a few years in a special response unit in Boston before I transferred here. Comes in handy occasionally."

After several minutes of tactical driving, they turned onto Ocean Drive, the coastal road that curved along the northern edge of town. The black SUV was nowhere in sight.

"I think we lost them," Lila said, releasing her death grip on the door handle.

"For now," Marcus agreed cautiously. "But we can't assume we're in the clear. Jennings knows this town as well as we do."

They continued north, the road hugging the coastline with the vast Atlantic on their right, glittering in the late afternoon sun. Eventually, Marcus turned into the entrance of Lighthouse Point Apartments, a modern complex built to resemble a collection of upscale beach cottages. A security gate barred the entrance, but Marcus had a key fob that opened it automatically.

"You weren't kidding about the security," Lila observed as the gate closed behind them. The complex was beautifully maintained, with manicured lawns, flowering shrubs, and neat footpaths connecting the various buildings. It seemed a world away from the quaint, slightly weathered charm of downtown Seabreeze Shores.

"One of the reasons I chose it," Marcus admitted as he parked in a numbered space beside a two-story building painted a soft coastal blue. "That, and the ocean view. Let's get inside."

They moved quickly from the car to the building entrance, Marcus scanning the area for any sign of pursuit. His apartment was on the second floor, at the end of a carpeted hallway decorated with tasteful nautical art. The door was solid, with a deadbolt and a modern electronic lock that required both a key and a code.

"Welcome to my humble abode," Marcus said with a touch of self-consciousness as he ushered Lila inside, locking the door securely behind them.

Lila wasn't sure what she had expected of Marcus's personal space. Something spartan and impersonal, perhaps, reflecting his professional demeanor. What she found instead was a surprisingly comfortable home that spoke of a man with more depth than his sometimes rigid exterior suggested.

Venom in Vanilla

The open-plan living area was dominated by a wall of windows overlooking the ocean, filling the space with natural light and expansive views. The furnishings were modern but inviting—a deep blue sectional sofa topped with carefully arranged throw pillows, a solid oak coffee table bearing a few well-thumbed books on maritime history, and a dining area with a glass-topped table and four chairs.

What surprised her most were the personal touches: framed black-and-white photographs of coastal scenes that had an artistic quality suggestive of the photographer's eye rather than store-bought decoration; a collection of antique fishing lures displayed in a shadow box; a bookshelf filled with an eclectic mix of murder mysteries, historical biographies, and classic literature.

"You took these photos?" Lila asked, moving to examine a particularly striking image of waves crashing against Seabreeze Shores' lighthouse.

Marcus nodded, setting the portfolio of evidence on the dining table. "Photography's a hobby. Helps clear my mind when cases get complicated. Something about focusing on composition and light... it's meditative."

"They're beautiful," Lila said sincerely, noting the careful framing and dramatic use of shadow in each image. This glimpse into Marcus's creative side fascinated her—another layer beneath the professional detective.

"Thank you," he replied, seeming genuinely pleased by her appreciation. "Make yourself comfortable. I'm going to call my State Police contact for an update on their ETA, then check in with the station to see if there's any official explanation for Jennings' behavior."

While Marcus made his calls from the kitDabney area, Lila explored the apartment further, noting small details that revealed aspects of his character: a chess board set up mid-game against an invisible opponent; a collection of local coffee mugs suggesting he supported small businesses; a yoga mat rolled neatly in the corner, hinting at an unexpected practice.

The spare bedroom he had mentioned was simply but thoughtfully furnished with a full-sized bed covered in a navy blue quilt, a bedside table with a reading lamp, and a small desk beneath the window. It looked ready for guests, though Lila wondered how often Marcus actually had visitors. The bathroom between the two bedrooms was immaculate, stocked with high-end but unfussy toiletries—the choices of a man who valued quality but avoided ostentation.

By the time she returned to the living area, Marcus had completed his calls and was organizing the documents from Daisy's portfolio on the dining table, creating a methodical arrangement that presumably made investigative sense to him.

"State Police will be here within thirty minutes," he reported. "They've coordinated with the county prosecutor's office and have authorization to question Jennings and secure evidence. In the meantime, I've photographed each document and sent the images to my secure cloud storage, in case anything happens to the originals."

"Smart," Lila nodded approvingly. "What about my family and Elsie? Were you able to check on them?"

"I spoke with Officer Jensen at the station. He confirmed that Jennings left your shop about fifteen minutes ago, apparently in a hurry. Your mother, brother, and Elsie are all still there and appear to be fine, though Jensen said they seemed concerned about you."

Relief flooded through Lila. "Should I call them? Let them know I'm safe?"

Marcus considered this, his expression thoughtful. "Not yet. If Jennings is monitoring phone activity, a call could give away our location. Once the State Police arrive and the situation is more secure, you can contact them."

Lila nodded, understanding the caution even as she hated the thought of her family worrying. "So now we wait?"

"Now we wait," Marcus confirmed. "And review what we know, see if there are connections we've missed." He gestured to the organized documents on the table. "Care to join me? Fresh eyes might spot something important."

They settled at the dining table, side by side, working through the historical evidence Daisy had provided. Samuel Jennings' journal proved particularly revealing, with entries spanning several years that detailed the family's involvement with Marigold Holdings, their stake in various development projects, and the increasingly desperate measures they had taken to overcome resistance.

"It's all about legacy for them," Lila observed, reading an entry where the elder Jennings lamented that locals couldn't see the 'greater vision' for Seabreeze Shores' future. "They genuinely believe they're improving the town, even if it means destroying what makes it special."

"That's often how corruption begins," Marcus replied, making notes as they worked. "With a belief that the ends justify the means. Small compromises lead to bigger ones, until eventually, murder seems like a reasonable solution to a problem."

As they worked, the setting sun cast the apartment in a golden glow, the ocean beyond the windows a rippling canvas of amber and rose. Lila found herself increasingly aware of Marcus beside her—the subtle citrus and cedar notes of his cologne, the thoughtful furrow of his brow as he analyzed documents, the surprising gentleness of his hands as he carefully handled the fragile journal pages.

At one point, they both reached for the same document, their fingers brushing. The brief contact sent a jolt of awareness through Lila, and she looked up to find Marcus watching her, his green eyes reflecting something beyond professional interest.

For a breathless moment, neither moved nor spoke. Then, with deliberate care, Marcus reached out and tucked a strand of hair behind Lila's ear, his fingers lingering against her cheek. "You've been extraordinary through all of this," he said softly. "Most people would have crumbled under the pressure, the revelations about their family, the danger."

Lila's heart hammered in her chest, her skin tingling where he'd touched her. "I don't feel extraordinary," she admitted. "Mostly I'm terrified and trying not to show it."

"That's what courage is," Marcus replied, his voice low. "Feeling the fear and continuing anyway."

He was so close now that she could see the faint scar near his right eyebrow, the flecks of gold in his green eyes, the slight unevenness of his stubble along his jaw. Without conscious thought, she leaned toward him, drawn by an invisible pull that seemed both inevitable and surprising.

Marcus hesitated, his professional boundaries warring visibly with personal desire. Then, with a soft exhale that might have been surrender, he closed the distance between them, his lips meeting hers in a kiss that started gentle but quickly deepened with the release of tension neither had fully acknowledged until now.

Lila's hand found its way to the nape of his neck, fingers threading through his dark hair as she responded to the kiss with an eagerness that surprised even her. Marcus's arm circled her waist, drawing her closer as the careful restraint he'd maintained throughout their investigation finally gave way to genuine feeling.

When they eventually pulled apart, both slightly breathless, a smile tugged at the corner of Marcus's mouth—not the reserved, professional smile she'd seen before, but something warmer, more personal. "I've been wanting to do that since you stormed into my office demanding answers about Elsie," he confessed.

"Even though I was furious with you?" Lila asked, amused and touched by the admission.

"Especially then," he replied, tucking another strand of hair behind her ear. "Your loyalty, your determination to protect your friend... it was impressive. Challenging, but impressive."

Lila laughed softly. "And here I thought I was just being difficult."

"Oh, you were definitely that too," Marcus teased, his hand still warm against her waist. The moment felt surreal—tender connection in the midst of danger and revelation, personal feelings emerging despite professional circumstances.

The sharp ring of Marcus's phone shattered the intimate atmosphere. His expression immediately shifted back to professional focus as he checked the screen. "It's the State Police," he reported, rising from his chair to answer. "Detective Cole."

Lila watched as he listened intently, his expression growing increasingly serious. "Understood," he said finally. "We'll stay put until you arrive. And Lieutenant? Be careful. Jennings knows this town better than any of us."

He ended the call, turning to Lila with renewed urgency. "They're ten minutes out, but there's a complication. Sheriff Jennings has issued an all-points bulletin for both of us—he's claiming we've stolen evidence in an active investigation and assaulted Daisy Clark at the historical society."

"What?" Lila exclaimed, shocked by the audacity of the lie. "Is Daisy okay?"

"The lieutenant says she's fine—shaken but unharmed. She's already told the State Police that Jennings fabricated the assault claim. "But it means every local officer is now looking for us, and Jennings has effectively turned the tables—painting us as the criminals while he maintains the appearance of law and order."

Lila sank back into her chair, the gravity of their situation hitting her anew. "So we're fugitives now? In our own town?"

"Temporarily," Marcus assured her, his tone steady despite the tension evident in his posture. "Once the State Police arrive with the county prosecutor, Jennings' authority will be superseded. But until then, we need to stay hidden and protect this evidence." He gestured to the documents spread across the dining table.

"What about the kiss?" Lila asked, the question slipping out before she could reconsider it.

Marcus blinked, momentarily thrown by the sudden shift in topic. "I... what about it?"

"Was it just adrenaline? The stress of the situation?" Lila pressed, needing clarity despite the sirens of their circumstances. "Because if we survive this, I'd like to know where we stand."

A slow smile spread across Marcus's face, unexpected warmth in the midst of crisis. "Lila Montgomery," he said, taking her hand, "that kiss had nothing to do with adrenaline and everything to do with you. And when this is over, I'd very much like to take you to dinner somewhere without murder evidence on the table or a corrupt sheriff hunting us down."

The simple sincerity of his response melted something inside Lila, a tension she hadn't realized she'd been carrying. "I'd like that too."

Their moment of connection was interrupted by lights sweeping across the apartment windows—headlights from vehicles turning into the complex. Marcus moved quickly to the window, peering cautiously around the edge of the curtain.

"Two unmarked sedans," he reported. "Could be State Police, but could also be Jennings or his deputies. Stay back from the windows."

He pulled out his service weapon, checking it with practiced efficiency before moving to the door to listen. Lila felt her heart hammering in her chest, the reality of their danger crystallizing in the sight of the gun in Marcus's hand.

Footsteps sounded in the hallway outside, then a firm knock at the door. "Detective Cole? Lieutenant Ramirez, State Police. We spoke on the phone."

Marcus and Lila exchanged glances. "How do we know it's really them?" she whispered.

"We don't," Marcus replied grimly. Then, raising his voice, he called, "Identification through the peephole, Lieutenant."

There was a pause, then the sound of something being held up to the peephole. Marcus checked carefully, then visibly relaxed. "It's them," he confirmed, holstering his weapon before unlocking the door.

Lieutenant Ramirez was a compact, serious-looking woman in her forties, with close-cropped salt-and-pepper hair and intelligent dark eyes that missed nothing as she entered the apartment, followed by two male officers. She wore a bulletproof vest over her button-down shirt, and her badge hung on a chain around her neck.

"Detective Cole," she greeted Marcus with a professional nod before turning to Lila. "Ms. Montgomery? I'm Lieutenant Elena Ramirez. My team has secured the building perimeter. I understand you have evidence connecting Sheriff Jennings to two homicides?"

"Yes," Marcus confirmed, leading her to the dining table where the documents were arranged. "Historical society records, a journal belonging to Samuel Jennings—the Sheriff's father—and investigative notes from a former officer suggesting Samuel Price's death in 1995 wasn't an accident."

Lieutenant Ramirez examined the evidence with methodical care, occasionally asking clarifying questions as Marcus and Lila explained the connections between the 1995 development project and Graham Fox's recent murder. Her expression remained professionally neutral, but Lila noted the slight widening of her eyes when she read the damning entry in Samuel Jennings' journal.

"This is substantial," she acknowledged finally, straightening up from the table. "Certainly enough for us to question Sheriff Jennings and secure the department's records relating to both cases." She turned to one of her officers. "Davidson, photograph everything, then secure these documents for transport."

The officer nodded, pulling out a camera and beginning the process of documenting each piece of evidence in situ before collection.

"What about the warrant for our arrest?" Lila asked, the thought of being labeled a criminal in her hometown still disturbing her. "Sheriff Jennings has the whole department looking for us."

"Already handled," Lieutenant Ramirez assured her. "The county prosecutor has temporarily suspended Sheriff Jennings' authority pending investigation. Local officers have been instructed to stand down and report to State Police command. That said," she added with a pointed look at Marcus, "you both need to come with us to give formal statements. And Detective Cole, your department will want to review your conduct in this investigation."

Marcus nodded, accepting the professional consequences of his actions without complaint. "Understood. What about Ms. Montgomery's family and friends? Sheriff Jennings was at her shop earlier, possibly using them as bait to draw us out."

"We have officers on the way there now," Ramirez confirmed. "They'll ensure everyone's safety and take statements regarding Sheriff Jennings' behavior." She checked her watch. "We should move. The Sheriff was last seen at the department, but he's not answering radio calls. We need to locate him before he realizes the extent of our involvement."

As Officer Davidson finished documenting and carefully packing the evidence, Lieutenant Ramirez's radio crackled with an update. She listened intently, her expression growing grave.

"Change of plans," she announced. "Our team at Salted Caramel's reports that Sheriff Jennings returned there approximately ten minutes ago. He's currently inside with Ms. Montgomery's mother, brother, and friend. Officers are maintaining surveillance but have been instructed not to engage until we arrive, given the potential for hostage situations."

Lila felt the blood drain from her face. "He's holding my family? We need to go there now!"

"We will," Ramirez assured her, "but we do this by the book. Jennings is potentially armed and dangerous, and your family's safety is the priority. That means we need a tactical approach, not an emotional one."

"Lieutenant," Marcus interjected, his voice level despite the tension evident in his stance, "I know the layout of Salted Caramel's intimately at this point. There's a back entrance through the alley that might allow us to approach unseen. And Jennings knows me—he might be more willing to negotiate if I'm present."

Ramirez considered this, clearly weighing the risks against the potential benefits of Marcus's involvement. "You can accompany us, Detective, but you follow my lead. Is that clear? One hint that personal feelings are clouding your judgment, and you're out."

"Crystal clear," Marcus agreed immediately.

"What about me?" Lila asked, stepping forward. "That's my family in there. I'm coming too."

"Absolutely not," Ramirez replied firmly. "You're a civilian and a potential target. You'll remain with Officer Dabney in a secure location until this is resolved."

"With all due respect, Lieutenant," Lila countered, drawing herself up to her full height, "Sheriff Jennings is in my shop because he's looking for me. If I don't show up, who knows what he might do to my family? I'm not suggesting I participate in any tactical operation, but my presence nearby might be useful in resolving this without violence."

Ramirez and Marcus exchanged glances, a silent communication passing between the two law enforcement professionals. Finally, Ramirez sighed. "You remain in the command vehicle, out of sight, unless specifically instructed otherwise. And you wear a vest at all times. Agreed?"

"Agreed," Lila nodded quickly, relief flooding through her at not being left behind.

They moved with efficient purpose after that, Officer Dabney bringing in bulletproof vests for both Lila and Marcus while Ramirez coordinated with her team via radio. Within minutes, they were heading down to the waiting vehicles, the evidence securely packed and in Davidson's custody.

The ride back to town was tense and largely silent, each occupant of the unmarked police sedan lost in their own thoughts. Lila sat in the back beside Marcus, drawing comfort from his solid presence despite the anxiety churning in her stomach. At one point, he reached over and took her hand, giving it a reassuring squeeze. The gesture, simple though it was, steadied her racing heart.

"Your family will be alright," he said quietly, for her ears alone. "Jennings is desperate, but he's not stupid. He knows harming them would only make his situation worse."

Lila nodded, trying to believe it. "I just keep thinking about how I got them into this mess. If I hadn't started investigating Graham Fox's death..."

"Then a murderer would have gone free," Marcus finished firmly. "And your father's involvement in the 1995 development would have remained a shadow over his memory, rather than being understood in context. You did the right thing, Lila. Sometimes doing the right thing has consequences we couldn't anticipate, but that doesn't make it wrong."

His words resonated with her, echoing what she'd learned about her father's decision to back out of the Maritime Ventures deal after Samuel Price's death. Jack Montgomery had chosen to bear a heavy financial burden rather than be complicit in wrongdoing. Perhaps that capacity for moral courage, even at personal cost, was part of his legacy to her.

As they approached Main Street, Lieutenant Ramirez directed the driver to take a circuitous route to avoid being spotted, eventually bringing them to a command post established in the municipal parking lot behind Town Hall, one block from Salted Caramel's. Several more State Police vehicles were already there, along with officers in tactical gear receiving briefings from their superiors.

"Command center's in the mobile unit," Ramirez explained, leading them to a large van equipped with communications equipment. "We've established phone contact with the shop and confirmed that Sheriff Jennings is inside with three civilians—Eva Montgomery, Kyle Montgomery, and Elsie Winters. No injuries reported, but Jennings is armed and has stated he wants to speak with you, Ms. Montgomery, and Detective Cole."

"Has he made any specific demands?" Marcus asked, his professional demeanor fully in place despite the personal stakes.

"Just the conversation, so far," Ramirez replied. "He claims he can explain everything if you'll hear him out. Classic stalling tactic while he figures out his next move." She turned to an officer monitoring communications. "Any update on the building surveillance?"

"Team Two reports all exits covered, ma'am," the officer responded. "Thermal imaging shows four individuals in the main shop area, seated at what appears to be a table or counter. One standing figure pacing nearby, presumably Jennings. No immediate signs of restraints or physical duress on the seated figures."

"Good," Ramirez nodded. "Let's establish direct communication." She picked up a secure phone, dialing a number and waiting. After a moment, she spoke: "Sheriff Jennings, this is Lieutenant Elena Ramirez, State Police. I understand you want to speak with Detective Cole and Lila Montgomery."

She listened briefly, then covered the mouthpiece. "He wants visual confirmation that you're both here and unharmed. Says he doesn't trust us not to trick him."

"We can do a video call," Marcus suggested. "Show him we're here without exposing our exact location."

Ramirez considered this, then nodded. "Set it up," she instructed one of her team members. Within minutes, a tablet was configured for a secure video call, and Ramirez handed it to Marcus. "Keep it tight on your faces, nothing in the background that might identify your location."

Marcus positioned the tablet so that both he and Lila were in frame but nothing else was visible. Ramirez initiated the call, and after a moment, Sheriff Jennings' face appeared on the screen. He looked haggard, his usually neat appearance disheveled, a thin sheen of sweat on his forehead. Behind him, Lila could make out the familiar interior of her shop, though the angle prevented her from seeing her family.

"Detective Cole," Jennings acknowledged, his voice strained. "And Lila. Good to see you both. I've been worried about your safety after that unfortunate misunderstanding at the historical society."

"Cut the act, Sam," Marcus replied, his tone firm but controlled. "We know about your father's involvement in Samuel Price's death. We know about the connection between Maritime Ventures in 1995 and Coastal Ventures today. And we have evidence suggesting you killed Graham Fox to prevent him from exposing these connections."

Jennings' expression hardened. "You don't understand. None of you do. This town was dying in 1995. The fishing industry was collapsing, tourism was seasonal at best. The development would have saved Seabreeze Shores, provided year-round employment, security. My father saw that vision, and I've carried it forward."

"By killing anyone who gets in your way?" Lila couldn't help interjecting, anger bubbling up despite her best intentions to remain calm. "Graham Fox was trying to expose a murder your family committed twenty-five years ago, so you silenced him. That's not vision, Sheriff. That's corruption."

"You sound just like your father," Jennings scoffed, bitterness evident in his tone. "Jack had the chance to be part of something transformative, but he lost his nerve when things got complicated. And now you're following in his footsteps, clinging to some romantic notion of what this town should be instead of what it could become."

"Let my family and Elsie go," Lila demanded, ignoring his provocations. "They have nothing to do with this."

"Actually, they have everything to do with it," Jennings countered, shifting the tablet so that Eva, Kyle, and Elsie came into view. They sat at one of the shop's tables, looking tense but unharmed. "Your family legacy is intertwined with mine, Lila. Your father's decision to back out of the 1995 deal set off a chain reaction that's culminated in this moment. It's poetic, really."

"There's no poetry in murder, Sheriff," Marcus interjected, his voice hard. "Let them go, and we can talk about an arrangement. The State Police are willing to hear your side of the story."

A hollow laugh escaped Jennings. "My side? My side died with my father's reputation when that deal fell apart. He was positioned to transform this town, to secure our family's legacy for generations. Instead, he died a bitter, broken man, watching as Seabreeze Shores stagnated in its quaint mediocrity."

"So Graham Fox was what—your chance to fulfill your father's vision?" Lila asked, beginning to understand the twisted logic driving Jennings' actions.

"Fox wasn't supposed to be a problem," Jennings admitted, his guard seemingly lowering as he warmed to the topic. "When Lawrence Caldwell contacted me about reviving the development plans, I saw it as divine intervention—a second chance to realize what should have happened decades ago. Fox was just the local representative, presenting the plans to property owners."

"But Fox discovered the truth about Samuel Price's death," Marcus prompted, keeping Jennings talking while subtly signaling to Ramirez, who was directing her team via written notes.

"That meddling law student he hired—Nina West," Jennings practically spat the name. "She uncovered Officer Reed's unofficial investigation, started asking questions about my father's connection to Maritime Ventures. When Fox confronted me with what they'd found, threatened to expose it all..." He trailed off, the implication clear.

On the edges of the tablet screen, Lila could see her mother's expression change—a subtle shift that she recognized immediately. Eva Montgomery was planning something. A lifetime of reading her mother's moods and signals allowed Lila to interpret the quick glance Eva directed at Kyle, the almost imperceptible nod toward the ice cream counter.

"Sheriff," Lila said, deliberately drawing Jennings' attention back to the tablet, away from her family. "What happened to Nina West? Is she still alive?"

The question clearly caught Jennings off guard. "What? Yes, she's fine. I simply... encouraged her to leave town. Paid her to forget what she'd found. Fox was less amenable to financial persuasion. He had principles." The last word dripped with contempt.

While Jennings focused on the tablet screen, Lila could see Kyle slowly reaching beneath the counter, where her father had installed a silent alarm button years ago after a late-night break-in. It connected directly to the police station—useless in this situation, with Jennings being the Sheriff—but the movement suggested Kyle had something else in mind.

"So you killed Fox to protect your family legacy," Marcus stated, not as a question but as confirmation, keeping Jennings engaged in their conversation.

"I protected this town's future," Jennings corrected, a fervent light in his eyes. "Fox's death was regrettable but necessary. The development plans can still proceed once this unfortunate situation is resolved. Lawrence Caldwell remains committed to the vision, with or without Fox."

Lieutenant Ramirez held up a note for Marcus and Lila to see: *Team in position at back entrance. Distraction needed in 30 seconds.*

Marcus gave a nearly imperceptible nod, then addressed Jennings again. "And what's your plan now, Sam? You must realize this can't end well. You're holding three innocent people hostage, you've confessed to murder on a recorded video call, and the State Police have secured the evidence linking your family to Samuel Price's death."

"I have leverage," Jennings insisted, though uncertainty had begun to creep into his voice. "As long as I have them," he gestured to Eva, Kyle, and Elsie, "I can negotiate terms. I'm not asking for much—just safe passage out of town and a head start before you come looking for me."

As he spoke, Lila noticed Kyle's hand emerge from beneath the counter, now holding something small and metallic—the CO_2 canister used to charge the shop's whipped cream dispensers. With deliberate slowness, he began unscrewing the top, preparing to release the pressurized gas.

"We can discuss terms," Marcus was saying, expertly keeping Jennings' attention on the tablet. "But first, I need your word that Eva, Kyle, and Elsie are unharmed and will remain that way throughout negotiations."

"Of course they're unharmed," Jennings scoffed. "What kind of monster do you think I am? I've known them for years. Eva and I were on the PTA together when our kids were in school. Kyle used to mow my lawn in high school. This isn't personal."

"Murder is always personal, Sheriff," Lila interjected, watching as Kyle positioned the canister, ready to release its contents. "Just like family legacy."

In the background of the video, Kyle suddenly twisted the canister valve, sending a loud hiss of escaping gas directly at Jennings. The sheriff started, turning instinctively toward the noise—and in that moment of distraction, Eva lunged forward, knocking the tablet from his hand while Elsie upended the table, creating a barrier between them and Jennings.

The video call dissolved into chaos—shouts, the crash of furniture, a glimpse of tactical officers bursting through the back door of the shop. Then the connection cut out entirely, leaving Lila and Marcus staring at a blank screen.

"Team One reports subject is down and secured," came the voice of the communications officer. "No injuries to hostages. Repeat, all hostages safe and unharmed."

Lila sagged against Marcus, relief washing through her in a dizzying wave. She hadn't realized how tightly wound she'd been until the tension suddenly released, leaving her trembling. His arm came around her shoulders, steadying her.

"Your family is quite resourceful," he observed, a note of admiration in his voice. "That was quick thinking with the CO_2 canister."

"Kyle always was good at improvising," Lila replied with a shaky laugh. "And my mother hasn't changed a bit—still taking charge in a crisis."

Lieutenant Ramirez approached, holstering her weapon. "Sheriff Jennings is in custody, no shots fired. Your family performed an impressive civilian assist, Ms. Montgomery. They'll be brought here momentarily for medical evaluation, then we'll need statements from everyone."

Sure enough, within minutes, the side door of the command van opened to admit Eva, Kyle, and Elsie, escorted by State Police officers. Lila rushed to embrace them, tears of relief stinging her eyes as she held her mother tightly, then her brother, then her best friend.

"Are you all okay?" she asked, scanning them for any signs of injury. "I was so worried!"

"We're fine, honey," Eva assured her, her composure remarkable given what she'd just experienced. "Nothing damaged but the furniture. Your father would be proud of how Kyle handled himself."

Kyle grinned, the adrenaline of the situation still evident in his slightly wild eyes. "Those summers working at the soda fountain finally paid off. Never thought I'd use a whipped cream charger as a weapon, though."

Elsie, normally so vivacious, seemed subdued, clinging to Lila's hand as if afraid she might disappear. "When Sheriff Jennings came to the shop asking about you, we knew something was wrong. He kept saying he just wanted to talk, but his hand never left his gun." She shuddered at the memory. "Then he got that call saying they'd found you, and everything changed. He became... different. Harder, colder. Like a mask had slipped."

"You're safe now," Lila assured her, squeezing her hand. "All of you are. And Jennings can't hurt anyone else."

Marcus, who had been conferring with Lieutenant Ramirez, joined their group. "The State Police will need statements from each of you, but it can wait until tomorrow. For tonight, they'll arrange accommodation at the Harborview Hotel—neutral ground, with security, until this is fully resolved."

"What about my shop?" Lila asked, practical concerns reasserting themselves now that the immediate danger had passed. "It's a crime scene now, isn't it?"

"Temporarily," Marcus confirmed. "The forensics team will process it tonight, and with any luck, you should be able to reopen within a day or two. Lieutenant Ramirez has agreed to expedite things, given the importance of Salted Caramel's to the town's economy."

Eva studied Marcus with the shrewd gaze of a mother assessing a potential suitor. "You seem to have taken a personal interest in my daughter's business, Detective Cole," she observed, a knowing smile playing at the corners of her mouth.

Marcus met her gaze directly, his usual professional reserve softening. "I've taken a personal interest in your daughter, Mrs. Montgomery. With her permission, of course."

Lila felt heat rise to her cheeks at this public acknowledgment of their changing relationship, but she couldn't suppress a smile. "It's a recent development," she explained to her family's curious faces.

"Not that recent," Kyle countered with a grin. "Anyone with eyes could see it developing for days. The real question is, does the detective appreciate your signature vanilla bean ice cream as much as your investigative skills?"

"I haven't had the pleasure yet," Marcus admitted. "Though I'm looking forward to it, once things settle down."

"Oh, you must try it," Eva insisted, momentarily forgetting the evening's trauma in her enthusiasm for her daughter's culinary talents. "Lila uses an infusion technique her father developed—steeping the vanilla beans in cream overnight rather than simply mixing in extract. Makes all the difference in the world."

As her mother launched into a detailed explanation of the Montgomery family's ice cream philosophy, Lila caught Marcus's eye over Eva's shoulder. The warm amusement in his gaze, the slight quirk of his mouth that suggested he was genuinely enjoying her mother's culinary lecture, touched something deep within her. In the midst of chaos and revelation, something new and precious was taking root.

Lieutenant Ramirez eventually interrupted their family moment to coordinate transportation to the Harborview Hotel. As they prepared to leave the command center, Lila found herself standing slightly apart with Marcus, a brief private moment before they rejoined the others.

"So," she said softly, "what happens now? With the case, I mean."

"Jennings will be processed and charged with Graham Fox's murder, along with obstruction of justice and multiple counts of attempted murder for today's hostage situation," Marcus replied. "The evidence from the historical society, combined with his confession during the video call, makes for a strong case. The State Police will also reopen the investigation into Samuel Price's death, though after twenty-five years, that may be more difficult to prove definitively."

"And what about us?" Lila asked, gathering her courage to address the sudden shift in their relationship amid the turmoil of the case.

Marcus's expression softened, the professional detective giving way to the man who had kissed her with such unexpected tenderness just hours ago. "That depends on you," he said, his voice low enough that only she could hear. "I meant what I said earlier. When this is over, I'd like to take you to dinner. Somewhere quiet, where we can talk about something other than murder evidence and corrupt sheriffs."

"I'd like that," Lila replied, a smile warming her face despite the exhaustion of the day. "Though I have to warn you, in Seabreeze Shores, 'quiet' is a relative term. Everyone will be watching and speculating."

"I can handle a little local gossip," Marcus assured her with a smile that transformed his usually serious face. "After all, I've just helped solve the town's biggest mystery in decades. Surely that earns me some goodwill."

"More than some," Lila agreed. "You might even achieve honorary local status. In another decade or two."

His laugh, warm and genuine, sent a pleasant shiver through her. "I suppose I'll have to stick around and earn my stripes, then."

"I suppose you will," Lila replied, her heart lighter than it had been in days despite the ordeal they'd just survived.

As they rejoined the others and prepared to leave for the safety of the Harborview Hotel, Lila couldn't help but reflect on how much had changed in just a week. Graham Fox's death had set in motion a cascade of revelations—about her father's past, about the town's history, about her own resilience in the face of danger. And somehow, in the midst of uncovering old secrets, something new and unexpected had blossomed—a connection with Marcus that held the promise of a future neither of them had anticipated when they first met over vanilla ice cream and murder.

The mysteries of Seabreeze Shores' past had been revealed, its secrets brought to light after decades hidden in shadow. And as one chapter of the town's history closed, Lila found herself looking forward to writing the next—with a certain detective possibly featuring prominently in the narrative.

Chapter 8
Secrets in the Shadows

Morning light filtered through the gauzy curtains of room 312 at the Harborview Hotel, casting soft patterns across the king-sized bed where Lila Montgomery had finally fallen into an exhausted sleep just before dawn. The events of the previous day—the revelations at the historical society, the confrontation at her shop, Sheriff Jennings' arrest—had left her mind racing long after the State Police had secured her family in the elegant waterfront hotel.

The gentle chime of her phone roused her from a dream involving ice cream that mysteriously transformed into evidence files. Lila fumbled for the device on the nightstand, blinking sleep from her eyes as she checked the screen. A text from Marcus:

Morning. Meeting with State Police in 30 min. Coffee after? Need to discuss new information.

Lila smiled despite her exhaustion. Even in text messages, Marcus maintained his efficient, somewhat formal communication style—though the invitation for coffee suggested their relationship continued to evolve beyond the professional.

She texted back: *Yes to both. Lobby in 25?*

His response came immediately: *See you then.*

The prospect of seeing Marcus provided the motivation Lila needed to drag herself from the comfortable bed. The hotel had provided toiletries and a change of clothes—simple but elegant Harborview Hotel-branded items that would suffice until she could return to her apartment. After a quick shower that helped clear the fog of too little sleep, Lila dressed in the provided navy slacks and white blouse, grateful that the hotel's emergency clothing options weren't limited to bathrobes and t-shirts.

The mirror reflected a woman who looked remarkably composed considering the circumstances—only the shadows beneath her hazel eyes hinted at the stress of recent days. Lila applied minimal makeup, ran a brush through her dark waves, and headed for her mother's adjoining room to check in before meeting Marcus.

Eva Montgomery was already awake and dressed, sitting by the window with a cup of room service tea, gazing out at the harbor view that gave the hotel its name. At sixty-two, Eva remained striking, her silver-streaked hair pulled back in its usual neat style, her posture as straight as it had been when Lila was a child. Only the slight tremor in the hand holding her teacup betrayed any lingering effects from yesterday's hostage situation.

"Morning, Mom," Lila greeted her, bending to kiss her cheek. "How did you sleep?"

"Well enough, considering," Eva replied, setting down her cup. "These fancy hotel mattresses are a bit too soft for my taste. Give me my own bed any day."

"The State Police said we might be able to go home today, once they've completed their initial investigation," Lila offered, taking the seat opposite her mother.

Eva studied her daughter with knowing eyes. "You're meeting with your detective this morning?"

"He's not *my* detective, Mom," Lila protested automatically, though she couldn't prevent the slight flush that colored her cheeks. "And yes, he's briefing the State Police, then we're getting coffee to discuss the case."

A knowing smile played at the corners of Eva's mouth. "Mmhmm. Just the case, I'm sure." Before Lila could formulate a response, her mother continued, "He seems like a good man. Intense, but solid. Your father would have approved."

The mention of her father sobered Lila. "What do you think Dad would make of all this? Finding out Sheriff Jennings' family was responsible for Samuel Price's death all those years ago?"

Eva sighed, her gaze returning to the harbor where fishing boats were heading out for their morning catch, just as they had for generations. "Your father suspected something wasn't right about Samuel's accident. That's why he backed out of the deal, took on that debt rather than be part of something he believed was corrupt. But proof? That would have given him peace, I think. Validation that his instincts were correct, that the sacrifice was worthwhile."

"I wish he could have known," Lila said softly. "That his decision ultimately helped expose the truth, even all these years later."

"He knows," Eva said with quiet conviction. "Wherever he is, Jack Montgomery knows his daughter finished what he started." She reached across to squeeze Lila's hand. "Now, you'd better get going. Don't keep your detective waiting."

"Not *my* detective," Lila muttered again, but she was smiling as she kissed her mother goodbye and headed for the elevator.

The Harborview Hotel's lobby was an elegant space of polished marble and nautical touches—model ships in glass cases, paintings of historic vessels, brass accents that gleamed in the morning light streaming through floor-to-ceiling windows. A State Police officer stood discreetly near the entrance, a reminder that the events of yesterday remained very much active.

Marcus was waiting near the concierge desk, in conversation with Lieutenant Ramirez. He wore a fresh suit—charcoal gray today, with a deep blue tie that brought out flecks of similar color in his green eyes. Somehow, despite the chaos of the previous day and what must have been an equally short night, he looked alert and professional.

He spotted Lila as she approached, and something in his expression softened momentarily before returning to its professional mask. "Ms. Montgomery," he greeted her, the formality clearly for

Lieutenant Ramirez's benefit. "I was just updating the Lieutenant on developments overnight."

"Developments?" Lila asked, glancing between them.

Lieutenant Ramirez nodded crisply. "We've located Nina West, the researcher who was working for Graham Fox. She's on her way back to Seabreeze Shores to provide a formal statement. And the forensics team completed their processing of your shop earlier this morning—you should be able to reopen by tomorrow, assuming everything checks out."

"That's wonderful news," Lila said, relief evident in her voice. Each day Salted Caramel's remained closed meant lost income during the crucial summer season. "Thank you for expediting things."

"Detective Cole was quite insistent about the importance of your business to the community," Ramirez replied with the barest hint of knowing amusement. "Now, if you'll excuse me, I need to check in with the team at the station. Sheriff Jennings' arraignment is scheduled for this afternoon." With a professional nod to them both, she departed, leaving Lila and Marcus alone in the busy lobby.

"There's a coffee shop across the street," Marcus suggested. "Less chance of being overheard than the hotel restaurant."

Lila nodded, acutely aware of the curious glances from hotel staff who had undoubtedly connected them to the police presence and the rumors already circulating through town. In Seabreeze Shores, news traveled faster than the tides, and by now, everyone would know about Sheriff Jennings' arrest and the Montgomery family's involvement.

They crossed the street to The Daily Grind, a small café that catered more to locals than tourists, with mismatched furniture, local artwork on the walls, and a menu offering uncomplicated but excellent coffee and fresh-baked goods. The morning rush had passed, leaving only a few tables occupied by people lingering over laptops or newspapers.

Marcus selected a table in the back corner, positioned so they could see the entrance while maintaining some privacy. The waitress, a college-aged girl with multiple ear piercings and bright blue hair, took their order—a strong black coffee for Marcus, a vanilla latte for Lila, and two blueberry muffins still warm from the oven.

"So," Lila began once they were alone, "you found Nina West?"

Marcus nodded, keeping his voice low despite their relative isolation. "State Police located her in Boston late last night. She left Seabreeze Shores abruptly after Sheriff Jennings threatened her—not with physical harm, but with ruining her career. She's a law student at Boston University, and Jennings implied he had connections who could ensure she never passed the bar."

"But now she's coming back? To testify against him?"

"With Jennings in custody and the State Police guaranteeing her safety, yes," Marcus confirmed. "Her testimony will be crucial in establishing the connection between Graham Fox's murder and the 1995 case. She was researching both for Fox when she uncovered evidence suggesting Samuel Price's death wasn't an accident."

Their coffee arrived, along with the promised muffins, steam still rising from the tender pastries studded with plump blueberries. Lila took a grateful sip of her latte, the rich warmth helping to chase away the last vestiges of too little sleep.

"There's something else," Marcus continued, breaking off a piece of his muffin but not eating it, a sign of his preoccupation. "The forensics team found additional evidence when processing your shop. A fingerprint on one of the freezer handles that doesn't match you, your family, Elsie, or any of your regular employees. They're running it through the database, but preliminary analysis suggests it's been there since around the time of Fox's death."

Lila frowned, trying to recall who might have accessed the freezer. "Delivery people sometimes put stock away if I'm busy with customers. Or it could be from a customer who reached for their own ice cream—it happens occasionally when we're really slammed and people get impatient."

"Possibly," Marcus acknowledged. "But combined with something else we found, it becomes more significant." He leaned forward slightly, lowering his voice further. "During the search of Sheriff Jennings' office, State Police discovered a burner phone hidden in his desk. The call logs show a conversation with an unidentified number at 3:17 PM on the day of Fox's death—approximately 40 minutes before the estimated time of death."

"So Jennings called someone right before Fox was killed," Lila said slowly, connecting the dots. "Someone who might have left a fingerprint in my shop's freezer. You think Jennings had an accomplice?"

"It's a possibility we have to consider," Marcus confirmed, his expression grave. "Sheriff Jennings was on duty that afternoon, documented at the station by multiple witnesses during the estimated time of Fox's murder. He could have orchestrated the killing without being physically present."

The implication sent a chill through Lila despite the café's warm atmosphere. "If Jennings had an accomplice, they're still out there. Someone who was in my shop, who might still be in town."

"Exactly," Marcus nodded. "Which is why I want you and your family to remain at the Harborview under State Police protection until we've identified all parties involved. Jennings isn't talking—claiming he wants his lawyer present for any further questioning—but Nina West's testimony might help us identify potential accomplices."

Lila broke off a piece of her muffin, though her appetite had diminished with this new information. "So we're still in danger."

"Potentially," Marcus admitted, not sugarcoating the situation. "But the State Police presence is substantial, and Lieutenant Ramirez is coordinating directly with the county prosecutor. Whoever Jennings was working with has to realize the net is closing."

"Unless they're planning to finish what Jennings started," Lila pointed out. "Silencing anyone who knows about the connection between Fox's death and the 1995 case."

"That's why we're taking precautions," Marcus assured her. He hesitated, then reached across the table to cover her hand with his. The gesture was surprisingly intimate for someone usually so reserved in public. "I won't let anything happen to you or your family, Lila."

The warmth and conviction in his voice sent a flutter through her chest that had nothing to do with fear. "I know," she said softly, turning her hand to briefly squeeze his before they both withdrew, aware of their public setting.

"There's one more development," Marcus continued, returning to his professional tone though his eyes remained warm. "The search warrant for Jennings' home turned up a key and some notes referencing an old warehouse near the marina—the abandoned Seabreeze Cannery building. Lieutenant Ramirez has authorized a search, scheduled for this afternoon. I'm on the team, and she's agreed that your local knowledge might be valuable, if you're willing to accompany us."

"The old cannery?" Lila frowned slightly, picturing the dilapidated structure that had stood empty for at least fifteen years. "It's been abandoned since the fishing industry declined. Why would Jennings have a key to it?"

"That's what we intend to find out," Marcus replied. "According to property records, it's owned by a shell company that might trace back to Marigold Holdings. If Jennings was working with them on the new development, it could have served as a meeting place away from prying eyes."

"Or a place to store incriminating evidence," Lila suggested, her mind racing with possibilities. "When do we go?"

"Two o'clock," Marcus said. "Lieutenant Ramirez wants daylight for the search, and we need to wait for the warrant to be formally processed."

"I'll be ready," Lila promised, her exhaustion forgotten in the face of this new lead. Despite the danger, she couldn't deny the thrill of being included in the investigation, of feeling like an active participant in uncovering the truth rather than a passive bystander.

Marcus studied her for a moment, a slight furrow appearing between his brows. "You know, most people would be looking for ways to distance themselves from danger at this point. Not volunteering to explore abandoned buildings connected to a murder case."

"I'm not most people," Lila replied with a small smile. "Besides, this case has been about my family from the beginning—my father's involvement in the 1995 deal, Graham Fox's death behind my shop, Sheriff Jennings using my mother and brother as hostages. I need to see it through."

"I understand that need," Marcus nodded, and something in his tone suggested he truly did. "Just promise you'll follow protocol during the search. Stay with the group, don't touch anything without forensic clearance, and if there's any sign of danger—"

"I'll run directly to safety and leave the heroics to the professionals," Lila finished for him, her smile widening slightly. "I may be curious, Marcus, but I'm not foolish."

The use of his first name seemed to affect him, a subtle softening around his eyes that most people would miss but that Lila was beginning to recognize as his emotional tell. "Good," he said simply.

They finished their coffee and muffins, the conversation shifting to lighter topics—Lila's plans for reopening the shop, Marcus's experience adjusting to small-town life after years in the city, mutual observations about Seabreeze Shores' quirky residents. In these moments, it was almost possible to forget the circumstances that had brought them together, to imagine this was simply a morning coffee date between two people exploring a new connection.

Almost, but not quite. Reality reasserted itself when Marcus's phone buzzed with a message from Lieutenant Ramirez, requesting his presence at the station to review Nina West's travel arrangements. They walked back to the Harborview together, their hands occasionally brushing in a way that seemed both accidental and deliberate.

"I'll meet you in the lobby at 1:30," Marcus said as they paused outside the hotel entrance. "Wear practical shoes. The cannery has been abandoned for years—the flooring could be unstable in places."

"Should I be worried that you're suddenly concerned with my footwear?" Lila teased, trying to lighten the moment.

A smile tugged at the corner of his mouth. "Professional advice only, Ms. Montgomery. Though I have noticed you favor impractical but charming sandals that would be hazardous in a derelict building."

"I'll find something suitable," she promised, touched by his attention to such details. "See you at 1:30."

As Marcus departed for the police station, Lila returned to her hotel room to update her mother and brother on the latest developments. Eva was predictably concerned about the warehouse search, while Kyle was disappointed he couldn't join them—Lieutenant Ramirez had limited civilian involvement to Lila, given her direct connection to the case.

"Besides," Lila reminded her brother as he sulked, "someone needs to stay with Mom and Elsie. I'd feel better knowing you're here with them."

"Playing bodyguard while you get all the excitement," Kyle muttered, though there was no real heat in his complaint. "Fine, but you'd better tell me everything when you get back. And be careful, Lila. Abandoned buildings are no joke—rotting floors, rusty nails, who knows what else."

"Between you and Marcus, I've been thoroughly warned about the structural dangers," Lila assured him. "I'll be with State Police the entire time. Nothing is going to happen."

At precisely 1:30, Lila met Marcus in the lobby. She had changed into jeans, a light long-sleeved shirt to protect against potential rusty surfaces, and sturdy walking shoes borrowed from Elsie, whose feet were fortunately the same size as her own. Marcus gave her outfit an approving nod as she approached.

"Lieutenant Ramirez is meeting us there with the forensics team," he explained as they walked to his unmarked police car. "Nina West's flight lands at 4:30, so we have a limited window for the initial search."

The drive to the abandoned cannery took only ten minutes, but it felt like crossing into a different world. While downtown Seabreeze Shores had evolved into a charming tourist destination, the industrial section of the harbor remained a testament to the town's faded fishing glory—weathered docks, empty processing facilities, and the looming presence of the Seabreeze Cannery building, its red brick façade darkened by decades of salt air and neglect.

Lieutenant Ramirez was already on site with a team of four State Police officers and two forensic technicians. The area had been cordoned off with police tape, and an officer stood guard at the perimeter, checking credentials as they approached.

"Detective Cole, Ms. Montgomery," Ramirez greeted them with a professional nod. "We've done an exterior assessment and secured the perimeter. No signs of recent activity outside, but that doesn't mean the interior hasn't been used."

She handed them both pairs of latex gloves and small flashlights. "Standard protocol—touch nothing without documenting it first. The building has no electricity, so we're working with portable lights and daylight through the windows. Ms. Montgomery, you stay with Detective Cole at all times. If he says leave, you leave immediately. Clear?"

"Crystal," Lila agreed, pulling on the gloves and tucking the flashlight into her pocket. Despite the circumstances, she couldn't deny a flutter of excitement at being included in an official police search.

The main entrance to the cannery was secured with a heavy padlock that showed signs of recent use—no rust on the mechanism, the keyhole clear of debris. Ramirez produced the key found in Jennings' home, and it turned smoothly in the lock, confirming their suspicions about its purpose.

"Stay alert," Ramirez instructed as they prepared to enter. "We don't anticipate anyone inside, but standard caution applies."

The door opened with a protesting groan of hinges long unused, revealing a cavernous main floor that had once housed the cannery's processing lines. Dust motes danced in shafts of light streaming through grimy windows high above, illuminating abandoned equipment draped in cobwebs and the ghostly outlines of workstations long deserted. The air smelled of salt, rust, and the faint, lingering scent of fish that seemed permanently embedded in the walls.

"Main floor appears unused," one of the officers reported after a preliminary sweep. "Dust undisturbed except for small animal tracks. No sign of human activity."

"Check the offices," Ramirez directed, pointing to a row of doors along the far wall. "That's where any meetings or document storage would likely occur."

The team moved methodically through the space, flashlight beams cutting through the gloom. Lila stayed close to Marcus as instructed, her senses heightened by the eerie atmosphere of abandonment. The cannery had been a bustling operation in her childhood, providing jobs for many local families. Seeing it empty and decaying was a stark reminder of how much Seabreeze Shores had changed, even as it retained its charming exterior for tourists.

The offices at the back of the building were in marginally better condition than the main floor, having been somewhat protected from the elements. Dust coated everything here as well, but there were subtle signs of disturbance—cleaner patches on desks where items might have recently sat, scuff marks on the floor suggesting chair movement.

"We've got something," called one of the forensic technicians from the largest office—presumably once belonging to the cannery manager. "Recent activity in this room. Multiple sets of footprints in the dust, documents recently moved on the desk based on dust patterns."

Everyone converged on the office, where the technician was carefully photographing the scene before any evidence was disturbed. Lila hung back in the doorway with Marcus, watching as Ramirez supervised the methodical documentation.

"There," Marcus murmured, pointing to a filing cabinet in the corner. "The dust is completely cleared from the handles. Someone's been accessing those files regularly."

Ramirez had noticed the same thing. "Let's get that cabinet opened and documented," she directed the technicians. "Contents photographed in situ before removal."

While the forensics team worked, Lila's attention was drawn to something else—a large map of Seabreeze Shores pinned to the wall, partially hidden behind a swinging dry-erase board that had protected it from the worst of the dust. Red pins marked several locations along the waterfront, including her shop, the B&B, Elliot's fishing dock, and other Harbor Act properties. Yellow strings connected some pins to others, creating a web of relationships that made little sense at first glance.

"Marcus," she said quietly, drawing his attention to the map. "Look at this. They've marked all the Harbor Act properties, including mine."

Marcus studied the map with professional interest. "Those yellow connections could represent ownership links or legal relationships. And look—there are dates written beside some pins." He leaned closer, careful not to touch the potential evidence. "The dates correspond to property transfers or business license renewals. They've been tracking property status changes for years."

Lieutenant Ramirez joined them, her expression grim as she assessed the map. "This confirms long-term planning. Marigold Holdings or their subsidiaries have been positioning themselves for this development for decades, not just since Graham Fox arrived in town."

"But why mark my shop?" Lila asked, noticing that Salted Caramel's had multiple markings, including a question mark and what appeared to be a dollar figure—significantly higher than the property's market value.

"Probably for the same reason they targeted Mira's B&B," Marcus reasoned. "Your Harbor Act rights make your property essential to their plans. The high figure suggests they were prepared to pay well above market value to secure it."

"Just like they did in 1995," Lila murmured, reminded again of how history was repeating itself. "My father turned them down then, even with financial incentives."

"And they likely assumed you would do the same," Marcus nodded. "Which might explain why Fox was killed behind your shop specifically—a warning, perhaps, or an attempt to pressure you through fear."

Before Lila could respond, one of the technicians called out from the filing cabinet she was processing. "Lieutenant, you need to see this. Hidden compartment in the back of the bottom drawer."

They gathered around as the technician carefully extracted a slim leather portfolio from a concealed space built into the rear of the cabinet. Inside were documents protected by plastic sleeves—property deeds, legal agreements, and most significantly, a handwritten letter dated just three days before Graham Fox's death.

Lieutenant Ramirez read it aloud, her voice neutral despite the damning content:

"'Fox knows too much. His researcher found Reed's old investigation notes. Containment essential before meeting with county officials next week. Use established protocol, guarantee deniability. Location should send appropriate message to remaining holdouts. L.C.'"

"L.C.," Marcus repeated. "Lawrence Caldwell, CEO of Marigold Holdings."

"This is direct evidence linking Marigold Holdings to Fox's murder," Ramirez stated, carefully returning the letter to its protective sleeve. "And confirmation that the location—behind Ms. Montgomery's shop—was deliberately chosen to intimidate other property owners."

"But it doesn't clarify whether Jennings acted alone or had an accomplice," Lila pointed out, remembering the unidentified fingerprint in her freezer and the call from Jennings' burner phone. "Just that he was following orders from Lawrence Caldwell."

"The 'established protocol' suggests a standard procedure," Marcus observed. "Possibly the same method used for Samuel Price's death in 1995. And 'guarantee deniability' implies distance between those ordering the action and those executing it."

"Which supports our accomplice theory," Ramirez nodded. "Jennings creating an alibi at the station while someone else carried out the actual murder."

As the forensics team continued processing the office, photographing the map and securing the documents from the hidden compartment, Lila wandered back into the corridor, needing a moment to process what they'd found. The cannery felt oppressive now, the weight of decades of manipulation and conspiracy pressing down on her.

A faint noise from farther down the hallway caught her attention—something between a scratch and a thump, too deliberate for the random settling of an old building. Despite Marcus's instructions to stay close, Lila found herself moving toward the sound, flashlight in hand.

"Hello?" she called softly, the beam of her light revealing a door at the end of the corridor, partially ajar when it had been closed during their initial sweep. "Is someone there?"

No response came, but as she approached the door, she noticed fresh scuff marks in the dust on the floor—someone had recently entered or exited this room. Training her flashlight on the door handle, she saw it was clean of dust, unlike the surrounding surface.

Common sense told her to return to the group, to fetch Marcus or Lieutenant Ramirez before investigating further. But curiosity—the same trait that had drawn her into this case from the beginning—propelled her forward. She pushed the door open wider with her elbow, keeping her gloved hands free and her flashlight directed into the room.

Unlike the offices they had already explored, this room appeared to be a small conference space, with a table and chairs arranged around it. More significantly, it showed clear signs of recent use—coffee cups on the table with liquid still inside them, papers arranged in neat stacks, and a laptop computer open but powered down.

"Marcus!" Lila called, her voice echoing in the empty building. "Lieutenant Ramirez! I've found something!"

She stepped further into the room, careful not to disturb potential evidence but wanting to see what the papers contained. The beam of her flashlight passed over what appeared to be architectural drawings—plans for a resort complex that would transform the Seabreeze Shores waterfront beyond recognition.

The sound of hurried footsteps in the hallway told her the others had heard her call. But before they could reach her, another sound froze her in place—the unmistakable click of a door locking somewhere behind the conference room.

Lila swung her flashlight toward the noise, revealing another door she hadn't noticed initially, partially hidden behind a storage cabinet. It was closed now, but the dust disturbed in front of it confirmed someone had just passed through.

"Lila?" Marcus's voice came from the hallway, closer now. "What did you find?"

Before she could answer, her flashlight beam caught something else—a small device attached to the underside of the conference table, blinking with a steady red light. Recognition hit her a moment too late as years of watching crime shows with her father crystalized into terrible understanding.

"Bomb!" she shouted, turning to run just as Marcus appeared in the doorway. "There's a bomb under the table!"

Marcus's training took over instantly. He grabbed Lila's arm, pulling her into the hallway as he shouted to the others: "Explosive device in the conference room! Evacuate immediately! Move!"

The next moments passed in a blur of motion and sound—running footsteps, Ramirez's sharp commands to her team, the controlled urgency of professional law enforcement responding to a threat. Marcus kept his arm around Lila, practically carrying her at times as they raced toward the exit, the other officers securing evidence as they moved.

They had just reached the main floor of the cannery when the world exploded behind them. The blast threw them forward, a wave of heat and pressure followed by the deafening crash of collapsing structure. Dust and debris filled the air as the back section of the building crumbled, sending shockwaves through the remaining structure.

Marcus shielded Lila with his body as chunks of ceiling rained down around them, his arms tight around her as they huddled against a supporting column. The roar of destruction seemed to last forever, though in reality it was probably only seconds before an eerie silence fell, broken only by the creaking of damaged support beams and the distant sound of emergency sirens.

"Is everyone out?" Ramirez's voice cut through the dust, tight with tension but controlled. "Sound off!"

One by one, the team members responded, confirming they had made it to safety with the secured evidence. Lila and Marcus were the last to call out, having been the furthest inside when the explosion occurred.

"We need to move," Marcus said urgently, helping Lila to her feet. "The remaining structure is compromised. The whole building could come down."

They staggered toward the exit, choking on dust and supporting each other through the obstacle course of fallen debris. Daylight ahead beckoned like a promise, growing larger as they approached the main doors that now hung askew on damaged hinges.

Just as they reached the threshold, a secondary crash sounded from somewhere above them. Lila looked up to see a massive support beam breaking free from the ceiling, plummeting directly toward them. Marcus saw it too, and with a desperate surge of strength, he shoved her through the doorway to safety.

Lila stumbled into the open air, turning back just in time to see Marcus dive forward as the beam crashed down, catching him glancingly across the back and pinning his legs beneath additional debris that followed. His cry of pain cut through the din of collapsing structure, spurring Lila into action despite Lieutenant Ramirez's shouts for her to stay back.

"Marcus!" she cried, rushing back to the doorway where he lay half-buried in rubble, his face contorted in pain but conscious. "Don't move! We'll get you out!"

Two State Police officers joined her immediately, assessing the situation with professional calm despite the urgency. "The beam's unstable," one reported. "If we move it wrong, more debris could follow."

"Fire department and rescue are two minutes out," Ramirez called from where she was coordinating the perimeter security. "Hold position but be prepared to extract if the structure shows signs of further collapse."

Lila knelt beside Marcus, careful not to disturb the debris but needing to be close to him. His breathing was labored, dust coating his face, a cut on his forehead trickling blood into his eyes. But he was alive, conscious, those green eyes finding hers with a focus that belied his physical distress.

"Are you hurt?" he asked, his voice strained but clear.

Lila almost laughed at the absurdity of his concern for her while he lay trapped in rubble. "I'm fine. Thanks to you."

"The evidence—"

"Secured," she assured him, marveling at his dedication even in this moment. "Everyone made it out with the documents and photographs. Now just lie still. Help is coming."

The wail of approaching sirens grew louder, emergency vehicles converging on the scene with lights flashing. In the distance, Lila could see curious onlookers gathering, held back by the police perimeter—the explosive collapse of an abandoned building drawing attention even in a town accustomed to unusual events.

"Someone was in there," Marcus said, grimacing as he tried to shift his position. "In the conference room or beyond it. They triggered the device remotely when they realized we'd found their meeting place."

"Jennings' accomplice," Lila guessed, remembering the freshly disturbed dust, the locked door that had been open moments before. "They must have been monitoring the building, knew we were conducting a search."

"Or they were there for a meeting," Marcus countered, his detective's mind working despite his predicament. "The coffee cups were fresh. Someone was using that room regularly, recently."

A groaning sound from above cut their conversation short—another portion of the structure threatening to give way. The officers tensed, preparing to attempt an emergency extraction despite the risks.

"We need to move him now," one decided, signaling to his colleague. "On my count, we lift the beam just enough for Ms. Montgomery to help pull him clear. Ready?"

Lila positioned herself at Marcus's shoulders, prepared to drag him backward once his legs were freed. The beam was massive, but with adrenaline and desperation fueling them, the officers managed to lift it just enough to reduce the pressure on Marcus's trapped limbs.

"Now!" the officer commanded, and Lila pulled with every ounce of strength she possessed, dragging Marcus backward as he grimaced in pain but helped propel himself with his arms. Inch by excruciating inch, they extracted him from the debris, moving just in time as another section of ceiling collapsed exactly where he had been lying.

They retreated a safe distance from the building, which continued to settle and groan ominously. Paramedics converged on them immediately, transferring Marcus to a gurney despite his protests that he could walk. Lila stayed by his side, her hand finding his as the medical team assessed his injuries.

"Probable fracture of the left tibia," one paramedic reported, cutting away Marcus's pant leg to reveal significant swelling and bruising. "Multiple contusions, laceration to the forehead requiring stitches. Potential concussion. We need to transport immediately for x-rays and further assessment."

"Go with the evidence," Marcus told Lieutenant Ramirez, who had joined them once Marcus was safely extracted. "Whoever planted that device knows we found their operation. They'll be desperate now, might attempt to destroy other evidence or flee the jurisdiction."

"Already on it," Ramirez assured him. "The documents and photographs are on their way to the State Police lab under armed escort. We've set up roadblocks at all exits from Seabreeze Shores, and I've requested additional personnel to secure the perimeter. No one's getting in or out without our knowledge."

She paused, surveying the collapsing building with grim professionalism. "Fire department will secure the scene once the structure stabilizes. We'll conduct a secondary search when it's safe, though I suspect whoever planted that device is long gone."

"What about Nina West?" Lila asked suddenly, remembering the researcher whose flight was due to land soon. "If someone's trying to destroy evidence, she could be in danger too."

Ramirez nodded, already reaching for her radio. "I'll arrange additional security for her arrival. No one outside this team knows her flight details, but we can't be too careful."

The paramedics had finished their initial assessment and were preparing to transport Marcus to the county hospital in nearby Harbor Bay—Seabreeze Shores being too small to have more than a basic urgent care facility. As they raised the gurney, Marcus's hand tightened around Lila's.

"Go with your family," he told her, his professional mask slipping to reveal genuine concern. "Lieutenant Ramirez will assign officers to protect you all at the hotel. Don't go anywhere alone, not even in the hotel. Not until we know who else is involved."

"I'm coming with you," Lila replied firmly. The determination in her voice brooked no argument, surprising even herself with its intensity. "My family is safe at the Harborview with State Police protection. You're alone, and after what just happened, I'm not letting you out of my sight."

A ghost of a smile touched Marcus's dust-covered face, a brief acknowledgment of what her words revealed about her feelings. "Lieutenant?" he deferred to Ramirez, who was observing their exchange with a carefully neutral expression.

"Ms. Montgomery can ride in the ambulance," Ramirez decided after a moment's consideration. "I'll assign Officer Dabney to accompany you both to Harbor Bay Hospital and remain as security. The rest of the team will continue the investigation here." She fixed Lila with a pointed look. "But once Detective Cole is stable, you return to your family at the Harborview. No negotiation on that point."

Lila nodded her agreement, relief flooding through her at not being separated from Marcus in this moment. As the paramedics loaded him into the waiting ambulance, she climbed in behind them, taking a seat where she could maintain visual contact without interfering with their work.

Officer Dabney—a compact, serious woman in her thirties with a no-nonsense demeanor—joined them, positioning herself near the doors where she could monitor both the patient and any external threats. The ambulance pulled away with sirens wailing, the collapsing cannery building receding behind them as they headed out of Seabreeze Shores toward Harbor Bay.

Inside the ambulance, the paramedics worked efficiently, establishing an IV line, monitoring vital signs, and conducting a more thorough assessment of Marcus's injuries. He remained stoically quiet through their ministrations, though Lila could see the tightness around his mouth that betrayed his pain.

"BP's 140 over 90, pulse 88," one paramedic reported. "Elevated but within expected range given circumstances. Left tibia shows signs of compound fracture but no arterial involvement. Laceration on forehead approximately two inches, will require sutures. Multiple contusions to back and shoulders consistent with impact trauma."

The clinical assessment continued, the medics speaking in the abbreviated language of their profession. Lila half-listened, her focus primarily on Marcus's face, watching for signs of deterioration. Despite his injuries, his eyes remained alert, occasionally finding hers with a reassurance that seemed incongruous given their positions—him on a gurney receiving emergency care, her supposedly being comforted.

"You should call your mother," Marcus said during a lull in the paramedic's activities. "Let her know what happened and that you're safe."

Lila nodded, pulling out her phone. Officer Dabney had already advised Lieutenant Ramirez of their status via radio, but personal reassurance to her family was indeed necessary. She stepped as far away as the confines of the moving ambulance allowed, dialing her mother's number.

Eva answered on the first ring, her voice taut with worry. "Lila? Are you alright? We just heard about an explosion at the cannery. Kyle's been trying to get past the police barricade to find you."

"I'm fine, Mom," Lila assured her quickly. "We all got out. The building was rigged with an explosive device that someone triggered when they realized we were searching the place. Marcus was injured getting me to safety—not life-threatening," she added hastily, "but serious enough that they're taking him to Harbor Bay Hospital. I'm in the ambulance with him now."

"Oh, thank God you're not hurt," Eva breathed, the relief palpable even through the phone. "I'll call Kyle immediately and tell him to stand down before he gets himself arrested trying to reach you. How badly is Detective Cole injured?"

"Broken leg, cuts, maybe a concussion," Lila reported, glancing back at the gurney where the paramedics were adjusting Marcus's oxygen levels. "He'll be okay, but he'll need surgery for the leg and time to recover."

"And you're going to the hospital with him?" Eva's tone held a knowing quality that made Lila blush despite the circumstances.

"Yes," she confirmed. "Lieutenant Ramirez assigned an officer to stay with us as security. I'll come back to the Harborview once Marcus is stabilized."

"Be careful, sweetheart," Eva cautioned. "Whoever planted that bomb is clearly desperate. And based on what you've told me, they may have connections to people still in town."

"I will," Lila promised. "The State Police have roadblocks at all exits from Seabreeze Shores, and they're bringing in additional officers. Stay in the hotel with Kyle and Elsie, and keep the officers updated on your movements, even within the building."

After a few more words of reassurance, Lila ended the call and returned to Marcus's side. The ambulance had increased speed, suggesting they were now on the highway connecting Seabreeze Shores to Harbor Bay.

"Your family okay?" Marcus asked, his voice slightly stronger now that the IV pain medication was taking effect.

"Worried but safe," Lila replied, settling into her seat. "Kyle was trying to get past police lines to find me, which is exactly the kind of impulsive heroics I'd expect from him."

A faint smile touched Marcus's lips. "Seems to run in the family."

"I have no idea what you're talking about," Lila replied with mock innocence.

"Of course not. Racing back into a collapsing building to help extract me wasn't impulsive at all. Completely rational."

"It was rational," Lila insisted. "You saved my life, Marcus. Did you expect me to just stand by while you were trapped?"

143

The intensity in her voice seemed to catch him off guard. His expression softened, professional detachment giving way to something more personal. "No," he admitted quietly. "I'm beginning to understand that's not who you are."

The moment stretched between them, weighted with unspoken emotions made more potent by their shared brush with death. But before Lila could respond, the ambulance lurched violently, throwing her against her seat restraints as the vehicle swerved sharply.

"What's happening?" Marcus demanded, his body tensing despite his injuries.

The paramedic steadying himself against the equipment rack looked equally alarmed. "I don't know—"

Officer Dabney was already on her feet, moving with remarkable balance toward the partition separating the patient compartment from the driver's cabin. "Driver! Report!" she commanded, her hand moving instinctively to her holstered weapon.

Another violent swerve threw them all sideways, medical equipment crashing to the floor. Through the small window to the front cabin, Lila caught a glimpse of what had caused the erratic driving—a black SUV cutting directly in front of the ambulance, forcing it toward the shoulder of the highway.

"We're being forced off the road," Dabney reported tersely, bracing herself against the partition. "Everyone secure yourselves. This could get rough."

The ambulance's sirens wailed in protest as the driver fought to maintain control, but the SUV continued its aggressive maneuvers, clearly intent on stopping their progress. Lila gripped the edge of her seat, heart pounding as she realized the implication—someone was deliberately targeting them, most likely to silence Marcus before he could share what they'd discovered at the cannery.

"Officer, can you return fire if they shoot?" Marcus asked, his detective's mind already analyzing the tactical situation despite his prone position.

"Affirmative," Dabney confirmed, her expression grim. "But I'd need a clear target, and civilian vehicles on the highway complicate engagement protocols."

The ambulance lurched again, this time accompanied by the sickening crunch of metal against metal as the SUV made direct contact with their front fender. Through the cabin window, Lila saw the driver struggling with the steering wheel, his face a mask of concentration as he fought to prevent a rollover.

"They're trying to force us off at the Harbor Point curve," Dabney realized aloud. "It's a steep embankment—ambulance would roll multiple times if we go over."

Marcus was already working to free himself from the gurney restraints, his face pale with pain but his movements decisive. "We need to prepare for impact or forced stop. Lila, position yourself on the floor between equipment mounts for maximum protection. Paramedics, secure loose equipment and prepare for possible patient transfer under fire."

The professionally calm instructions galvanized everyone into action despite the chaos of the violently swaying ambulance. Lila slid to the floor as directed, wedging herself into a protected alcove between mounted cabinets. The paramedics secured equipment and additional medical supplies, their training overcoming their obvious fear.

Officer Dabney had moved to a position where she could observe both the cabin window and the rear doors, her weapon now drawn but held in a ready position rather than aimed. "I've called for backup," she reported. "State Police units are en route but at least five minutes out."

"We don't have five minutes," Marcus replied grimly, having managed to free himself from the gurney despite his injuries. He slid to the floor near Lila, positioned to shield her with his body despite his broken leg and numerous contusions. The protective gesture wasn't lost on her, even in the midst of their peril.

The ambulance swerved violently one final time, then began to slow as the driver apparently realized their best chance was to stop on their own terms rather than be forced off the road. The deceleration pressed them all forward, equipment straining against its moorings.

"They're stopping in front of us," Dabney reported, peering through the cabin window. "Two men exiting the SUV. Armed with—" She ducked suddenly as a shot shattered the small window, sending glass shards spraying into the compartment. "Handguns, likely 9mm. Driver's hit!"

The ambulance jerked to a complete stop, the engine still running but no one now controlling it. Through the partition, Lila could see the driver slumped over the steering wheel, blood visible on his uniform. The paramedics moved immediately toward the cabin, medical instincts overriding self-preservation.

"Stay back!" Dabney ordered sharply. "Secure this compartment. I'll engage the hostiles and attempt to draw fire away from the ambulance."

"You're outnumbered," Marcus protested, reaching for the backup weapon strapped to his ankle despite his injuries. "At least take this."

"Negative," Dabney replied firmly. "You maintain this position and protect Ms. Montgomery. If I can't neutralize the threat, you're the secondary line of defense." Her expression softened briefly. "It's been an honor, Detective Cole."

Before either Marcus or Lila could respond, Dabney was moving, pushing through the rear doors in a controlled exit that minimized her exposure. The crack of gunfire followed immediately, Dabney returning fire from the limited cover provided by the ambulance itself.

"We need to help her," Lila whispered, the sound of gunfire sending jolts of adrenaline through her system.

"We help by staying put and not becoming additional targets," Marcus replied, though the frustration in his voice made it clear he hated the passive role as much as she did. "Dabney is highly trained for exactly this scenario. Our job is to be ready if her position is overrun."

The paramedics had retreated from the cabin attempt, recognizing the futility of reaching their colleague with an active shooter situation outside. Instead, they had taken up protective positions near the remaining medical equipment, one of them clutching a portable defibrillator as if it might serve as a weapon in last resort.

The gunfire outside continued in sporadic bursts, suggesting Dabney was conserving ammunition while maintaining enough fire to keep their attackers from rushing the ambulance directly. Lila could hear shouts between the gunshots, though the words were indistinct through the vehicle's walls.

"Highway Patrol should have noticed the stopped emergency vehicle by now," Marcus murmured, more to himself than to Lila. "Even without Dabney's call for backup, standard protocol would route units to investigate."

"Unless they've been intercepted too," Lila suggested, the implications of that possibility chilling her. "If whoever is behind this has enough resources to coordinate an attack on a police-escorted ambulance, they might have contingencies to delay backup."

Marcus's expression confirmed her reasoning was sound, though he clearly wished it wasn't. "Which means we need to prepare for the possibility that Dabney can't hold them off indefinitely."

A sudden increase in gunfire from outside punctuated his statement, followed by a cry of pain that sounded horribly like Officer Dabney. The subsequent silence was somehow worse than the gunfire had been.

"They got Dabney," one of the paramedics whispered, his face pale with fear. "What do we do now?"

Marcus's expression hardened into the focused determination Lila had seen when he was pursuing leads in Fox's murder case. Despite his injuries, despite the pain evident in the tightness around his mouth, he projected calm authority.

"We prepare to defend this position," he stated, checking the ammunition in his backup weapon. "Doors are lockable from inside. Limited entry points works in our favor. And State Police backup is still coming, whether intercepted or delayed."

Lila realized with a chill that he was preparing for a last stand—injured, with limited ammunition, protecting three civilians against at least two armed attackers. The odds were not in their favor, yet he remained composed, his training overriding even the natural fear response such a situation would trigger.

Footsteps approached the ambulance, slow and deliberate. Not the hurried advance of law enforcement backup, but the measured pace of someone who believed they had all the time in the world. The rear doors of the ambulance rattled as someone tested the locks.

"Montgomery!" a voice called from outside, deep and unfamiliar. "We know you're in there with the detective. We don't want to hurt you—just hand over Cole and the evidence, and you can walk away. This isn't your fight."

Lila and Marcus exchanged glances, a silent communication passing between them. They both knew the promise was empty—anyone willing to attack an ambulance and shoot a police officer wouldn't leave witnesses, regardless of what they claimed.

"Harbor Bay Hospital dispatchers will have noted our failure to arrive," Marcus called back, playing for time. "State Police units are already en route. Whatever you're planning, you won't get away clean."

A cold laugh answered him. "We've got at least ten minutes before anyone else arrives. More than enough time to finish this and be gone. Last chance, Montgomery. Open the doors, or we start shooting through them. Your choice."

"Don't respond," Marcus whispered to Lila, shifting position to better shield her despite his broken leg. "They're trying to establish your exact position before firing."

The paramedics had moved as far from the doors as possible, crouching behind the gurney for minimal protection. One of them, a young man barely out of his twenties, was visibly trembling, while his older colleague maintained a grim composure that spoke of prior experience with violence.

"Time's up," the voice outside announced. "Don't say we didn't give you options."

Lila tensed, expecting a hail of bullets through the ambulance doors. Instead, she heard something far more terrifying—the sound of liquid splashing against the vehicle's exterior, followed by the distinctive odor of gasoline.

"They're going to burn us out," the older paramedic realized aloud, horror dawning on his face. "Or straight up burn the ambulance with us inside."

Marcus's expression confirmed the assessment, his eyes darting around the confined space for any possible avenue of escape. The ambulance had only two exits—the rear doors now being doused with accelerant, and the cabin doors, which would require them to pass the wounded or dead driver and expose themselves directly to the gunmen.

"Options?" Lila asked quietly, refusing to give in to the panic clawing at her throat.

"Limited," Marcus admitted, his voice equally low. "Ambulance framework is reinforced, but interior fittings are flammable. Once they ignite the accelerant, we have maybe two minutes before smoke inhalation becomes critical, less until flames breach the compartment."

The splashing sound continued, suggesting their attackers were being thorough in their application of the gasoline. Lila's mind raced, cataloging and discarding potential solutions with increasing desperation.

The older paramedic had moved to a supply cabinet, retrieving what appeared to be emergency breathing apparatus—helpful against smoke, but useless against actual flames.

"Last warning!" the voice outside called, now tinged with sadistic anticipation. "Come out now, or burn. Your choice, but make it quick. I've got a lighter right here."

The situation was crystallizing into terrible clarity: they were trapped, outgunned, with an injured detective, two civilian paramedics, and at least two armed attackers willing to commit murder in broad daylight. Whatever evidence they had discovered at the cannery, whatever threat Marcus posed to their operation, these people were determined to eliminate it permanently.

And yet, despite the overwhelming odds, Lila found herself experiencing not just fear but a surprising strain of anger. These people had killed Graham Fox, had been involved in Samuel Price's death decades earlier, had corrupted Sheriff Jennings, and were now threatening more lives to protect their development plans. The sheer callousness of it—valuing profit over human life to such an extreme—kindled a resistance in her that burned hotter than her fear.

"The oxygen tanks," she whispered suddenly, the idea forming even as she spoke. "If they light the gasoline..."

Marcus's eyes widened fractionally as he followed her reasoning. "The explosion could kill us all," he cautioned, though she could see he was already calculating the angles, the timing, the desperate gamble she was proposing.

"If we don't try something, we're dead anyway," Lila replied with grim certainty. "At least this way we have a chance."

The younger paramedic had overheard their exchange. "Are you suggesting we detonate our own oxygen supply? That's insane!"

"No," Marcus corrected, his tactical mind having refined the idea already. "We create a controlled pathway for the pressurized oxygen to vent when the fire reaches a specific point. Directional force, if we position it correctly, could blow out the cabin partition."

"Giving us an escape route through the front," the older paramedic realized, already moving toward the oxygen equipment. "It's risky as hell, but he's right—it's better than burning alive."

"We need to move fast," Marcus urged, his voice tight with controlled urgency. "They'll light the accelerant any second."

What followed was a desperate race against time—the paramedics quickly disconnecting an oxygen cylinder and positioning it according to Marcus's instructions, Lila gathering what medical supplies might be useful for their escape attempt, Marcus himself retrieving Dabney's fallen weapon from where they could see it through the shattered partition window.

"Ready?" Marcus asked, his gaze meeting Lila's with an intensity that communicated far more than the simple question. If this failed, if their desperate gambit resulted in a catastrophic explosion rather than a controlled breach, these might be their final moments together.

"Ready," she confirmed, something passing between them in that shared look—regret for possibilities unexplored, determination to survive against the odds, and perhaps most surprisingly, a connection that had formed with remarkable speed and depth during their short acquaintance.

"On my signal, everyone move to the forward position, as low to the floor as possible," Marcus directed. "When the oxygen ignites, we'll have seconds at most to exit through the cabin."

The distinctive click of a lighter sounded from outside, followed immediately by the whoosh of gasoline igniting. Flames licked up the sides of the ambulance, visible through the small windows, their orange glow casting sinister shadows inside the compartment.

"Now!" Marcus commanded, all of them scrambling toward the front of the ambulance as the temperature inside began to rise with alarming speed. The oxygen cylinder had been positioned to direct its force toward the partition when the heat triggered its pressure release valve.

Smoke began seeping in through the seals around the doors, acrid and choking. The younger paramedic pulled his shirt over his nose and mouth, while the older one distributed the emergency breathing apparatus he'd retrieved earlier. The fire's roar grew louder, hungry flames consuming the accelerant and beginning to attack the ambulance itself.

"It's getting hot enough," the older paramedic warned, eyeing the oxygen cylinder with professional knowledge of its tolerances. "Pressure valve should blow any—"

The rest of his sentence was lost in a deafening explosion as the oxygen cylinder's safety valve finally yielded to the rising heat. The directed force blasted through the partition exactly as Marcus had calculated, the concussive wave stunning them all momentarily despite their preparation.

Ears ringing, vision blurred by smoke and debris, Lila felt Marcus pull her forward toward the newly created escape route. The ambulance's cabin was now accessible, though the unconscious or dead driver remained slumped over the steering wheel. Outside, she could hear confused shouting from their attackers, who clearly hadn't expected this development.

"Through the driver's side door," Marcus directed, his voice barely audible above the roar of the flames and the ringing in their ears. "Stay low, use the ambulance for cover, and run for the tree line. Don't stop for anything."

The older paramedic went first, carefully maneuvering past his colleague to reach the door handle. A quick check outside, then he was moving, half-falling from the elevated cab to the asphalt below. The younger paramedic followed, terror giving him speed despite his earlier panic.

"Your turn," Marcus told Lila, his grip on her arm firm but gentle despite the desperate circumstances. "I'll be right behind you."

Lila hesitated, unwilling to leave him behind with his injuries. "We go together," she insisted, already positioning herself to help support his weight.

"Lila—" he began, but whatever argument he intended to make was cut short by another explosion—the ambulance's fuel tank this time, rupturing from the intense heat of the gasoline fire. The vehicle lurched violently, throwing them both against the dashboard.

Through the windshield, now cracked from the heat, Lila could see their attackers regrouping, weapons raised as they realized their quarry might be escaping. One man—tall, expensively dressed despite the incongruity of his appearance at a violent crime scene—was directing the other toward the front of the ambulance.

"We need to move now," Marcus urged, grimacing against the pain of his broken leg but somehow managing to pull himself upright using the steering wheel for leverage. Together, they forced open the driver's side door, heat from the spreading fire washing over them in suffocating waves.

Gunfire erupted as soon as the door opened, bullets pinging against the ambulance's exterior. Their attackers had spotted the escape attempt and were determined to prevent it. Lila ducked instinctively, pulling Marcus down with her.

"We're pinned," Marcus stated grimly, assessing their deteriorating situation with professional detachment. "Fire behind, gunmen ahead. Limited cover between here and the tree line."

The ambulance groaned ominously beneath them, the structure compromised by heat and multiple explosions. They couldn't stay where they were—the vehicle would become their coffin within minutes as flames consumed the remaining oxygen and structural integrity failed.

"There," Lila pointed through the windshield, indicating a shallow drainage ditch that ran alongside the highway, offering minimal but potentially life-saving cover. "If we can reach that ditch, we can move toward those emergency vehicles."

For in the distance, blue and red lights were finally visible, approaching rapidly from the direction of Harbor Bay—the backup that had been delayed but not prevented. Their attackers had noticed too, their shots becoming more frantic as they realized their window of opportunity was closing.

"On three," Marcus agreed, positioning himself to move despite his injuries. "One, two—"

A new sound cut through the chaos—the distinctive report of high-powered rifles, different from the handguns their attackers had been using. State Police snipers, deploying from the arriving vehicles, had established firing positions and were engaging the gunmen.

"Police! Drop your weapons!" amplified voices commanded through bullhorns. "You are surrounded! Lay down your weapons and place your hands on your heads!"

Their attackers' response was predictably violent—more gunfire, now directed at the approaching law enforcement rather than the ambulance. In the momentary shift of attention, Marcus seized their opportunity.

"Now!" he urged, and together they tumbled from the ambulance, Lila supporting as much of Marcus's weight as she could manage while they half-ran, half-crawled toward the drainage ditch. The paramedics were already there, having reached safety during the initial confusion of the exploding oxygen tank.

They collapsed into the shallow depression just as the firefight intensified behind them. The well-dressed man who had been directing the attack was now retreating toward a second vehicle that had been hidden from their view, while his companion provided covering fire against the advancing State Police units.

"Stay down," Marcus instructed, though the command was hardly necessary—none of them were in any hurry to raise their heads into the exchange of gunfire. The drainage ditch offered minimal protection, but it was enough to keep them below the line of fire as law enforcement methodically advanced on their attackers.

Lila's heart pounded against her ribs, adrenaline and fear creating a cocktail that made every sensation painfully sharp—the rough gravel digging into her palms, the heat of the burning ambulance still radiating against her back, the ragged sound of Marcus's breathing beside her as he fought through the pain of his injuries.

One of the State Police officers had spotted them in the ditch and was now directing a medical team in their direction, the professionals moving in the crouched manner of those accustomed to operating in dangerous conditions. The firefight was winding down, the attackers either neutralized or in retreat, pursued by additional units.

"Detective Cole! Ms. Montgomery!" The officer reached them, dropping to a knee beside the drainage ditch. "Are you injured? We have medics standing by."

"Broken leg, multiple contusions," Marcus reported tersely, professional even in extremis. "The paramedics may have smoke inhalation. Officer Dabney is down, condition unknown, position approximately twenty meters south of the ambulance."

The officer relayed this information into his radio, and within moments, medical personnel were helping them from the ditch. Marcus was transferred to a backboard despite his protests that he could walk with assistance, his pallor and the visible deformation of his left leg making his claims obviously false.

Lila stayed by his side as they were moved toward a safe triage area established behind the State Police vehicles. All around them, organized chaos unfolded—firefighters battling the fully engulfed ambulance, tactical teams securing the perimeter, medical personnel triaging the injured.

"The man in the suit," Marcus was saying to Lieutenant Ramirez, who had arrived with the backup units. "Tall, gray hair, expensive watch.

He was directing the attack. Have units pursue the secondary vehicle, black sedan, heading south on Highway 1."

Ramirez was already relaying the information, her efficiency impressive as she simultaneously coordinated the crime scene response and collected Marcus's observations. "We have units in pursuit. Preliminary ID on the shooter we neutralized suggests Coastal Ventures security detail. No ID, but equipment is high-end, professional."

"Lawrence Caldwell," Lila interjected, the realization crystalizing as she recalled the well-dressed man's commanding presence. "The CEO of Marigold Holdings. That's who was directing the attack."

Ramirez's expression sharpened with interest. "You're certain? You could identify him?"

"I've seen his photograph in business publications," Lila confirmed. "And the initials in the letter we found at the cannery—L.C. It has to be him."

"Which means this goes higher than Jennings, higher than local corruption," Marcus added, wincing as a paramedic stabilized his broken leg. "Marigold Holdings' executive leadership is directly involved in eliminating witnesses and evidence."

"We'll put out an APB for Caldwell immediately," Ramirez decided, already turning to relay the instructions to her team. "And increase security for all witnesses, especially Nina West when she arrives. If they're willing to attack a police-escorted ambulance in broad daylight, they're desperate enough to try anything."

As the medical team prepared Marcus for transport in a new ambulance—this one with significantly heavier police escort—Lila found herself experiencing a curious mixture of exhaustion and hyperawareness. The immediate danger had passed, but the implications of what they'd discovered were only beginning to unfold.

The development plans, the murders spanning decades, Sheriff Jennings' corruption—all of it connected to Marigold Holdings and its ruthless pursuit of profit. And now Lawrence Caldwell himself had emerged from the shadows, directly participating in an attempted murder rather than merely ordering it from a safe distance. Whatever evidence they had uncovered at the cannery must be damning indeed to provoke such a desperate response.

"You should go with your family," Marcus told her as they prepared to load him into the ambulance. His face was pale from pain and blood loss, but his eyes remained intensely focused on hers. "The State Police will secure the hospital, but Caldwell is still out there. He knows you can identify him now."

"I'm not leaving you," Lila replied with quiet certainty. The hours since they'd first met in her ice cream shop seemed impossibly distant now, as if they belonged to different people in a different lifetime. Something had fundamentally shifted between them during their shared ordeal—a connection forged in danger that felt unbreakable in this moment.

Marcus studied her face, perhaps recognizing the futility of arguing with her determined expression. "Lieutenant Ramirez won't like it," he warned, though without much conviction.

"Lieutenant Ramirez doesn't have to like it," Lila countered. "But she's practical enough to recognize that keeping us together simplifies her security logistics."

A ghost of a smile touched Marcus's lips despite his evident pain. "You make a compelling argument, Ms. Montgomery."

"I thought we were past formalities, Detective Cole," she responded, matching his tone despite the gravity of their circumstances.

Before he could reply, Lieutenant Ramirez approached, her expression grim. "We've got a problem," she announced without preamble. "The evidence from the cannery—documents, photographs, everything—was in a transport vehicle intercepted en route to the State Police lab. Two officers down, evidence missing. This was a coordinated attack on multiple fronts."

The implication landed heavily between them. Without the physical evidence, their case against Lawrence Caldwell and Marigold Holdings rested primarily on witness testimony—vulnerable to legal challenges, character assassination, and the passage of time.

"Nina West becomes even more crucial now," Marcus observed, his detective's mind working despite his injuries and the chaos surrounding them. "Her testimony about what Fox discovered could be the key to linking Caldwell to both murders."

"Her flight lands in fifteen minutes," Ramirez confirmed. "I've diverted additional units to secure her arrival and transport to a safe location. But given what's happened here..." She didn't need to complete the thought. The ruthlessness and resources demonstrated by their opponents were now abundantly clear.

As the medical team finally loaded Marcus into the waiting ambulance, Lila climbed in beside him, ignoring the questioning look from Ramirez. Some battles weren't worth fighting, and she suspected the Lieutenant had more urgent concerns than where Lila Montgomery chose to sit during a medical transport.

"We'll rendezvous at Harbor Bay Memorial," Ramirez told them, securing the ambulance doors herself. "Security detail is already in place. No stops, no detours, direct route only." These last instructions were directed at the new driver, who nodded with appropriate gravity.

As the ambulance pulled away, lights flashing but sirens silent—no need to announce their movement more than necessary—Lila found herself watching the receding chaos through the rear windows. The burning hulk of the first ambulance, the State Police vehicles forming a protective perimeter, the medical teams treating the injured including Officer Dabney, who had apparently survived her wounds.

"We're still missing something," Marcus said quietly, drawing her attention back to him. The IV pain medication was finally taking effect, softening the lines of tension around his mouth but doing nothing to dull the sharp intelligence in his eyes. "Caldwell wouldn't risk exposing himself directly unless he was truly desperate. There must be more to what Fox discovered, something beyond what we've found so far."

"Maybe Nina West knows," Lila suggested, adjusting the thin blanket the paramedics had draped over Marcus to combat shock. "If she was researching for Fox, she might have uncovered something we haven't yet."

"If she makes it to the safe house," Marcus replied grimly. "Given the coordination of these attacks, I'm concerned they may have compromised her travel arrangements as well."

The implication chilled Lila despite the ambulance's regulated temperature. If Caldwell's resources extended to intercepting police transports and coordinating multiple simultaneous attacks, what might be awaiting Nina West when her flight landed?

As the ambulance sped toward Harbor Bay Memorial Hospital, its police escort maintaining vigilant formation around them, Lila couldn't shake the feeling that they were racing toward not just medical treatment for Marcus, but toward another confrontation—one where the stakes were even higher than their own survival.

Lawrence Caldwell was still out there, growing more desperate with each passing hour. And desperate men with unlimited resources were perhaps the most dangerous adversaries of all.

The remainder of the journey to Harbor Bay Memorial passed in tense silence, the ambulance crew focused on monitoring Marcus's condition while Lila divided her attention between him and the world outside, half-expecting another attack despite their police escort. By the time they reached the hospital's emergency entrance, her nerves were stretched to breaking point, every sudden movement or loud noise triggering an adrenaline spike.

The hospital had been notified of their arrival and the security concerns surrounding it. A team of medical professionals waited at the ambulance bay, ready to transfer Marcus directly to a treatment area, while uniformed State Police officers established a visible security presence throughout the emergency department.

"We need to keep moving," one of the officers told Lila as the medical team whisked Marcus away for immediate assessment. "You'll be placed in a secure waiting room adjacent to the treatment area. Lieutenant Ramirez's orders."

Lila allowed herself to be guided through the bustling emergency department, noting the strategic positioning of officers at all entrance points. The "secure waiting room" turned out to be a small conference space normally used for family consultations during medical crises, now repurposed with a police officer stationed directly outside the door.

"Can I get you anything, ma'am?" the officer asked, his young face serious beneath his State Police cap. "Water? Coffee?"

"Water would be good," Lila admitted, suddenly aware of her parched throat and the lingering smell of smoke clinging to her clothes and hair. "And any news on Detective Cole's condition when it becomes available."

"Yes, ma'am. I'll arrange that immediately."

Left alone in the sterile conference room, Lila finally had a moment to process the events of the past few hours. The cannery explosion, Marcus's injuries, the ambulance attack—it seemed impossible that all of it had happened in a single afternoon. Her hands trembled slightly as delayed shock began to set in, and she clasped them together on the table to still the movement.

Her phone had been damaged during their escape from the burning ambulance, the screen cracked and unresponsive. She needed to contact her family, let them know she was safe, but would have to rely on the officers for that now. The isolation was unsettling after the constant activity and danger of the day.

The officer returned with a bottle of water and a hospital-issued sweatshirt. "Thought you might want this, ma'am. The emergency staff noticed you had smoke exposure." He placed both items on the table respectfully. "I've requested an update on Detective Cole, but it might be a while. He's been taken directly to surgery for the leg fracture."

"Thank you," Lila said, grateful for the small kindnesses. "Is there any way I can get a message to my family? My phone was damaged in the... incident." The word seemed absurdly inadequate for what they'd experienced, but she lacked the energy to find a more accurate description.

"Of course. I can have someone contact them directly. They're still at the Harborview Hotel in Seabreeze Shores, correct?"

"Yes. Please let them know I'm safe and will call as soon as I can." She hesitated, then added, "And could you find out if Nina West's flight has landed? She's a key witness in our case, expected to arrive this afternoon."

The officer's expression shifted subtly—a micro-expression of concern quickly masked by professional neutrality. "I'll inquire about Ms. West's status, ma'am. Please try to rest. This room is secure."

After he left, Lila sipped the water gratefully, the cool liquid soothing her smoke-irritated throat. She pulled on the hospital sweatshirt over her dust-and-smoke-stained clothes, drawing modest comfort from its clean softness against her skin. The digital clock on the conference room wall showed 4:45 PM—Nina's flight should have landed fifteen minutes ago.

Time passed with excruciating slowness in the quiet room. Lila alternated between sitting and pacing, her mind replaying the day's events on an endless loop, searching for patterns or connections they might have missed. The map at the cannery with its marked properties, the hidden documents implicating Lawrence Caldwell, Sheriff Jennings' role as local enforcer for Marigold Holdings' plans—it all connected, but something still seemed to be missing from the full picture.

At 5:23 PM, according to the unforgiving conference room clock, the door opened to admit Lieutenant Ramirez. The State Police officer's usual crisp appearance had suffered somewhat—smudges of soot on her uniform, a small tear in her sleeve, hair escaping from its usually neat arrangement—but her manner remained professionally composed.

"Ms. Montgomery," she greeted Lila, taking the seat across from her at the conference table. "Detective Cole is in surgery. The orthopedic team is optimistic, but he'll be facing significant recovery time. No life-threatening injuries, though the smoke exposure is being monitored."

Relief flooded through Lila at the relatively positive prognosis. "Thank you for letting me know. Have you heard anything about Nina West? Her flight should have landed almost an hour ago."

Something flickered in Ramirez's eyes—a tightening that immediately set off warning bells in Lila's mind. "That's actually why I'm here," the Lieutenant said carefully. "There's been a complication."

"What kind of complication?" Lila asked, already dreading the answer.

"Ms. West never boarded her flight in Boston," Ramirez reported, her tone neutral but her expression grave. "According to airport security footage, she arrived at the terminal but was approached by two men in suits who showed identification—likely false credentials. She left with them voluntarily approximately ninety minutes before her scheduled departure."

"They took her," Lila realized, cold dread settling in her stomach. "Caldwell's people got to her before she could testify."

"It appears that way," Ramirez confirmed. "Boston PD is investigating, but given the sophistication we've seen in their other operations today, I'm not optimistic about finding her quickly. These people are professionals, with resources and contingency plans."

The implications were chilling. Without the physical evidence from the cannery and without Nina West's testimony, their case against Lawrence Caldwell and Marigold Holdings was significantly weakened. They still had what they'd discovered at the historical society and Sheriff Jennings in custody, but Jennings had already demonstrated loyalty to his employers by refusing to cooperate.

"So what now?" Lila asked, frustration edging her voice. "They're just going to get away with multiple murders spanning decades because they can afford to hire enough thugs and lawyers?"

"Justice can be delayed, Ms. Montgomery, but it rarely stays denied indefinitely," Ramirez replied, though without the confident conviction such a statement might normally carry. "We're setting up a dedicated task force for this case, bringing in federal resources since it now spans multiple jurisdictions. Lawrence Caldwell's direct involvement in today's attack has elevated this beyond a local matter."

The assurance should have been comforting, but Lila had seen too much in the past few days to take bureaucratic promises at face value. "And in the meantime? What about my family? What about everyone else involved in this case? Are we just supposed to wait for the next attack?"

"We've increased security at the Harborview for your family," Ramirez answered, her patience admirable given Lila's barely contained frustration. "Ms. Winters and your brother and mother are safe. And you'll remain under protection here at the hospital until Detective Cole is stabilized, after which we'll reassess the situation."

Before Lila could respond, a knock at the door interrupted them. Ramirez rose to answer it, exchanging quiet words with someone in the hallway before returning to the table with renewed tension evident in her posture.

"There's been another development," she said, resuming her seat. "Mira Douglas is missing."

"Missing?" Lila echoed, struggling to process this new complication. "The B&B owner? Since when?"

"Since this morning, apparently. Her assistant reported it when she failed to return from what was supposed to be a brief errand. Given everything else happening today, the report was delayed in reaching my team." Ramirez checked her notes. "Initial investigation shows her car is still at the B&B, but security cameras captured her getting into a black SUV at approximately 8:15 this morning. The vehicle matches the description of the one involved in the ambulance attack."

The pieces began connecting in Lila's mind. "They took her too. But why? What does Mira have to do with any of this? I mean, yes, her B&B was on Harbor Act land, but so are lots of properties."

"That's what we need to determine," Ramirez agreed. "Her connection to this case may be more significant than we initially thought. The timing suggests Caldwell's organization was moving to eliminate potential witnesses or complications even before we discovered the evidence at the cannery."

A memory surfaced in Lila's exhausted mind—the contract Elsie had found in Graham Fox's briefcase, the one offering Mira Douglas twice the market value for her B&B. "The contract," she said aloud. "Fox was offering Mira an extremely generous deal for the B&B. We assumed it was because of the Harbor Act rights, but what if there was something more? Something specific about that property?"

Ramirez leaned forward, interest sharpening her gaze. "What are you thinking?"

"I don't know exactly," Lila admitted, the theory forming even as she spoke. "But the historical society records showed that the B&B was partially built on reclaimed harbor land, which gave it certain rights under the Harbor Act. But it's also one of the oldest buildings in town, with a direct lineage to the original harbor master's office from the 1800s."

"Historical significance," Ramirez murmured, echoing the notation that had been found in Graham Fox's notebook regarding Salted Caramel's. "You think there's something about the building itself? Something beyond its legal status?"

"It's worth investigating," Lila suggested. "Especially since they've now taken Mira. There must be a reason they specifically targeted her today, of all days."

Ramirez was already on her feet. "I'll have a team search the B&B immediately. If there's something there that connects to this case, we need to find it before Caldwell's people return to clean up any remaining evidence."

As Ramirez moved to the door, Lila called after her. "Lieutenant? What about Detective Cole?"

"I've assigned two officers to his room in post-op," Ramirez assured her. "They'll remain there throughout his hospital stay. And you'll be escorted to see him as soon as he's out of surgery." She hesitated, then added with surprising gentleness, "He was asking for you, you know. Before they took him into surgery. That's not standard procedure for a detective discussing a witness."

The implication hung in the air between them—an acknowledgment of the personal connection that had developed between Lila and Marcus throughout their investigation. "He saved my life," Lila said simply. "More than once today."

"And you saved his," Ramirez countered. "The paramedics reported that your idea with the oxygen tank prevented them all from burning alive in that ambulance. That kind of shared experience... it creates bonds that aren't easily broken."

With that surprisingly insightful observation, the Lieutenant departed, leaving Lila once again alone with her thoughts in the sterile conference room. The digital clock continued its relentless march, now showing 5:47 PM. Somewhere in the hospital, Marcus was undergoing surgery for injuries sustained protecting her. Her family remained under guard at the Harborview Hotel, probably frantic with worry despite whatever reassurances the State Police had provided.

And Lawrence Caldwell was still free, his organization now holding both Nina West and Mira Douglas—two women who possessed information that could potentially expose decades of corruption and murder. The stakes had escalated far beyond what any of them could have imagined when Graham Fox's body was discovered behind Salted Caramel's less than a week ago.

At 6:30 PM, the door opened again, this time admitting a hospital staff member in surgical scrubs accompanied by one of the State Police officers.

"Ms. Montgomery? Detective Cole is out of surgery and asking for you. If you'll come with us, we'll take you to the recovery area."

Lila rose immediately, grateful for the chance to see Marcus and confirm his condition for herself. The officer led her through a maze of hospital corridors, security checkpoints requiring badge access at several points emphasizing the precautions being taken. Finally, they arrived at a private room in the post-surgical recovery wing, another officer already stationed outside the door.

"He's still groggy from anesthesia," the staff member cautioned as they prepared to enter. "Try not to excite or agitate him. The surgery went well, but he needs rest to begin healing properly."

Lila nodded her understanding, then followed the nurse into the dimly lit room. Marcus lay in the hospital bed, his left leg immobilized in a cast and elevated on pillows, an IV line delivering fluids and medication, and monitoring equipment tracking his vital signs with soft, rhythmic beeps. His face was pale against the white hospital pillow, the cut on his forehead now neatly sutured, but his eyes were open and alert despite the lingering effects of anesthesia.

"Lila," he said, his voice rougher than usual but unmistakably relieved. "You're okay."

"I'm fine," she assured him, moving to the chair positioned beside his bed. "You're the one who decided to play hero and get yourself pinned under a collapsing building."

A ghost of his usual smile touched his lips. "Occupational hazard. Did everyone else make it out?"

"Yes. The paramedics are being treated for smoke inhalation but should be fine. Officer Dabney survived her injuries—she's in surgery now." Lila hesitated, then decided he deserved the complete update despite his condition. "Nina West never made it onto her flight. Caldwell's people intercepted her at the Boston airport. And Mira Douglas is missing too, apparently taken this morning in a similar vehicle to the one that attacked our ambulance."

Marcus absorbed this information with a slight furrowing of his brow, his detective's mind clearly working despite the post-surgical haze. "They're eliminating witnesses. Closing ranks." He shifted slightly in the bed, wincing as the movement disturbed his injured leg. "The evidence from the cannery?"

"Gone," Lila confirmed. "Intercepted en route to the State Police lab. Ramirez says they're setting up a task force, bringing in federal resources."

"That will take time," Marcus observed, frustration evident despite his weakened state. "Time Caldwell will use to further cover his tracks."

"Ramirez is sending a team to search the B&B," Lila told him. "I suggested there might be something there—some reason beyond the Harbor Act rights that made the property valuable enough for Caldwell to abduct Mira."

"Good thinking," Marcus approved, his eyes growing heavier as the medication in his IV continued to work through his system. "Historical significance... there's something we're still missing..." His voice trailed off, fatigue and medication finally overcoming his determination to remain alert.

"Rest," Lila urged gently, reaching out to touch his hand where it lay on the blanket. "We'll figure it out."

His fingers curled weakly around hers, the gesture communicating what his fading consciousness could not. As his breathing deepened and evened out in sleep, Lila remained beside him, their hands still connected, finding unexpected comfort in the simple human contact amid the chaos their lives had become.

She must have dozed off herself, exhaustion finally claiming her after the adrenaline and stress of the day. The sound of the door opening roused her, and she blinked awake to find Lieutenant Ramirez entering the room, her expression taut with barely contained excitement.

"Ms. Montgomery," she said quietly, mindful of the sleeping patient. "We found something at the B&B. Something I think you need to see."

Lila carefully disentangled her fingers from Marcus's, relieved when he didn't stir. "What is it?"

"A hidden room," Ramirez replied, her voice low but intense. "Behind a false wall in the basement. And inside, records dating back to the 1800s—shipping manifests, property deeds, and what appears to be evidence of substantial financial fraud spanning generations."

"Financial fraud?" Lila echoed, struggling to connect this to the development plans and murders they'd been investigating.

"Not just any fraud," Ramirez clarified. "Evidence suggesting that the original harbor lands—the ones covered by the Harbor Act—were acquired through systematic theft from the town's founding families. If these documents are authenticated, they could invalidate the entire legal foundation of current property ownership along the waterfront."

The implications hit Lila with stunning force. "Which would make the Harbor Act protections meaningless. Caldwell wouldn't need to buy the properties or eliminate holdouts if he could prove the current owners' claims were based on fraudulent acquisitions in the first place."

"Exactly," Ramirez confirmed. "And based on the meticulous organization of these records, it appears Mira Douglas was well aware of their significance. The question is whether she was working with Caldwell or against him."

"Against," Lila decided immediately, the pieces falling into place. "She refused to sign the contract selling the B&B to Coastal Ventures. If she'd been working with Caldwell, she would have taken the money and handed over the evidence. Instead, she kept it hidden, protected it."

"Until today," Ramirez noted grimly. "Now both she and the evidence are in Caldwell's hands. We only found the hidden room because it was left open in their haste—they must have taken the originals and missed some duplicates in their rush."

A chill ran through Lila as she processed the expanding scope of the conspiracy. What had begun as an investigation into a single murder now encompassed historical fraud, multiple kidnappings, and a legal battle that could reshape the entire ownership structure of Seabreeze Shores' waterfront.

"What happens now?" she asked, glancing at Marcus's sleeping form, wishing he were awake to help make sense of these new revelations.

"Now," Ramirez replied with grim determination, "we find Mira Douglas and Nina West before Caldwell forces them to authenticate or destroy those records. Because with the evidence from the cannery gone, their testimony combined with the duplicate records we found at the B&B may be our only chance to bring Caldwell to justice for everything—the fraud, the development scheme, Graham Fox's murder, and potentially Samuel Price's death as well."

As Lieutenant Ramirez outlined the next steps in their investigation, Lila's gaze remained on Marcus, his features relaxed in drug-induced sleep, unaware of the new complications in a case that seemed to grow more dangerous with each revelation. The quiet beeping of his monitoring equipment provided a rhythmic counterpoint to Ramirez's tactical planning, a reminder of how close they'd all come to becoming additional victims in Lawrence Caldwell's ruthless pursuit of profit.

And somewhere beyond the hospital's secured perimeter, Caldwell himself was orchestrating his endgame, holding two key witnesses and evidence that could either secure his victory or ensure his destruction. The next twenty-four hours would determine which outcome prevailed—and whether justice for Graham Fox, Samuel Price, and the town of Seabreeze Shores would finally be served after decades of manipulation and murder.

As Lila listened to Ramirez's plans, she couldn't shake the feeling that the most dangerous confrontation still lay ahead—and that despite all the protection surrounding them, they remained vulnerable to a man whose resources and ruthlessness had already proven formidable. The game of shadows and secrets was entering its final phase, with lives hanging in the balance and a killer determined to silence anyone who threatened his ambitions.

The warning Marcus had given her echoed in her mind: Trust no one.

Chapter 9
Breaking Point

The Harborview Hotel's executive suite had been transformed into an impromptu command center by dawn the following morning. State Police officers moved efficiently between makeshift workstations, coordinating search efforts for Nina West and Mira Douglas while monitoring Lawrence Caldwell's known properties and associates. Lieutenant Ramirez stood at the center of the operation, her crisp professionalism undiminished despite having been awake for nearly thirty hours straight.

Lila sat at a small desk near the windows, a cup of untouched coffee growing cold beside her as she pored over copies of the documents found in Mira Douglas's hidden room. After spending the night at Harbor Bay Memorial Hospital—refusing to leave Marcus despite Ramirez's initial insistence—she had reluctantly agreed to return to the Harborview when it became clear that Marcus would remain sedated for at least twelve hours following his surgery.

"Anything useful in those records?" Eva Montgomery asked, approaching with a fresh cup of coffee to replace Lila's neglected one. Despite the strain of recent days, Eva maintained her composed demeanor, her silver-streaked hair neatly styled, her clothes immaculate—finding dignity and control where she could in circumstances beyond her power to change.

"Maybe," Lila replied, rubbing her tired eyes. "These property transactions from the 1890s show a pattern of acquisitions by the Caldwell family's company—though it wasn't called Marigold Holdings back then. A series of purchases from families who had apparently fallen on hard times, all at prices well below market value."

"That's suspicious but not necessarily illegal," Eva observed, settling into the chair beside her daughter. "Opportunistic business practices have a long history, especially in towns dependent on fluctuating industries like fishing."

"True, but look at this," Lila pointed to a faded letter included among the documents. "A correspondence between Thomas Caldwell—presumably Lawrence's ancestor—and the Harbor Commissioner, outlining a scheme to artificially depress local fishing yields by restricting access to prime waters. The families who sold their waterfront properties did so after seasons of diminishing catches, catches that were being deliberately sabotaged."

Eva studied the letter with a deepening frown. "So the Caldwells have been manipulating Seabreeze Shores for generations, not just in recent decades. But why would Mira Douglas have these records? What's her connection to all this?"

Before Lila could offer a theory, Lieutenant Ramirez approached their table, her expression indicating new developments.

"We've identified the vehicle that transported Mira Douglas," she announced without preamble. "Traffic cameras tracked it to a private airfield outside Harbor Bay. FAA records show a private jet registered to a subsidiary of Marigold Holdings departed for the Cayman Islands at 10:17 yesterday morning."

"The Caymans," Lila repeated, the implications clear. "Banking privacy laws, limited extradition. They're holding her—and probably Nina West—outside our jurisdiction."

"Exactly," Ramirez confirmed. "We're working with international law enforcement, but these processes are slow, especially when dealing with corporations that maintain elaborate legal shields."

"So Caldwell gets away with it," Eva said quietly, her voice tinged with the resignation of someone who had seen justice delayed or denied before. "Just like in 1995 when Samuel Price died."

"Not necessarily," Ramirez countered, her determined expression belying the obstacles she'd just outlined. "Lawrence Caldwell made a critical error yesterday—he personally participated in the attack on the ambulance transporting Detective Cole. We have multiple officers who can place him at the scene, and Ms. Montgomery's identification of him from prior photographs adds weight to their testimony."

"But without Mira Douglas or Nina West to connect him to Graham Fox's murder, how do you prove the larger conspiracy?" Lila questioned, frustration edging her voice. "He'll claim he was acting emotionally, that he believed Detective Cole had falsely accused him and reacted poorly. His lawyers will negotiate it down to assault or reckless endangerment, and the murders will remain unsolved."

Ramirez's expression didn't change, but something in her eyes suggested Lila had touched a nerve. "Which is why we need to find additional evidence or testimony linking Caldwell directly to Fox's murder. We're focusing our investigation on individuals who might have knowledge of the operation but weren't valuable enough to extract from the country—lower-level associates, employees of Coastal Ventures who might have witnessed incriminating conversations or actions."

"Frank Mitchell," Lila suggested suddenly, the name surfacing from her exhausted mind. "He owns the general store next to my shop, and his property is also on Harbor Act land. He admitted to me that he had already signed an agreement with Graham Fox, unlike most other waterfront property owners who were holding out."

"We've already brought Mr. Mitchell in for questioning," Ramirez replied with a slight nod of approval at Lila's reasoning. "He's being cooperative but claims his interactions were solely with Fox, never directly with Caldwell or anyone claiming to represent Marigold Holdings."

A thought occurred to Lila as she considered the timeline of events. "What about Elliot Price? The fisherman whose father died in that supposed accident in 1995. We haven't really investigated his connection to all this."

"Price has been under surveillance since Sheriff Jennings' arrest," Ramirez informed her. "His movements have been consistent with his normal routine—boat out before dawn, return mid-afternoon, brief stops at local establishments. Nothing to suggest involvement in Caldwell's organization."

"Or he's very good at maintaining his cover," Lila countered, the lack of sleep making her more willing to voice suspicions. "His father's death would have given him plenty of reason to hate the Caldwells and their development plans. Maybe he's been playing a long game, working his way into their confidence while planning some kind of revenge."

Ramirez considered this perspective with professional objectivity. "It's a theory worth exploring. I'll have officers bring him in for a formal interview today." She checked her watch. "I should get back to the command post. The county prosecutor is arriving within the hour to review our evidence against Caldwell and determine if it's sufficient for an arrest warrant."

After Ramirez departed, Eva studied her daughter's exhausted face with maternal concern. "You need to rest, Lila. You've been going non-stop since yesterday morning. Even detectives sleep occasionally."

"I'll rest when Marcus—Detective Cole—is out of danger and we've found Nina and Mira," Lila replied stubbornly, though she couldn't stifle the yawn that followed her declaration. "Besides, I couldn't sleep right now if I tried. Too much adrenaline."

"At least eat something," Eva insisted, pushing a plate of pastries toward her. "You can't function on coffee alone, despite what your brother might believe."

At the mention of Kyle, Lila glanced around the suite. "Where is Kyle, anyway? And Elsie?"

"Elsie is resting in her room—the poor girl was completely overwhelmed by yesterday's events. Kyle convinced the officers to let him go to your shop briefly with an escort. He wanted to check that everything was secure and ready for when you eventually reopen." Eva's tone was carefully neutral, but Lila detected an undercurrent of worry.

"You're concerned about him being out there," Lila observed. "Even with police protection."

"I'm concerned about all of us," Eva admitted. "This Lawrence Caldwell has shown he's willing to go to extraordinary lengths to protect his interests. And while I have faith in Lieutenant Ramirez and her team, I can't help feeling that we're still missing something important—some piece of the puzzle that would make everything else make sense."

The observation resonated with Lila's own unease. Despite the progress they'd made in uncovering the conspiracy, there remained gaps in their understanding—motivations and connections that continued to elude them. Why had Mira Douglas kept those historical records hidden for so long, only to be taken now? What had Graham Fox discovered that made him dangerous enough to kill? And how did it all connect to her father's involvement in the 1995 development plans?

Her phone—a replacement provided by the State Police after her original was damaged in the ambulance attack—buzzed with an incoming message. It was from Harbor Bay Memorial Hospital, informing her that Marcus Cole was awake and recovering well from surgery. A wave of relief washed through her, momentarily displacing her exhaustion and worry.

"Good news?" Eva asked, noting her daughter's changed expression.

"Marcus is awake," Lila confirmed, a small smile touching her lips despite everything. "The doctors say he's doing well."

"Marcus, is it?" Eva observed with knowing gentleness. "Not Detective Cole anymore?"

Lila felt a flush warm her cheeks. "It's been an intense few days. We've been through a lot together."

"Clearly," Eva agreed, without the teasing Lila might have expected. Instead, her mother's expression held understanding and a hint of concern. "Just be careful, sweetheart. Not about your feelings—those are what they are. But about the situation. This case has already proven dangerous in ways none of us could have anticipated. And while your detective seems like a good man, his first priority has to be solving the case."

"I know that," Lila assured her, though the reminder stung slightly. "We both understand the priorities here. Whatever's developing between us... it can wait until this is resolved."

Eva patted her hand gently. "I just don't want to see you hurt—physically or emotionally. Now, are you going to go see him?"

"Lieutenant Ramirez wanted me to stay here, where the security is established," Lila replied, though her desire to check on Marcus personally was evident in her tone.

"I suspect she'll make an exception, provided you take an appropriate escort," Eva suggested. "And it might be beneficial for the investigation if you can update Detective Cole on the latest developments. He might see connections we're missing."

The thoughtful rationalization was so clearly designed to give Lila a professional excuse to visit Marcus that she couldn't help smiling at her mother's transparent effort. "I'll ask her."

To Lila's mild surprise, Ramirez agreed readily to the proposed hospital visit, assigning two officers to accompany her. "Detective Cole's perspective would indeed be valuable," the Lieutenant acknowledged. "And your presence might help his recovery. Medical studies consistently show that patient outcomes improve with the support of..." She trailed off, perhaps realizing the unusually personal nature of her commentary. "In any case, keep the visit brief. We'll continue analyzing the documents here."

The drive from Seabreeze Shores to Harbor Bay took just under thirty minutes, the State Police vehicle maintaining a careful surveillance pattern to detect any potential tails or threats. Lila used the time to organize her thoughts, preparing to brief Marcus efficiently on the latest developments while also mentally preparing herself for his condition. The last time she'd seen him, he'd been pale and groggy from anesthesia, his normally sharp features softened by medication and pain.

Harbor Bay Memorial Hospital's security had been enhanced since yesterday's events, with uniformed officers at all entrances and ID checkpoints established at key access points. Lila and her escorts were ushered through these security measures with professional courtesy, their credentials having been communicated in advance by Lieutenant Ramirez.

Marcus had been moved from the recovery area to a private room in the orthopedic ward, with an officer stationed directly outside his door. The guard nodded in recognition as Lila approached, confirming her identity before allowing her to enter while her escorts remained in the hallway.

The hospital room was brighter than the recovery area had been, sunlight streaming through partially opened blinds, illuminating Marcus as he sat propped against pillows, his casted leg elevated on a support, a hospital breakfast tray pushed half-eaten to the side. He looked up as she entered, and the way his expression brightened upon seeing her sent a warm flutter through Lila's chest despite her exhaustion.

"You look terrible," he greeted her, though the warmth in his eyes belied the blunt assessment.

"Charming as always, Detective," Lila replied, settling into the visitor's chair beside his bed. "Especially coming from someone who recently treated a collapsing building like a gymnastics obstacle."

A smile tugged at the corner of his mouth. "Touché. How bad is it really? Ramirez has been suspiciously vague in her updates."

Lila hesitated, torn between the desire to shield him from additional stress during his recovery and the professional respect that demanded honesty. The latter won out. "Nina West never made her flight—she was intercepted at Boston airport by men posing as officials. Mira Douglas was abducted yesterday morning and traced to a private jet that flew to the Cayman Islands. The evidence from the cannery was intercepted and stolen during transport. And the duplicates we found at Mira's B&B suggest a fraudulent land scheme dating back to the 1890s that could potentially invalidate current waterfront property ownership."

Marcus absorbed this rapid-fire briefing with a deepening frown, his mind visibly processing each element despite the pain medication that occasionally clouded his eyes. "Caldwell's consolidating his position," he concluded. "Removing witnesses, securing evidence, preparing legal countermeasures in case the fraud is exposed."

"That's our assessment as well," Lila agreed. "Ramirez is hoping to secure an arrest warrant based on Caldwell's direct involvement in the ambulance attack, but without connecting him to Fox's murder specifically, he might escape the more serious charges."

"What about Jennings? Is he still refusing to cooperate?"

"Completely stonewalled, according to Ramirez. His attorney has advised him to say nothing until a formal deal is offered, and the prosecutor is reluctant to deal when we already have him on attempted murder from the hostage situation at my shop."

Marcus shifted slightly in the bed, wincing as the movement disturbed his injured leg. "What about the historical records from Mira's B&B? Anything specific that might give us leverage?"

"That's actually why I wanted to see you," Lila admitted, retrieving copies of key documents from her bag. "We've identified a pattern of manipulative business practices by the Caldwell family dating back to the 1890s, including artificially depressing local fishing yields to force families to sell waterfront properties. But we're still missing the connection to Mira Douglas herself. Why did she have these records? Why keep them hidden? And what made her valuable enough for Caldwell to extract from the country rather than simply..." She couldn't quite bring herself to say 'eliminate.'

"Rather than silencing her permanently," Marcus completed the thought with professional detachment. "Let me see what you've found."

Lila handed over the documents, watching as Marcus reviewed them with the methodical attention to detail that had impressed her from their first meeting. Despite his injured state and the medication flowing through his system, his mind remained sharp, identifying patterns and connections with remarkable speed.

"Look at this," he said after several minutes, indicating a notation on one of the property deeds. "The Douglas family name appears here, but not as owners of the B&B property. They owned adjacent land that was acquired by the Caldwell corporation in 1907, described as 'under duress and protest' according to this marginal note."

Lila leaned closer to examine the faded handwriting. "So Mira's family lost property to the Caldwells over a century ago? That might explain why she kept these records—a family grudge passed down through generations."

"More than a grudge," Marcus suggested, turning to another document. "This legal filing from 1910 shows an attempt by Edward Douglas to contest the sale, claiming fraud and coercion. The case was dismissed by a local judge, but Edward apparently didn't give up. There are notes here about his continued investigation into the Caldwell family's business practices."

"Which might explain why Mira had all these records," Lila realized, excitement building as the connection formed. "She inherited not just property but her ancestor's mission to expose the Caldwells' fraudulent acquisition of waterfront land."

"And when Graham Fox started researching the town's history for leverage in his development plans, he may have approached Mira for information about the B&B's background," Marcus continued, following the logical chain. "Instead, she shared these records with him, revealing the larger pattern of fraud that could potentially undermine the entire development."

"So Fox wasn't killed because he opposed the development," Lila concluded, the pieces finally aligning. "He was killed because he discovered evidence that could destroy not just the current project but the Caldwell family's entire claim to the waterfront properties they've acquired over generations."

"Exactly," Marcus nodded, his expression grave. "And if these records can be authenticated, they wouldn't just stop the current development—they could potentially force the return of fraudulently acquired properties to the descendants of the original owners, or to the town itself. Billions in real estate and future development rights are at stake."

The magnitude of the motivation clarified the extreme measures Caldwell had taken—the multiple murders, the abductions, the attack on a police-escorted ambulance in broad daylight. This wasn't just about one development project; it was about preserving a family empire built on a century of fraud.

"We need to find Mira Douglas," Lila stated, the urgency clear in her voice. "She's not just a witness; she's been gathering evidence against the Caldwells for years, possibly her entire life. She must know more than what was in that hidden room."

"International recovery will be challenging," Marcus cautioned, though his expression suggested he shared her sense of urgency. "The Cayman Islands aren't known for their cooperation in financial investigations, and Caldwell has likely taken precautions to keep her hidden and isolated."

"There must be something we can use as leverage," Lila insisted, rising from her chair to pace the small hospital room. "Someone who knows Caldwell's operation from the inside, someone who might be willing to talk in exchange for consideration."

Marcus watched her movement, his eyes tracking her with a mixture of professional assessment and something more personal that she wasn't quite ready to define. "What about Sheriff Jennings?" he suggested after a thoughtful pause. "His cooperation has been secured through traditional legal channels, but perhaps a different approach might be effective."

"What do you mean?" Lila asked, pausing in her pacing.

"Jennings isn't just a corrupt official; he's a local who's spent his entire life in Seabreeze Shores. His father before him was involved with the Caldwells, but they were also part of the community. There might be emotional leverage there that a standard plea deal doesn't address."

"You think I should talk to him?" Lila realized, understanding the implication. "As someone connected to the town's history, to my father's involvement in the 1995 deal?"

"It's worth considering," Marcus replied carefully. "Jennings has known your family for decades. That personal connection might reach him in ways that formal interrogation hasn't."

Lila resumed her pacing, considering the suggestion. It made tactical sense, but the thought of facing the man who had held her mother and brother hostage, who had been involved in Graham Fox's murder and potentially Samuel Price's death decades earlier, sent a cold knot of anxiety through her stomach.

"I'd need Ramirez's approval," she said finally. "And preparation—questions designed to elicit specific information rather than just general cooperation."

"I can help with that," Marcus offered, already reaching for a notepad on his bedside table. "If you're willing to try, I think it could make a difference. Jennings may be loyal to Caldwell, but his connection to Seabreeze Shores is lifelong. That kind of emotional tie can sometimes outweigh financial allegiance, especially when faced with the prospect of spending decades in prison far from home."

As they began outlining potential approaches, Lila found herself studying Marcus with newfound appreciation. Despite his injuries, despite the pain medication that occasionally clouded his expression, his mind remained incisive and strategic. More than that, he was trusting her with a critical interview, recognizing her unique position to reach Jennings in ways conventional law enforcement might not.

Their planning session was interrupted by a gentle knock at the door. One of Lila's State Police escorts entered, his expression suggesting urgent news.

"Ms. Montgomery, we've received word from Lieutenant Ramirez. Your brother has failed to check in at the designated time. His police escort reports that he gave them the slip at your ice cream shop approximately forty-five minutes ago."

Lila felt her blood run cold. "What do you mean, 'gave them the slip'? They were supposed to be protecting him!"

"According to the report, Mr. Montgomery claimed he needed to retrieve something from the shop's basement storage area. When he didn't return after several minutes, the officer checked and found a rear exit that wasn't on the building plans. A delivery entrance that had been sealed over but apparently reopened recently."

"Kyle wouldn't just disappear without a reason," Lila insisted, fear and confusion warring in her voice. "Especially not with everything that's happening. He knows how dangerous this situation is."

"Lieutenant Ramirez has dispatched additional units to search the area," the officer assured her. "And they're reviewing security camera footage from neighboring businesses to determine his direction of travel."

Marcus was already reaching for the phone beside his bed. "I need to speak with Lieutenant Ramirez immediately," he said, his voice carrying the unmistakable authority of a senior detective despite his hospital-bound state. "And I want roadblocks established at all exits from Seabreeze Shores, with particular attention to the marina and private boat launches."

As the officer moved to comply with these directives, Lila sank back into the visitor's chair, her mind racing with possibilities, none of them reassuring. Kyle was impulsive, yes, but not reckless enough to deliberately evade police protection during an active murder investigation. Unless...

"He found something," she realized aloud, the pieces connecting in her mind. "At the shop. Something he didn't want to share with the police, at least not immediately."

"Something he thought might put him in danger if the wrong people knew he had it," Marcus agreed, his expression grim as he waited for the phone connection to Lieutenant Ramirez. "Which means he's potentially carrying evidence that could make him a target for Caldwell's organization."

The implications didn't need stating. If Kyle had discovered something significant enough to warrant slipping away from police protection, he had effectively painted a target on his back for the same people who had abducted Nina West and Mira Douglas—and who had nearly killed Lila and Marcus just twenty-four hours earlier.

Lieutenant Ramirez came on the line, and Marcus immediately launched into a series of targeted questions and directives, his detective's mind fully engaged despite his physical limitations. Lila half-listened, her thoughts centered on her brother, mentally tracing his potential movements through Seabreeze Shores. Where would Kyle go if he'd found something important? Who would he trust with information he wasn't willing to share with the State Police?

A memory surfaced—Kyle as a teenager, hiding a bottle of stolen rum from their father in the one place Dad never looked: the old tree fort they'd built together at the edge of the Gardner family's orchard. The Gardners were gone now, their property sold to developers years ago, but the orchard remained, an undeveloped green space on the outskirts of town that locals still used for picnics and unofficial community events.

"The orchard," she said suddenly, interrupting Marcus's conversation with Ramirez. "Kyle might have gone to the old Gardner orchard. We had a hideout there as kids, a place we kept secrets from our parents."

Marcus relayed this information immediately, then covered the mouthpiece to speak directly to Lila. "Ramirez is redirecting units to the orchard now. She wants you to remain here under protection until Kyle is located."

"That's not happening," Lila replied firmly, already gathering her things. "He's my brother. If he's in danger because of something connected to my shop, I need to help find him."

The look Marcus gave her combined understanding with professional concern. "At least wait for proper backup and a coordinated approach. Running into a potential ambush won't help Kyle."

Before Lila could respond, Marcus's attention returned to the phone, his expression changing as he received new information. "When?" he asked sharply. "And you're certain of the identification? ... Yes, I understand. Keep me updated." He hung up, his face grim as he turned back to Lila.

"What is it?" she demanded, recognizing the look of a detective with bad news to deliver.

"Security cameras at the marina captured footage of Kyle boarding a boat approximately thirty minutes ago. He wasn't alone. The quality isn't great, but Ramirez's team believes he was accompanied by Elliot Price."

"Elliot?" Lila echoed, confusion replacing her initial fear. "That doesn't make sense. Why would Kyle go anywhere with Elliot?"

"We don't know if it was voluntary," Marcus reminded her gently. "The footage isn't clear enough to determine if Kyle was under duress. But it does show Price's fishing boat leaving the marina and heading out into open water shortly afterward."

The implications crashed over Lila like an icy wave. Elliot Price, whose father had died in a suspicious boating accident orchestrated by the Caldwells in 1995. Elliot, who had inherited his father's land and likely his grudge against the developers. Elliot, who had known the Montgomery family for decades and would have had ample opportunity to gain Kyle's trust.

"We've been looking at this all wrong," she whispered, the pieces rearranging in her mind. "What if Elliot isn't working for Caldwell? What if he's been operating independently all this time, pursuing his own agenda connected to his father's death?"

Marcus was already reaching for the phone again. "Lieutenant Ramirez needs this perspective immediately. If Price is working against Caldwell rather than for him, his motivations and likely actions change significantly." He paused, studying Lila's face with a mixture of concern and admiration. "Your instincts have been solid throughout this investigation. What's your read on Price's intentions toward your brother?"

Lila considered the question carefully, trying to set aside her personal fear to analyze the situation objectively. "Elliot knew our father well. They were fishing partners for years after Samuel Price died. If Kyle found something at the shop—something connected to the development plans or the historical fraud—Elliot might see him as an ally rather than a target."

"Or he might see him as leverage," Marcus suggested, the detective in him considering all possibilities. "Something to trade for whatever endgame he's pursuing against Caldwell."

Before Lila could respond, her phone buzzed with an incoming text message. Her breath caught when she saw it was from Kyle's number:

Safe with Elliot. Found something big at shop. Meeting Mira's contact who has proof against Caldwells. Don't trust police—some still loyal to Jennings. Will contact when safe. TRUST NO ONE.

"It's from Kyle," she told Marcus, showing him the message. "He says he's safe with Elliot, that they're meeting someone who has evidence against the Caldwells. And he says not to trust the police because some officers might still be loyal to Jennings."

Marcus read the message carefully, his expression troubled. "This complicates things significantly. If there's a leak within local law enforcement feeding information to Caldwell's organization, it could explain how they've stayed ahead of our investigation."

"Should I respond?" Lila asked, her thumb hovering over the keyboard. "Try to get more information about where they're going?"

"No," Marcus decided after a moment's consideration. "If his phone has been compromised, any response might put him in additional danger. But we need to get this information to Ramirez immediately, with all appropriate operational security measures."

As Marcus placed the call to Ramirez, Lila read Kyle's message again, focusing on one particular phrase: "Mira's contact." If Kyle and Elliot were meeting someone connected to Mira Douglas, someone who might have additional evidence against the Caldwells, it suggested a wider network of resistance than they had previously suspected. Perhaps Mira's abduction had triggered contingency plans she had established precisely for such a situation.

The thought brought a glimmer of hope amid the worry. If Mira had been systematically gathering evidence against the Caldwells for years, she might have secured backup documentation, perhaps distributed it among trusted allies as insurance against exactly the kind of corporate muscle now being deployed against her.

"Lieutenant Ramirez is implementing communication protocols to identify potential leaks," Marcus reported after finishing his call. "She's also deploying Coast Guard assets to locate Price's fishing boat, but with a significant head start and his lifetime of experience in local waters, it could be challenging to find them quickly."

"So we wait," Lila said, frustration evident in her voice as she sank back into the visitor's chair. "While my brother is out there with Elliot Price, meeting some mysterious contact who may or may not actually be connected to Mira Douglas."

"Not exactly," Marcus replied, his tone shifting subtly. "Ramirez agreed that you should proceed with the Jennings interview we discussed. If there are indeed officers still loyal to him feeding information to

Caldwell, Jennings might be our best chance to identify them. And if Elliot Price is working against Caldwell, Jennings might know something about his operation as well."

"You think Jennings will talk to me?" Lila asked skeptically. "After everything that's happened?"

"I think he might," Marcus nodded. "Especially if he believes Caldwell has abandoned him—left him to face charges alone while extracting more valuable assets like Mira Douglas to safe haven in the Caymans. Men like Jennings operate on personal loyalty. Once that's broken, their own self-interest typically prevails."

Lila considered the strategy, finding both logic and hope in the approach. If Jennings could be persuaded to cooperate, he might provide the leverage they needed against Caldwell. And he might know something about Elliot Price's independent agenda that could help them locate Kyle.

"When?" she asked simply.

"Immediately," Marcus replied. "Ramirez is arranging the interview now, with appropriate security measures. And Lila," he added, his tone softening slightly as he reached for her hand, "he responds best to emotional appeals. Share your genuine concern for Kyle. Let him see the human impact of his actions. Men like Jennings often compartmentalize the consequences of their choices—putting a face and a name to those consequences can be powerful."

The personal touch—his fingers warm around hers, the genuine concern in his eyes—grounded Lila amid the swirling chaos of the situation. Despite everything—his injuries, the professional demands of the case, the complex web of corruption they were untangling—Marcus Cole remained present and connected in a way that steadied her when she needed it most.

"I'll make him talk," she promised, squeezing Marcus's hand briefly before releasing it and rising to her feet. "Whatever it takes to find Kyle and stop Caldwell."

As she moved toward the door, Marcus called after her. "Lila. Be careful. Whatever game Elliot Price is playing, whatever Jennings might reveal—we're still missing pieces of this puzzle. And incomplete information can be more dangerous than none at all."

The warning followed her as she left the hospital room, escorted by the State Police officers who would transport her to the secure facility where Sheriff Jennings was being held pending trial. Throughout the drive, Lila mentally prepared for the confrontation ahead, organizing what she knew about the former sheriff, his connection to her family, and the leverage they might use to secure his cooperation.

But beneath the tactical preparation, a current of fear ran deep—fear for Kyle, out on open water with a man whose true motivations remained unclear; fear for Mira Douglas and Nina West, in the hands of a corporation willing to kill to protect its secrets; and fear that despite all they had uncovered, they might still be missing the most dangerous element of all.

As the secured State Police facility came into view, Lila steeled herself for the interview ahead. Whatever Jennings knew, whatever secrets still remained hidden in the tangled history of Seabreeze Shores, she was determined to uncover the truth—for Kyle, for Marcus, for her father's memory, and for a town that had lived too long under the shadow of corruption and murder.

The time for half-measures and caution had passed. They had reached the breaking point, and only the raw truth, however painful or dangerous, could guide them through what lay ahead.

Chapter 10
The Truth Revealed

The County Detention Center sat at the edge of Harbor Bay, its modern façade belying the grim purpose within. Unlike the aging courthouse downtown with its classical columns and weathered stone, the detention center was all sleek angles and security features—cameras surveilling every approach, reinforced glass in precise geometric patterns, landscaping designed to eliminate hiding places rather than for aesthetic appeal.

Lila followed her State Police escort through a series of security checkpoints, each requiring more stringent identification protocols than the last. The weight of the situation pressed down on her with each sealed door that closed behind them—Kyle somewhere out on the water with Elliot Price, Marcus confined to a hospital bed with his injuries, and she about to confront the man who had once been Seabreeze Shores' most trusted authority figure, now revealed as a corrupt enforcer for generations of corporate fraud.

"Interview Room Three has been prepared as Lieutenant Ramirez requested," the facility officer informed them as they reached the final security station. "Sheriff Jennings has been advised of Ms. Montgomery's visit but not its purpose. The room is monitored with both audio and visual recording, and officers will be stationed directly outside."

Lila nodded her understanding, though her attention had caught on a detail. "He's still being called 'Sheriff'?"

The officer's expression remained professionally neutral. "Officially, his status is suspended pending the outcome of his case. Until formal removal proceedings are completed, the title remains."

The bureaucratic technicality struck Lila as absurdly inappropriate given the circumstances, but she kept this observation to herself. Lieutenant Ramirez had briefed her thoroughly on the approach to take with Jennings—find the balance between his potential resentment toward Lawrence Caldwell for abandoning him and his lifelong connection to Seabreeze Shores. Appeal to his local loyalties, his knowledge of the Montgomery family, his potential desire to salvage some small piece of his reputation in the community he'd served for decades.

Interview Room Three was antiseptically bland—beige walls, a simple table bolted to the floor, four matching chairs, and a large mirror that undoubtedly concealed an observation area. Sam Jennings already sat at the table when Lila entered, his hands resting on the surface rather than cuffed as she had half-expected. He wore a standard-issue orange jumpsuit that seemed to hang on his frame, as if he'd lost weight in the short time since his arrest.

"Lila," he greeted her, his voice carrying the same folksy tone she'd known all her life, though now it seemed like a performance rather than genuine warmth. "This is an unexpected visit. I figured you'd be the last person who'd want to see me after our... misunderstanding at your shop."

"Misunderstanding?" Lila echoed, taking the seat across from him. "Is that what you call holding my family hostage at gunpoint, Sam?"

A flicker of genuine shame passed across his face before the practiced mask of the small-town sheriff returned. "Things got out of hand. I never intended for anyone to get hurt. I just needed time to explain my side of things before that State Police lieutenant took over."

Lila studied him, seeing beyond the façade for perhaps the first time. Sam Jennings had been a fixture in Seabreeze Shores throughout her life—presenting awards at school assemblies, leading the Memorial Day parade, stopping by Salted Caramel's for his regular scoop of butter pecan every Wednesday afternoon. The disconnect between that familiar figure and the man implicated in murder, corruption, and hostage-taking was still difficult to reconcile.

"I'm not here about what happened at my shop," she said finally. "I'm here about Kyle."

Wariness immediately replaced Jennings' practiced affability. "Your brother? What about him?"

"He's missing," Lila stated bluntly. "Last seen boarding Elliot Price's fishing boat with something he found at my shop—something connected to the Caldwell development plans and possibly to Graham Fox's murder."

Jennings sat back slightly, his expression now genuinely surprised. "Elliot Price? Why would he..." He trailed off, something calculating entering his gaze. "What exactly do you think I know about this, Lila?"

"I think you know a lot more than you've admitted about Lawrence Caldwell's operations in Seabreeze Shores. I think you know who in the local police might still be feeding information to Caldwell's organization. And I think you might know what game Elliot Price is playing—whether he's working for Caldwell, against him, or running his own agenda entirely."

Jennings was quiet for a long moment, his weathered fingers tapping a slow rhythm on the table as he considered his response. "That's quite a shopping list of information you're after. What makes you think I'd share any of it, even if I knew?"

"Because Caldwell left you to take the fall," Lila replied simply. "He extracted Mira Douglas and Nina West to the Cayman Islands but left you here to face multiple felony charges alone. He abandoned you after decades of loyal service from both you and your father."

Something hardened in Jennings' eyes at the mention of his father. "You don't know anything about my father's relationship with the Caldwells."

"I know more than you think," Lila countered, producing copies of the documents found in Mira Douglas's hidden room. "I know your father helped Samuel Jennings orchestrate the 'accident' that killed Samuel Price in 1995 when he refused to sell his waterfront property. I know the Caldwell family has been systematically defrauding the property owners of Seabreeze Shores for more than a century. And I know your family has been instrumental in helping them maintain that fraud through intimidation, corruption, and occasionally murder."

Jennings didn't reach for the documents, his gaze fixed on Lila's face instead. "You sound just like your father," he said quietly. "Jack had the same self-righteous tone when he backed out of the 1995 deal. As if he hadn't been perfectly willing to profit from it until things got complicated."

"My father made mistakes," Lila acknowledged, refusing to be baited. "But he tried to make them right, even at significant personal cost. That's why I'm here, Sam. To give you the same opportunity. Help us find Kyle. Help us stop Caldwell before more people die for his family's century of fraud."

"And what do I get in return?" Jennings asked, the calculating look returning to his eyes. "A slightly more comfortable cell? A mention at my sentencing about my cooperation? You'll forgive me if that doesn't seem particularly motivating."

Lila had anticipated this response, had prepared for it during her drive from the hospital. "You get to preserve whatever small shred of your legacy in Seabreeze Shores might still be salvageable. The town where your family has lived for generations, where your children grew up, where people trusted you to protect them. You get to look in the mirror and know that when the moment came to choose between loyalty to a corrupt corporation and loyalty to your community, you finally made the right choice."

The appeal landed with surprising impact, something vulnerable flickering across Jennings' face before he could suppress it. For a moment, Lila glimpsed the man beneath the corrupt sheriff—someone who had begun his career with genuine intentions before being drawn into his father's corrupt arrangements with the Caldwells, someone who had rationalized each compromise as necessary for the greater good of a town that needed economic development to survive.

"Elliot Price is dangerous," Jennings said finally, his voice lower now, as if sharing a confidence rather than providing official information. "Not in the way Caldwell is dangerous—with money and hired muscle and corporate lawyers. Price is dangerous because he's got nothing left to lose. His father died fighting the Caldwells, his family's tradition of fishing is dying with the declining industry, and he's been planning his revenge for twenty-five years."

"Revenge against Caldwell?" Lila prompted when Jennings paused.

"Against the entire Caldwell operation," Jennings clarified. "Including those of us who helped them. He approached me about ten years ago, tried to recruit me to help expose the corruption. Said he had evidence of what really happened to his father but needed someone with authority to act on it. I reported the conversation to Lawrence Caldwell, and we arranged for Price to be discredited—financial problems, some minor legal issues, enough to ensure no one would take his accusations seriously."

"But you didn't eliminate him," Lila observed. "Like you did with Graham Fox when he discovered too much."

Jennings didn't deny the implied accusation. "Price was local. Deeply connected. His disappearance would have raised too many questions. Fox was an outsider, easier to dismiss as a tragic accident. And I didn't—" He stopped, reconsidering his words. "The directive regarding Fox came directly from Lawrence Caldwell. I merely... facilitated certain aspects."

"By ensuring the investigation ruled his death an accident," Lila finished for him. "Just like you did with Samuel Price twenty-five years earlier."

"The past can't be changed," Jennings replied, a note of defensiveness entering his tone. "What matters now is what Price might be planning. If he's taken your brother, it's because Kyle found something Price believes can be used against Caldwell's organization. Something significant enough to risk exposing his operation after all these years of careful planning."

"What operation?" Lila pressed. "What has Elliot been doing all this time?"

Jennings leaned forward slightly, lowering his voice though the room was certainly monitored. "Building a case. Gathering evidence. Forming alliances with others who've been harmed by the Caldwells over the years. I never knew the full extent, but I heard rumors—a network of people sharing information, documenting the pattern of fraud and intimidation, preparing for the moment when they could finally expose the entire century-long scheme."

"And Mira Douglas?" Lila asked. "Was she part of this network?"

"Almost certainly," Jennings nodded. "The Douglas family has had a grudge against the Caldwells for generations. There were rumors that Edward Douglas—Mira's great-grandfather—had compiled extensive documentation of the Caldwells' fraudulent land acquisitions before his mysterious death in 1912. If Mira continued that work, collected that evidence..."

"Then she would be an invaluable ally to Elliot Price," Lila finished, the connections forming rapidly in her mind. "And now she's been taken by Caldwell's people, which might have forced Price to accelerate whatever plan he's been developing."

"With your brother somehow caught in the middle," Jennings confirmed grimly. "Price wouldn't harm Kyle deliberately—the Prices and Montgomerys have been friendly for generations. But he wouldn't hesitate to use him as leverage if necessary, especially now that Mira's been taken."

"Leverage against whom?" Lila asked, though she was beginning to suspect the answer.

"Against you," Jennings replied simply. "Or more specifically, against Detective Marcus Cole and the State Police investigation. Price doesn't trust law enforcement—with good reason, given my involvement and the deep corruption in local policing. If Kyle found evidence that could expose Caldwell once and for all, Price would want to control how and when that evidence is revealed. He'd need to ensure it isn't intercepted or buried by Caldwell's remaining allies in the system."

"Kyle's text mentioned 'Mira's contact,'" Lila recalled. "Someone with proof against the Caldwells. Do you know who that might be?"

Jennings shook his head. "Mira kept her network compartmentalized for security. But there was one name that surfaced occasionally in discussions—Olivia Reed. Thomas Reed's daughter."

"Thomas Reed?" The name triggered a distant memory from their investigation. "The rookie officer who initially investigated Samuel Price's death and was reassigned when he found evidence of sabotage?"

"The same," Jennings confirmed. "After he resigned from the force, he left town, but his daughter returned about five years ago. She's been working as a marine biologist at the coastal research station north of

Seabreeze Shores. I always suspected she might be continuing her father's investigation, but we never found proof."

The pieces were falling into place with dizzying speed. Kyle's work in marine biology would have brought him into contact with the coastal research station. He might have known Olivia Reed professionally, might even have suspected her connection to the historical investigation without realizing its significance until he found whatever evidence had prompted his hasty departure.

"Where would Price take Kyle if they were meeting Olivia Reed?" Lila asked urgently.

Jennings considered this, his expression thoughtful. "The research station itself would be too public. And Price wouldn't risk his boat being seen near known locations if he's making a move against Caldwell. There's an abandoned lighthouse on Gull Point, about five miles up the coast. It's remote, easily defended, and has clear sightlines in all directions. If I were planning a secure meeting to exchange sensitive information, that's where I'd choose."

Lila rose immediately, the urgency of the situation overriding any desire to continue the interview. "One last question, Sam. Which officers in the local department are still loyal to Caldwell? Who's been feeding him information about the investigation?"

Jennings hesitated, the calculus of self-preservation visibly working behind his eyes. Finally, he sighed. "Deputy Chief Wallace. He's been on Caldwell's payroll for at least fifteen years. And Officer Jensen at the State Police outpost—he's Wallace's brother-in-law, recruited more recently but positioned to access state-level intelligence."

"Thank you," Lila said, surprised by the sincerity in her own voice. "This will help us find Kyle and stop Caldwell."

As she turned to leave, Jennings called after her. "Lila. Be careful with Price. He's not a killer by nature, but he's been consumed by this vendetta for decades. And people who've sacrificed everything for revenge sometimes lose perspective on collateral damage."

The warning followed Lila as she exited the interview room, its ominous tone reinforcing the stakes of the situation. Her State Police escorts were waiting in the hallway, their expressions professionally neutral despite having undoubtedly monitored the entire conversation.

"I need to speak with Lieutenant Ramirez immediately," Lila told them, already moving toward the exit. "And someone needs to inform

Detective Cole about what we've learned regarding Elliot Price's operation and the potential location of Kyle."

"Lieutenant Ramirez is waiting in the secure conference room," one of the officers informed her. "And Detective Cole has been kept updated throughout your interview."

The efficiency of the State Police operation was both reassuring and slightly unsettling. As they escorted her from the detention center to a waiting vehicle, Lila found herself wondering how much of what she'd just learned had already been suspected or known by Ramirez and her team. Had the interview with Jennings been as much about confirming their existing theories as it was about developing new leads?

Lieutenant Ramirez was indeed waiting in the facility's conference room, surrounded by maps and communications equipment. She looked up as Lila entered, her expression grim but focused.

"Good work with Jennings," she said without preamble. "We've already dispatched a Coast Guard vessel to the Gull Point lighthouse, and aerial surveillance is en route. If your brother and Price are there, we'll locate them within the hour."

"What about Olivia Reed?" Lila asked. "If she's Mira's contact, bringing evidence against the Caldwells, we need to ensure her safety as well."

"Ms. Reed is currently unaccounted for," Ramirez replied, her tone carefully neutral. "She didn't report for work at the research station today, and her residence appears to have been vacated in a hurry. We're operating under the assumption that she's either with Price and your brother, or she's been intercepted by Caldwell's organization."

The latter possibility sent a chill through Lila. "And the officers Jennings identified? Deputy Chief Wallace and Officer Jensen?"

"Both have been quietly isolated from operational information while we verify Jennings' claims," Ramirez assured her. "If they've been feeding information to Caldwell, they won't be able to alert him to our current activities."

Lila nodded, relieved by the thoroughness of the State Police response but still anxious about Kyle's safety. "What's our next step? I want to be there when you find Kyle."

Ramirez studied her for a moment, clearly weighing operational security against Lila's personal stake in the situation. "We'll be establishing a forward command post near Gull Point," she decided finally. "You can accompany us there, but you'll remain with the command team, not the tactical unit making the approach. This is still an active law enforcement operation, Ms. Montgomery, not a family reunion."

"I understand," Lila agreed quickly, willing to accept any conditions that kept her close to the action. "When do we leave?"

"Immediately," Ramirez replied, already gathering her materials. "And Ms. Montgomery? Detective Cole has requested to join us at the command post, against medical advice. He's being transported by medical personnel as we speak."

The news that Marcus had somehow persuaded doctors to release him from the hospital so soon after surgery was both concerning and oddly reassuring. Despite his injuries, he was determined to see this through—to find Kyle, to stop Caldwell, to bring the entire conspiracy to justice. His dedication strengthened Lila's own resolve as they prepared to depart.

The journey to Gull Point took approximately forty minutes, following coastal roads that wound through increasingly remote terrain. The abandoned lighthouse came into view as they crested a final hill—a stark white tower perched on a rocky promontory, its once-proud beam long since extinguished, its keeper's cottage now a weathered shell beside it. The surrounding landscape was sparse and windswept, offering minimal cover for approach but also few hiding places for potential threats.

The State Police had established their command post in a concealed position approximately half a mile from the lighthouse, utilizing a natural depression in the terrain to hide vehicles and equipment from casual observation. As Lila exited the car, she was immediately struck by the increased security presence—tactical officers in body armor, communications specialists with advanced equipment, even a medical team standing by for any potential casualties.

And there, seated in a modified transport chair that accommodated his casted leg, was Marcus Cole. Despite the pallor of his complexion and the evident pain that creased the corners of his eyes, his mind was clearly fully engaged, conferring with a tactical officer over a detailed map of the lighthouse grounds. He looked up as Lila approached, relief briefly softening his professional expression.

"Your interview with Jennings was enlightening," he said by way of greeting. "Particularly the confirmation of Price's long-term operation against Caldwell."

"I'm more concerned about finding Kyle right now than unraveling the entire conspiracy," Lila replied, though the tremor in her voice belied her attempt at a businesslike tone. "Have your surveillance teams located him yet?"

"Confirmed approximately ten minutes ago," Marcus nodded, gesturing to a surveillance monitor that displayed a thermal image of the lighthouse keeper's cottage. "Three heat signatures inside—consistent with your brother, Price, and likely Olivia Reed. Coast Guard has established a perimeter to prevent any water-based approach or escape, and tactical teams are in position for a coordinated entry when Lieutenant Ramirez gives the order."

Lila studied the thermal image, trying to determine any details about the three figures inside the cottage. They appeared to be seated around what was probably a table, their postures suggesting conversation rather than confrontation. "They don't look like hostages," she observed cautiously. "More like people having a meeting."

"That aligns with our current assessment," Marcus agreed. "Based on Jennings' information and the surveillance, we believe this is indeed a planned rendezvous rather than a kidnapping. The question remains what evidence they're discussing and what action they intend to take with it."

Lieutenant Ramirez joined them, her expression suggesting new developments. "We've just received word from our team monitoring Lawrence Caldwell's movements. He boarded a private jet at Harbor Bay Airport thirty minutes ago, destination Nassau, Bahamas. He's running."

"After extracting Mira Douglas and Nina West to the Caymans," Marcus noted grimly. "Consolidating his resources and evidence beyond U.S. jurisdiction."

"But why now?" Lila questioned. "What's changed in the last few hours that would prompt him to flee after so aggressively defending his position yesterday?"

The answer hit them simultaneously—a realization that transformed their understanding of the entire situation.

"Whatever Kyle found," Marcus said slowly, "whatever he took from your shop that was valuable enough to risk slipping his police protection..."

"It must be something devastating to Caldwell's position," Lila finished. "Something he can't afford to have revealed under any circumstances."

"Enough to abandon his entire operation and flee the country," Ramirez added, already reaching for her radio. "We need to accelerate our timeline. If Caldwell is this desperate, he might have assets already en route to eliminate the evidence and any witnesses—including your brother and his associates."

The next several minutes passed in a blur of activity as Ramirez coordinated the tactical approach. Lila remained beside Marcus, drawing unexpected comfort from his steady presence despite the tension of the situation. When he reached for her hand during a particularly intense radio exchange, she grasped his fingers without hesitation, the simple human connection anchoring her amid the swirling uncertainty.

"Tactical teams in position," came the report over Ramirez's radio. "Awaiting your command."

Ramirez looked to Lila, a surprisingly compassionate moment from the otherwise strictly professional officer. "We'll bring your brother out safely," she promised. "But you need to prepare yourself for the possibility that whatever he's involved in is more complicated than we currently understand."

Lila nodded, tightening her grip on Marcus's hand as Ramirez gave the order to proceed. On the surveillance monitors, they watched as tactical officers began their coordinated approach to the lighthouse keeper's cottage, moving with the disciplined precision of extensive training.

"Movement inside," the surveillance officer reported suddenly. "Subjects appear to be reacting to something—possibly they've detected our approach."

The thermal images on the monitor showed the three figures inside the cottage now standing, moving rapidly in what appeared to be organized rather than panicked motions. One figure—taller than the others and likely Elliot Price—moved toward what would be the building's rear exit.

"Team Two, be advised, subjects may be attempting to exit via the rear of the structure," Ramirez directed into her radio. "Maintain non-lethal approach protocol. These are potential witnesses, not confirmed hostiles."

The tension in the command post was palpable as the tactical teams closed in on the cottage. Lila held her breath, her gaze fixed on the thermal image that likely represented Kyle, willing him to stay safe, to make no sudden movements that might be misinterpreted by the approaching officers.

And then, just as the tactical teams reached the cottage perimeter, something unexpected happened. The door of the cottage opened, and one of the figures stepped out, hands clearly raised in a gesture of surrender or cooperation.

"Subject exiting the main entrance," came the immediate report. "Male, early thirties, hands visible and raised. Matches description of Kyle Montgomery."

"That's Kyle," Lila confirmed, relief washing through her at this apparent voluntary surrender. "He's cooperating."

The thermal imaging was now supplemented by body camera footage from the tactical officers, showing Kyle standing calmly at the cottage entrance, his expression determined rather than fearful as he spoke to the approaching officers. Though the audio was indistinct at this distance, his body language suggested he had been expecting this confrontation and had prepared for it.

"Second subject exiting, female, mid-thirties," came the ongoing report. "Hands visible, carrying what appears to be a document case. Likely Olivia Reed based on preliminary visual confirmation."

The woman who emerged behind Kyle was slender and professional-looking despite the remote location, her dark hair pulled back in a practical ponytail, her movements deliberate and calm as she placed the document case on the ground as instructed by the tactical officers.

"Where's Price?" Ramirez demanded, noting that the third heat signature remained inside the cottage.

The answer came moments later as Elliot Price finally emerged from the building's rear exit, immediately surrounded by Team Two officers. Unlike Kyle and Olivia, his body language suggested tension and reluctance, though he offered no resistance as the officers secured him.

"All subjects in custody, Lieutenant," came the confirmation over the radio. "Area secure, no additional persons located in the structure. Document case has been secured and subjects are being transported to your location for preliminary questioning."

The relief in the command post was palpable as the operation concluded without violence or resistance. Lila sagged slightly against Marcus, the tension of the past hours suddenly catching up with her as the immediate threat to Kyle passed.

"You did it," she told him softly. "You found him."

"We found him," Marcus corrected, his own relief evident beneath his professional demeanor. "And now perhaps we'll finally get some answers about what's been happening in Seabreeze Shores for the past century."

It took approximately fifteen minutes for the tactical teams to return to the command post with their three detainees. Kyle was brought directly to Lila, the officers having been briefed on their relationship, while Olivia Reed and Elliot Price were escorted to separate debriefing areas for preliminary questioning.

"Lila," Kyle exclaimed as he reached her, pulling her into a fierce hug despite the tactical officers still flanking him. "Thank God you're okay. After everything that's happened, I wasn't sure—"

"I'm fine," Lila assured him, returning the embrace with equal intensity before pulling back to examine him for any signs of injury or distress. "But what were you thinking, slipping away from your police protection? And that cryptic text about not trusting the police? Do you have any idea how worried I've been?"

Kyle had the grace to look slightly abashed, though determination quickly replaced his momentary contrition. "I had to, Lila. After what I found hidden in Dad's old office at the shop, I couldn't risk it falling into the wrong hands. And Jennings wasn't the only corrupt officer in Seabreeze Shores—I couldn't be sure who might be feeding information to Caldwell."

"We know," Lila nodded. "Deputy Chief Wallace and Officer Jensen. Jennings confirmed it during my interview with him. But Kyle, what did you find that was worth taking such a risk?"

Kyle glanced around at the officers still present, his expression suggesting he remained cautious about sharing information too broadly. Noting his hesitation, Lieutenant Ramirez approached, her professional demeanor softened slightly by the successful resolution of the immediate crisis.

"Mr. Montgomery, I understand your concern about operational security," she said, directly addressing his unspoken wariness. "But we need to know what evidence you've discovered regarding Lawrence Caldwell and his organization. Especially given his apparent flight from U.S. jurisdiction this morning."

"Caldwell's running?" Kyle's surprise appeared genuine. "That actually makes sense, given what we found." He turned back to Lila. "It was in Dad's old filing cabinet at the shop, hidden in a false bottom I discovered while looking for the backup financial records after the shop was closed for Fox's murder investigation. A sealed envelope addressed to me, to be opened only if something happened to him."

"Dad left you a letter?" Lila asked, confused by this revelation. "Why wouldn't he have mentioned it to me or Mom?"

"Not just a letter," Kyle corrected. "Evidence. Proof that the Caldwell family's entire claim to the waterfront properties is based on fraudulent acquisitions dating back to the 1890s. Birth certificates, marriage licenses, and death certificates proving that the current 'Lawrence Caldwell' is actually not a Caldwell at all—he's Lawrence Mitchell, son of the family's former gardener, who assumed the identity of the real Lawrence Caldwell after his death in a boating accident in 1982."

The revelation landed with stunning force, transforming their understanding of the entire conspiracy. Not just fraud in acquiring properties, but identity theft at the highest level of the corporation—a false heir leading a multi-generational criminal enterprise.

"That's why he's been so desperate to acquire all the Harbor Act properties," Marcus realized, his detective's mind quickly processing the implications. "Not just for the development value, but because a thorough title search during major construction could expose the fraudulent chain of ownership. And once the identity theft was discovered, the entire Caldwell empire would be vulnerable to legal challenge."

"Exactly," Kyle confirmed. "Dad discovered this while researching the 1995 development deal. He confronted the fake Lawrence Caldwell privately, hoping to force him to abandon the project without exposing the fraud publicly. That's why he backed out of the deal so suddenly—not just because of Samuel Price's death, but because he'd discovered the lie at the heart of the Caldwell empire."

"And Caldwell used his debt to Maritime Ventures to keep him quiet," Lila concluded, the pieces finally aligning. "The financial pressure ensured Dad wouldn't expose what he knew, even as he refused to participate in the development."

"The debt was the leverage," Kyle agreed. "But Dad didn't trust Caldwell to honor their arrangement forever. So he compiled all the evidence and left it for me, with instructions to use it if anything suspicious ever happened in connection with another Caldwell development project."

"Like Graham Fox's murder behind your shop," Ramirez noted, her expression thoughtful as she processed these revelations. "But why contact Elliot Price instead of coming directly to law enforcement with this evidence?"

"Because Dad's letter specifically mentioned Elliot's father had been investigating the same fraud before his 'accident,'" Kyle explained. "And because Elliot had connections to a broader network of people who'd been gathering evidence against the Caldwells for decades. I needed to verify what I'd found against their research, make sure we had an airtight case before going public."

"Olivia Reed and Mira Douglas," Lila guessed, recalling the network Jennings had described.

"Among others," Kyle confirmed. "Mira had been maintaining her great-grandfather's records of the original fraudulent land acquisitions. Olivia had been documenting the environmental impact of the Caldwells' undisclosed industrial waste dumping along the coast—leverage to ensure certain officials remained cooperative. Together with Dad's evidence of the identity theft, we have enough to not only stop the current development but to potentially unravel the entire Caldwell corporate empire."

The scale of the conspiracy—spanning multiple generations and involving fraud, identity theft, environmental crimes, and murder—was almost incomprehensible. And yet, the pieces fit together with terrible clarity, explaining not only Graham Fox's murder but the decades of corruption and manipulation that had shaped Seabreeze Shores' development.

"Where is this evidence now?" Ramirez asked, her tone suggesting she already anticipated the answer.

"The original documents are in the case Olivia brought out of the cottage," Kyle replied. "But we've already digitized everything and distributed copies through secure channels. Even if Caldwell's organization managed to intercept or destroy the originals, the evidence is preserved and ready for release to appropriate authorities."

"Including the real Lawrence Caldwell's family," a new voice interjected. Olivia Reed had been brought to join their conversation, her expression suggesting a combination of relief and determination. "The legitimate heirs have been located in Europe, completely unaware that their cousin's identity had been stolen. They've been briefed and are prepared to pursue legal remedies once the evidence is publicly released."

The implications were staggering—not just criminal prosecutions for murder and fraud, but potentially the largest corporate identity theft case in history, with billions in assets at stake. No wonder the false Lawrence Caldwell had fled at the first indication that the evidence had been discovered.

"And Mira Douglas?" Lila asked, remembering the B&B owner who had been abducted to the Cayman Islands. "Is she safe?"

"As safe as she can be under the circumstances," Olivia replied with a slight smile. "What Caldwell doesn't realize is that Mira went voluntarily—allowing herself to be 'abducted' to gain access to Caldwell's offshore operations. She's been our deep-cover operative for years, working to document the international financial aspects of the fraud."

This final revelation completed the picture of an operation far more sophisticated and far-reaching than any of them had initially suspected. What had appeared to be a simple murder investigation had uncovered a century of fraud, a network of resistance spanning generations, and now an international effort to bring down one of the most elaborate corporate conspiracies in modern history.

"So what happens now?" Lila asked, looking between Lieutenant Ramirez, Marcus, and the others who had become entangled in this extraordinary case.

"Now," Ramirez said with uncharacteristic satisfaction, "we build the case methodically, coordinate with international authorities to locate and apprehend Lawrence Mitchell-Caldwell, and begin the process of unraveling decades of corruption and fraud. It won't happen overnight, but justice will finally come to Seabreeze Shores."

As the command post transformed into a processing center for the mountain of evidence and testimony now available, Lila found herself drawn to a quiet corner where Marcus sat, his professional demeanor still intact despite the obvious pain from his injuries and the exhaustion of the prolonged operation.

"How are you holding up?" she asked, taking the seat beside him.

"I've been better," he admitted with a wry smile. "But seeing this case finally break open makes it worthwhile. Your father would be proud of what you and Kyle have accomplished."

The mention of her father brought unexpected tears to Lila's eyes. "I wish he could have seen this. He carried that secret for so long, protecting us by keeping silent, even as the debt burdened our family for years."

"He found a way to ensure the truth would come out eventually," Marcus observed gently. "Through his children. That's a powerful legacy, Lila."

The simple truth of this observation resonated deeply. Jack Montgomery had indeed found a way to balance his responsibility to his family with his commitment to justice—not through dramatic confrontation, but through careful preparation for a moment he wouldn't live to see.

"What about us?" Lila asked, the question emerging before she could reconsider it. "When all this is over, when you're recovered and Seabreeze Shores is no longer an active crime scene... what happens with us?"

Marcus's expression softened, his professional mask slipping to reveal the man beneath—thoughtful, compassionate, and surprisingly vulnerable. "I was hoping to explore that question over dinner at Salted Caramel's," he replied. "I've heard they make exceptional vanilla ice cream. The owner has a special infusion technique, I'm told."

Despite everything—the exhaustion, the stress, the lingering anxiety of the past days—Lila felt a smile bloom across her face. "She does," she confirmed. "Though I hear the owner is quite selective about who she shares her special flavors with."

"I'm willing to earn that privilege," Marcus replied, reaching for her hand. "One scoop at a time."

The simple promise of normalcy—of ice cream and conversation and the gentle exploration of what existed between them—felt like the most precious gift amid the chaos of conspiracy and revelation. Before Lila could respond, Kyle appeared beside them, his expression suggesting both apology for the interruption and excitement about new developments.

"Lieutenant Ramirez just received word from the international task force," he reported. "They've located Nina West at a resort in the

Cayman Islands. She's safe and has agreed to provide testimony about her research for Graham Fox."

"And Mira Douglas?" Lila asked, not releasing Marcus's hand despite her brother's knowing glance at their entwined fingers.

"Still maintaining her cover within Caldwell's organization," Kyle confirmed. "But she's established secure communication with the task force and is providing real-time intelligence on his offshore operations. They're building a comprehensive case that spans multiple jurisdictions."

"What about the false Lawrence Caldwell?" Marcus inquired, his detective's mind still focused on the primary suspect despite his injuries and the personal moment that had been interrupted.

"His private jet filed a flight plan for Nassau but diverted mid-flight," Kyle explained. "Current intelligence suggests he may be heading for a country without extradition treaties with the United States. The task force has alerts at all potential destinations, but apprehension may take time."

"He'll be found eventually," Marcus said with the quiet confidence of someone who had spent his career pursuing justice. "Men like that—those who believe themselves untouchable—eventually make mistakes. They can't help themselves."

Lieutenant Ramirez approached their small group, her professional demeanor intact despite what must have been extraordinary fatigue after the intensive investigation. "We're wrapping up operations here," she informed them. "Mr. Montgomery, you'll need to provide a formal statement regarding the evidence you discovered, but that can wait until tomorrow. Ms. Montgomery, I've arranged for secure transport back to Seabreeze Shores for you and your family. And Detective Cole," she added with the barest hint of dry humor, "the medical team is becoming increasingly vocal about returning you to the hospital before your surgical team files kidnapping charges against me."

"I can't imagine why," Marcus replied, though the pallor of his complexion and the tightness around his eyes suggested the pain medication was wearing off. "I'm perfectly comfortable directing operations from a wheelchair."

"Of course you are," Ramirez agreed with surprising gentleness. "But even detectives need to follow medical advice occasionally. The case will still be here when you're recovered enough to return to active duty."

As the command post began to dismantle around them, Lila found herself experiencing an almost surreal sense of transition. The investigation that had consumed her life for the past week—transforming her understanding of her family's history, her town's development, and her own capacity for courage under pressure—was evolving from immediate crisis to systematic legal process. The adrenaline-fueled days of danger and discovery were giving way to statements, evidence processing, and the methodical construction of a landmark legal case.

The drive back to Seabreeze Shores passed in contemplative silence, Kyle beside her in the secure transport vehicle, both siblings processing the extraordinary revelations and considering their implications for the future. By the time they reached the Harborview Hotel, where Eva and Elsie were waiting under continued police protection, the sun was setting over the harbor, painting the familiar landscape in hues of gold and amber.

"I still can't quite believe it," Kyle admitted as they approached the hotel entrance. "That Dad knew all this time about the fake Lawrence Caldwell. That he protected us by staying silent, even as he prepared for the truth to eventually come out."

"It explains so much," Lila replied softly. "The extra jobs, the financial strain, his reluctance to expand the shop despite opportunities. He was carrying such a burden alone."

"Not entirely alone," Kyle corrected gently. "Mom must have known something. Remember how whenever anyone mentioned the Caldwells or Maritime Ventures, she would change the subject? She was protecting his secret too, in her way."

The observation cast their mother in a new light—not just as the supportive spouse but as an active partner in Jack Montgomery's silent resistance against the corruption that had shaped Seabreeze Shores. As they entered the hotel, Eva's expression upon seeing them confirmed Kyle's theory—relief at their safety, yes, but also a deeper understanding that suggested she had anticipated this day might eventually come.

"It's over, isn't it?" she asked simply, embracing them both. "Jack's evidence is finally being used?"

"You knew," Lila stated rather than asked, searching her mother's familiar face for confirmation.

"Not everything," Eva admitted. "Your father kept some details even from me, for my protection. But I knew he had discovered something dangerous about the Caldwells, something that forced him to back out of the development deal. And I knew he had made provisions for that information to be revealed if it ever became necessary."

"Why didn't you say something when all this started?" Kyle asked, no accusation in his tone, merely curiosity.

"Because your father was very specific about the timing," Eva explained, leading them to a quiet corner of the lobby. "The evidence was for Kyle, with instructions that it should only be used if another Caldwell development threatened the town. If I had mentioned it prematurely, before you found it yourself..." She shook her head. "I had to trust your father's judgment, even after he was gone."

The wisdom of Jack Montgomery's approach was evident now. By keeping the evidence hidden until absolutely necessary, by entrusting it specifically to Kyle with clear conditions for its use, he had ensured that when the moment came, the revelation would be supported by a network of additional evidence gathered independently by others like Mira Douglas, Olivia Reed, and even Elliot Price. Not one person's accusation that could be discredited or silenced, but a comprehensive case built across decades.

As the Montgomery family gathered in Eva's hotel suite, joined by Elsie who had remained loyally by Eva's side throughout the crisis, the conversation gradually shifted from the case itself to its implications for their lives moving forward. Salted Caramel's would reopen, of course, but now as a symbol of the town's resilience rather than just a beloved local business. And the development that had threatened the waterfront would never materialize, at least not under the Caldwell banner.

"What happens to all the waterfront properties if the Caldwell ownership is invalidated?" Elsie wondered, curled comfortably in an armchair with a cup of herbal tea. "Could the original families reclaim them after all these years?"

"That will be for the courts to decide," Kyle replied, his academic background emerging as he considered the legal complexities. "The case involves property fraud spanning more than a century, with multiple generations of ownership changes. The legitimate Caldwell heirs in Europe will have claims, as will the descendants of the original families. It could take years to fully resolve."

"But Seabreeze Shores will remain Seabreeze Shores," Lila stated with quiet certainty. "Not transformed into some generic resort destination that erases its history and character."

The conversation continued into the evening, the relief of resolution allowing for moments of laughter and reminiscence that had been impossible during the tension of the investigation. Plans were made for the shop's reopening, for Kyle's return to his research position (now with a unique publication opportunity regarding the environmental impact of the Caldwells' coastal industrial practices), for a proper family dinner once the immediate legal proceedings were completed.

It was nearly midnight when Lila's phone buzzed with a text message. She checked it discreetly, a small smile forming as she read:

Doctors finally relented and provided a proper phone charger. Surgery team less than thrilled about my field trip today. How are you holding up? – MC

She excused herself from the family gathering, stepping onto the suite's balcony overlooking the moonlit harbor to reply:

Family reunited and processing everything. Mom knew more than she let on. How's the leg? When can I visit? – LM

His response came quickly:

Leg's been better. Doctors insisting on at least three days of proper hospital rest before they'll consider releasing me. Apparently "chasing criminals with a fresh surgical repair" is frowned upon in medical circles. You're welcome anytime visiting hours permit. – MC

Lila leaned against the balcony railing, the sea breeze playing with her hair as she considered her response. The formal tone of their text exchange belied the moment they had shared at the command post—the acknowledgment of something developing between them that transcended the professional relationship of their initial meeting.

I'll bring ice cream. Vanilla bean, properly infused. Tomorrow afternoon? – LM

The three dots indicating his typing appeared immediately:

Nothing would aid my recovery more effectively. Medical science be damned. Tomorrow it is. – MC

She could almost see his smile through the message, the hint of dry humor that occasionally broke through his professional demeanor. As she tucked the phone back into her pocket, Lila found herself looking out over the familiar landscape of Seabreeze Shores—the harbor lights, the gentle curve of the waterfront, the silhouette of buildings that had stood for generations. The town would change, inevitably, as the Caldwell conspiracy unraveled and new truths came to light. But its essential character—the community that had sustained her family for generations—would endure.

Three Months Later~
Salted Caramel's had never been busier. The combination of summer tourism and the national attention generated by what the media had dubbed "The Caldwell Conspiracy" had transformed the modest ice cream shop into something of a local landmark. Visitors from across the country came to sample the famous vanilla bean ice cream and, if they were lucky, catch a glimpse of the owner who had helped unravel one of the most elaborate corporate fraud schemes in American history.

Lila wiped down the counter with practiced efficiency, having just served the last customers of a particularly hectic afternoon rush. The shop gleamed with fresh paint and new fixtures—a minor renovation undertaken after the official reopening, funded partly by the advance from the book deal she'd been offered to tell the full story of Graham Fox's murder and the century of corruption it had exposed.

The bell above the door jingled, and Lila looked up with her professional smile, ready to greet another customer. Instead, she found Marcus Cole standing in the entrance, a bouquet of wildflowers in one hand, his weight still slightly favoring his right leg despite the recent removal of his cast.

"Are those for me, or are you trying to butter up the staff for extra toppings?" she teased, coming around the counter to greet him properly.

"Purely strategic bribery," he replied with the smile that still made her heart skip—warmer and more frequent now that the case had been resolved and their relationship had developed beyond the professional boundaries of their first meeting. "Though I'm hoping they might earn me a private tasting of that new flavor you've been developing."

"The blackberry bourbon vanilla?" Lila asked, accepting the flowers with a quick kiss that she still found thrilling despite the growing familiarity between them. "It's almost ready. Another day of infusing should perfect the balance."

"I'm a willing test subject whenever you're ready," Marcus offered, following her behind the counter as she found a vase for the flowers. The casual ease with which he moved through her space reflected the evolution of their relationship over the past months—from detective and witness to partners in both the investigation and, increasingly, in life.

As Lila arranged the wildflowers, Marcus updated her on the latest developments in the case that continued to unfold across multiple jurisdictions. The false Lawrence Caldwell had been apprehended attempting to enter Venezuela, his distinctive appearance and expensive tastes ultimately betraying him despite elaborate identity precautions. Nina West had completed her formal testimony regarding Graham Fox's research, providing crucial links in the evidentiary chain. And Mira Douglas had finally emerged from her deep-cover role within the Caldwell organization, returning to Seabreeze Shores to a hero's welcome and the beginning of restoration work on her historic B&B.

"The legitimate Caldwell heirs have proposed a settlement regarding the waterfront properties," Marcus concluded, accepting the small dish of vanilla bean ice cream Lila had instinctively prepared for him. "They're suggesting a trust structure that would preserve the historical ownership while ensuring responsible development that maintains the town's character."

"That sounds remarkably reasonable given the circumstances," Lila observed, leaning against the counter beside him. "How is Sheriff Jennings taking all these developments?"

"About as well as can be expected," Marcus replied, savoring a spoonful of ice cream between responses. "His cooperation has been noted in the sentencing recommendations, but he's still facing significant prison time. The same can't be said for Deputy Chief Wallace, who continues to deny any wrongdoing despite overwhelming evidence to the contrary."

Their conversation drifted from the case to more personal matters—Marcus's physical therapy progress, Lila's plans for expanding Salted Caramel's menu for the fall season, the book she had begun writing with Kyle's assistance to document both the contemporary investigation and their father's role in preserving the crucial evidence.

"Have I mentioned how remarkable it is that you can discuss multiple homicides while creating perfect ice cream?" Marcus asked, watching as Lila efficiently served an elderly couple who had entered the shop despite the "Closed" sign she had flipped during their conversation.

"Multitasking is essential in both ice cream making and amateur detective work," she replied with a wink as she returned to his side. "Though I'm hoping to focus more on the former than the latter moving forward."

"No more investigating mysterious deaths or century-old corporate conspiracies?" Marcus teased, though there was genuine curiosity beneath the lightness of his tone.

"I think I'll leave that to the professionals," Lila decided, sliding onto the stool beside him. "Though I reserve the right to offer insights when particularly puzzling cases arise. I've discovered I have a knack for connecting seemingly unrelated details."

"That you do," Marcus agreed with surprising seriousness. "Your perspective was invaluable throughout the investigation. You saw connections I might have missed, understood the town's dynamics in ways an outsider never could."

The sincerity of the compliment warmed Lila more deeply than any casual flirtation might have. From Marcus—whose professional standards were exacting and whose praise was never offered lightly—such acknowledgment carried particular weight.

"We made a good team," she said simply.

"We still do," he corrected, reaching for her hand across the counter. "Which brings me to the other reason for my visit today, beyond the obvious pleasure of your company and exceptional ice cream."

Something in his tone—a hint of uncharacteristic nervousness beneath the composed exterior—caught Lila's full attention. "Oh?"

"I've been offered a position heading a new specialized investigation unit," Marcus explained, his thumb tracing absent patterns on her palm as he spoke. "The Caldwell case has prompted a comprehensive review of similar potential corporate conspiracies across the coastal region. The governor has authorized a task force to identify and investigate patterns of corruption, environmental crimes, and fraud that might otherwise escape traditional jurisdictional boundaries."

"That sounds perfect for you," Lila observed, genuinely pleased for him despite the hint of uncertainty his announcement triggered. A new position might mean relocation, a disruption to the relationship they had been carefully building over the past months. "Where would this task force be based?"

"That's the question I wanted to discuss with you," Marcus replied, his expression suggesting the conversation was about to take a more personal turn. "I've been given latitude to establish our headquarters in a location that provides strategic access to the coastal investigation areas. One option is Harbor Bay, with its existing law enforcement infrastructure. But another possibility..." He hesitated, then continued with careful precision, "Another possibility is Seabreeze Shores itself."

The implication hung between them—that his decision about the task force location was directly connected to their relationship, to the future they might build together in the town that had shaped her life and now, unexpectedly, his as well.

"Seabreeze Shores doesn't have much in the way of office space for a specialized investigation unit," Lila observed, her practical nature asserting itself even as her heart raced with the possibilities his words suggested.

"True," Marcus acknowledged with the hint of a smile. "But it does have exceptional ice cream. And I've grown rather attached to both the product and its maker."

The simple declaration—understated yet unmistakably meaningful—was quintessentially Marcus. No grand gestures or elaborate proclamations, just honest acknowledgment of what had developed between them and a practical proposal for nurturing it further.

"Are you saying you'd base your career decision on access to proper vanilla bean ice cream?" Lila asked, matching his tone while knowing they were discussing something far more significant.

"I'm saying I'd like to build something here," Marcus replied, his gaze steady on hers. "Professionally, yes. But more importantly, personally. With you, if that's something you might want too."

In the warm afternoon light of the shop that had been her family's legacy for generations, surrounded by the familiar sights and scents of a business that had weathered corporate conspiracies, murder investigations, and the everyday challenges of small-town commerce, Lila considered the extraordinary journey that had brought them to this moment. From their first meeting over Graham Fox's murder to the unraveling of a century of corruption and fraud, their lives had become intertwined in ways neither could have anticipated.

"I think," she said finally, shifting to face him more directly, "that Seabreeze Shores would benefit enormously from hosting your task force.

The town has a vested interest in addressing corporate corruption, after all." She paused, then added with deliberate softness, "And I have a vested interest in having you nearby. For extensive ice cream quality control purposes, of course."

The smile that spread across Marcus's face—unguarded and genuine in a way she had rarely seen during the intensity of the investigation—was answer enough. He leaned forward, closing the distance between them, and kissed her with a thoroughness that suggested ice cream was very much a secondary consideration in his decision-making process.

When they finally parted, the shop bathed in the golden light of approaching sunset, Lila couldn't help but reflect on how differently things might have turned out. If Graham Fox hadn't been killed behind her shop, if her father hadn't preserved the crucial evidence, if she and Marcus hadn't forged their unlikely partnership amid danger and revelation—Seabreeze Shores might have been transformed into just another generic resort development, its history and character erased by corporate greed.

Instead, the town stood at the threshold of a new chapter—one where long-buried truths had finally emerged, where justice had prevailed against seemingly insurmountable odds, and where connections both personal and communal had been strengthened through adversity.

"I should warn you," Lila told Marcus, her fingers still entwined with his, "that dating the local ice cream shop owner comes with certain responsibilities. Taste-testing experimental flavors, enduring endless food puns, occasional late nights during the summer rush..."

"I think I can handle those demands," he replied with mock seriousness. "My investigative training has prepared me for stakeouts of all kinds. Even those involving dessert."

As the sun dipped toward the horizon, painting Seabreeze Shores in hues of amber and gold, they remained together in the shop that had become both the starting point of their journey and, unexpectedly, the foundation for whatever might come next. The mystery that had brought them together had been solved, the century of secrets finally exposed to light. What remained was something entirely new—a future they would craft together, one scoop at a time.

1. Blackberry Mint Breeze

Inspired by Lila's experimental flavor for the Seabreeze Festival.

Ingredients:

- 2 cups heavy cream
- 1 cup whole milk
- 3/4 cup sugar
- 1 ½ cups fresh blackberries
- 1 tsp lemon zest
- 1/3 cup fresh mint leaves
- Pinch of salt

Instructions:

1. Simmer blackberries, sugar, and lemon zest until berries soften. Strain to remove seeds and set aside to cool.
2. In a saucepan, warm milk and mint leaves. Turn off heat, let steep 30 minutes, then strain.
3. Whisk in cream, cooled blackberry purée, and pinch of salt.
4. Chill mixture thoroughly, then churn in ice cream maker.
5. Serve with a fresh mint sprig and lemon zest curl.

2. Vanilla Orchid Legacy

Lila's signature vanilla bean tribute to her father.

Ingredients:

- 2 cups heavy cream

- 1 cup whole milk
- 3/4 cup sugar
- 2 vanilla beans, split and scraped
- 1 tsp vanilla extract
- Pinch of sea salt

Instructions:

1. Combine milk, cream, sugar, and vanilla beans in a pot. Simmer gently for 5 minutes, then steep for 30.
2. Remove pods, add extract and sea salt.
3. Chill mixture, then churn until soft-serve texture.
4. Freeze until firm. Garnish with edible vanilla orchid if available.

3. Seabreeze Salted Caramel Swirl

The shop's namesake flavor—rich, sweet, and kissed with sea air.

Ingredients:

- 1 cup sugar (for caramel)
- 1/4 cup water
- 1 ¼ cups heavy cream
- 1 cup whole milk
- 1 tsp sea salt flakes
- 3 egg yolks

Instructions:

1. Make caramel by heating sugar and water until deep amber. Carefully whisk in ¾ cup cream and salt. Let cool.

2. Whisk egg yolks with milk and remaining cream over low heat until custard coats a spoon.

3. Combine custard with caramel and chill.

4. Churn, then swirl extra thick caramel ribbons as you pack into a container.

4. Sunset Strawberry Cheesecake Cone

The flavor Lila served to beachgoing tourists.

Ingredients:

- 2 cups cream cheese, softened
- 1 ½ cups heavy cream
- 1 cup whole milk
- 1 cup strawberry purée
- 3/4 cup sugar
- 1 tsp vanilla extract
- 1 cup crushed graham crackers

Instructions:

1. Whip cream cheese, sugar, milk, and strawberry purée until smooth.

2. Fold in cream and vanilla.

3. Chill and churn, then layer in graham cracker crumbs.

4. Freeze until scoopable, then serve in waffle cones.

5. Boardwalk Bonfire S'mores Ice Cream

A cozy, smoky homage to Seabreeze Shores evenings.

Ingredients:

- 2 cups heavy cream
- 1 cup whole milk
- 3/4 cup brown sugar
- 1 tsp smoked sea salt
- 1 tsp vanilla extract
- 1 cup mini marshmallows
- 1 cup crushed graham crackers
- 3/4 cup dark chocolate chunks

Instructions:

1. Roast marshmallows under broiler until toasty.
2. Combine cream, milk, sugar, salt, and vanilla. Stir in toasted marshmallows.
3. Chill and churn. In the last minutes of churning, add graham crackers and chocolate.
4. Freeze until firm and serve by the seaside—or dream about it.

Patti Petrone Miller

Meet Patti, the creative force behind "Where the Magic Happens." More than just an author, Patti brings stories to life as the Executive Producer of an animated TV series based on her heartwarming tale "ELLIOT FINDS A HOME"—the story of a special dog with thumbs and his silent friend who prove that sometimes, actions speak louder than words.

Patti's writing journey has been nothing short of remarkable. A cherished author at Polygon Entertainment, she's danced her way onto the USA TODAY bestseller list and claimed Amazon's #1 spot multiple times. With 7 dozen books spanning from Urban Fantasy to Horror, Patti weaves tales that transport readers to worlds limited only by imagination.

Her life reads like an adventure novel filled with fascinating chapters:

At just 4 years old, she charmed audiences on "Romper Room" She shared memorable moments with Captain Kangaroo and Mr. Green Jeans She once enjoyed a train ride and sandwich with Sidney Poitier She high-fived President Nixon during a circus visit She attended school alongside magician David Copperfield She roller-skated with John Travolta before his rise to fame She warmed her hands and heart sharing cocoa with Abe Vigoda

Venom in Vanilla

When she's not crafting bestsellers, Patti embraces life as a teacher, grandmother, and devoted pet parent. Known affectionately as the "Queen of Halloween," this Wiccan High Priestess infuses her spooky stories with authentic magic that keeps readers spellbound.

Patti's books fly off shelves as quickly as they're stocked, so follow her social media to stay connected with this one-of-a-kind storyteller whose magical worlds welcome all who dare to dream.

www.ingramcontent.com/pod-product-compliance
Lightning Source LLC
LaVergne TN
LVHW041806060526
838201LV00046B/1152